ALSO BY ELIZABETH J. DUNCAN

PENNY BRANNIGAN MYSTERY SERIES

Murder Is for Keeps
Murder on the Hour
Slated for Death
Never Laugh as a Hearse Goes By
A Small Hill to Die On
A Killer's Christmas in Wales
A Brush with Death
The Cold Light of Mourning

SHAKESPEARE IN THE CATSKILLS MYSTERY SERIES

Ill Met by Murder
Untimely Death
Much Ado about Murder

The Marmalade Murders

The Marmalade Murders

A PENNY BRANNIGAN MYSTERY

Elizabeth J. Duncan

Minotaur Books

New York

THE MARMALADE MURDERS. Copyright © 2018 by Elizabeth J. Duncan. All rights reserved. Printed in the United States of America. For information, address St. Martin's Press, 175 Fifth Avenue, New York, N.Y. 10010.

www.minotaurbooks.com

The Library of Congress Cataloging-in-Publication Data is available upon request.

ISBN 978-1-250-10149-5 (hardcover)
ISBN 978-1-250-10150-1 (ebook)

Our books may be purchased in bulk for promotional, educational, or business use. Please contact your local bookseller or the Macmillan Corporate and Premium Sales Department at 1-800-221-7945, extension 5442, or by email at MacmillanSpecialMarkets@macmillan.com.

First Edition: April 2018

10 9 8 7 6 5 4 3 2 1

For Carol Putt

Acknowledgments

Thank you to my current editor, Hannah Braaten, for guiding this book through all the stages of publication, and to my agent, Dominick Abel, for his insightful suggestions that helped to shape the story.

I appreciate the practical contributions of Graham and Carole Bloxsome, and Eirlys Owen, and extend heartfelt thanks to Sheila Fletcher, and Sylvia and Peter Jones for proofreading the first-pass pages. They did a terrific job, but any errors or omissions are mine.

And, as always, special thanks to Lucas Walker and Riley Wallbank for their love and support.

I owe everything to St. Martin's Press, for making this series possible. It was a privilege to work with so many fine editors over the years: the late Ruth Cavin, Toni Kirkpatrick, Anne Brewer, and Melanie Fried.

And finally, to my readers who took the time to tell me how much they enjoyed the adventures of Penny Brannigan and her friends, thank you so much.

The Marmalade Murders

One

For three days it rained. Not the soft, gentle kind that's really more of a fine mist, but the hard, lashing kind that can turn a halfhearted trickle of a waterfall into a gushing torrent in minutes, and bring normally calm rivers to the brink of overflowing their banks with a sudden and terrifying ferocity.

And then, to the great relief of the organizing committee and exhibitors of the annual agricultural show, the rain stopped. On Wednesday morning, the late-August sun rose out of the mist, pale and hesitant at first, but then confidently resumed its rightful position, as if its absence had been merely a temporary inconvenience.

And on that sun-drenched Wednesday morning, Penny Brannigan gave Harrison, her handsome grey cat, a good-bye pat, locked the front door of her cottage on the edge of the North Wales market town of Llanelen, and set off on her walk to work.

She moved in a brisk, purposeful fashion, taking strong, confident steps. Her red hair, expertly trimmed into a well-shaped, blunt bob, lifted gently from the sides of her face as a light breeze ruffled it. Raising her eyes skyward, without slowing down, she marvelled at how the heavy pewter sky of yesterday had magically transformed into a brilliant, benign blue. She breathed deeply, filling her lungs with fresh, pure air, rinsed clean by the recent rain.

Her walk to work at the Llanelen Spa, which she co-owned with her friend and business partner Victoria Hopkirk, took her past open fields bordered by grey stone walls. And because of the freshly fallen rain, the grassy fields, here in the valley and on up into the hills, were an especially deep, bright shade of green. Vivid, even. Haydn Williams, a local farmer, had once explained to her that the striking green effect had to do with the plants' roots being able to absorb more nitrogen from the soil after a heavy rain.

Normally, the fields near Penny's home were dotted with grazing sheep, but today, the sheep were gone, replaced by several sturdy, mud-spattered four-wheel-drive farm vehicles. Men and women, close enough to be easily seen, but not close enough to speak to, tramped across the fields in groups of twos and threes, seemingly deep in conversation, occasionally pointing at the ground or opening their arms in broad, expansive gestures.

Penny recognized Haydn Williams, pacing in measured strides with a sturdy woman wearing a puffy green vest and a plaid skirt that just skimmed the tops of her dark green waterproof boots. When they were almost at the top of the field, they stopped, conferred, and the woman remained where she was as Haydn began walking slowly backward, a yellow tape measure unspooling between them.

Penny left them to their work, and without trying to acknowledge him, she continued on her way.

After a few minutes of pleasant walking along the bank of the River Conwy, she reached the graceful three-arched seventeenth-century stone bridge that represented the town. Its image was reproduced on postcards, mugs, tea towels, and countless other promotional items.

The river, glittering in the morning sun and swollen from the recent rain, had reached the high-tide mark, and Penny admired its fast-flowing energy as she waited for a gap in the traffic that would allow her to cross the two-lane road. A few cars speeding past in both directions and one lorry later, she darted across, then lifted the latch on the black wrought-iron gate that separated the path that led to the Spa from the pavement. The gate's hinges squeaked a mild protest as she swung it open, reminding her once again that they really must get that seen to.

"Morning, Penny." Receptionist Rhian Philips smiled from behind her desk as Penny opened the door. "Mrs. Lloyd's waiting to see you, if you can spare her a few minutes."

"Mrs. Lloyd? But she's not due until tomorrow, surely. Or has she changed her appointment? Maybe something's come up." Mrs. Lloyd was a regular customer with a standing appointment for a manicure every other Thursday, so her hands would look their best as she dealt the cards or played the dummy's hand at the over-sixties social club bridge night.

"No, not an appointment." Rhian lowered her voice, although there was no one else in the reception area to overhear. "She said it was a private matter."

"Oh, I see. Well, where is she? In the manicure studio?"

"No, she's waiting for you in the quiet room."

"Oh, right. Well, thanks. I'd better see what she wants."

The aptly named quiet room was a small space down the corridor, perfect for private conversations or a reflective moment alone. Decorated in soothing neutral colours of cream and taupe, it featured two comfortable chairs upholstered in chocolate brown faux suede arranged to face each other, a selection of smart women's magazines, and on a small shelf mounted under a watercolour of the Spa, painted by Penny herself, a grouping of unscented LED candles that flickered convincingly, providing atmosphere without the fire hazard. Mrs. Lloyd, sipping a latte from a tall glass, glanced at the door as Penny entered, and placed the magazine she had been browsing on the low table between the two chairs. A well-upholstered woman in her late sixties, Mrs. Lloyd wore her hair in soft grey curls that framed a round, relatively unlined face. She was blessed with a smooth English rose–type complexion that had aged well, thanks to a robust skin-care regime that involved lashings of cold cream at night and generous applications of moisturizer in the morning.

"Oh, there you are. Good," she said, folding her hands in her lap and leaning forward as Penny lowered herself into the chair opposite her. "Now, I know you've got a busy day ahead of you, so I'll come right to the point. I'm here to ask for your help. We're that desperate; you're our last hope. I can't think of anyone else to ask."

Penny groaned inwardly. She had a sinking feeling that

Mrs. Lloyd, who was terribly keen on community involvement, was about to ask her to do something she wouldn't want to do. Thoughts on how she could graciously say no without causing offence raced through her mind.

"When you say, 'we,' who's 'we'?" Penny asked with a cautious smile, hoping she was managing to hide her reluctance. "And why are you so desperate that I'm your last resort?"

"I'm just about to explain. It's the agricultural show, see. We need your help with something. Well, two things, if I'm honest, but let's take it one at a time."

"Oh, the agricultural show. Yes, I saw lots of activity in the fields when I walked by a few minutes ago. There seemed to be a lot of discussion going on. Haydn Williams and a woman I didn't recognize were pacing and measuring. Trying to work out where something should go, it looked like. A tent or pens for the animals, perhaps."

"Could be," agreed Mrs. Lloyd. "The grounds will be very soft and soggy. All that rain over the last few days has caused the organizing committee a lot of concern, I can tell you. Rain or shine, the show must go on. Trouble is, if it rains again, we're in trouble. I don't know if you remember, but a few years ago we had that atrocious weather on the day—high winds, and the rain was bucketing down. So no one came to the show except the folks with entries, and it was all a complete and utter disaster because we made no money from footfall through the gate. Normally, this is one of the biggest rural shows in the area. Hundreds of people turn out in good weather. The fields are full of parked cars. But not that year. And we still had to cover all the show expenses, which depleted our reserve funds, and we've only

5

just now built them back up to where they should be. You wouldn't believe how expensive it is to put on a show like that. That marquee costs six thousand pounds to rent, for one day. One day!"

"That seems like an awful lot of money for a marquee rental."

"Well, it's more like three days, what with setting up and taking down, and the thing is massive, and I suppose the fee includes all that, but certainly it doesn't come cheap. Still, there has to be one."

"Maybe that's what Haydn was doing—measuring up for the marquee. Are we talking about the big white marquee where the judging takes place?"

"That's the one. Well, some of the judging takes place there. The flowers and cakes and jams and such like. The animals stay outside in the fields where they belong. But the marquee also serves as the refreshment tent. But what am I like? I've gone way off topic. I came here to ask you to help out at the show."

Penny squirmed in her chair and, bracing for something she didn't want to hear, asked, "So how can I help? I haven't been to the agricultural show in years, and I don't know the first thing about sheep or cattle, so I'm not sure I'm the best person to be asking."

"Well, hear me out," replied Mrs. Lloyd. "First, the lady who used to do the judging of the children's pets is unfortunately no longer available, so I thought of you."

"Me? I didn't even know there is a children's pet competition. What do I know about judging children's pets?"

"You've got a cat, haven't you?"

"Well, yes, but . . ."

"There you are, then!" said Mrs. Lloyd triumphantly. "Good enough."

"Oh, that's how desperate you are, is it?"

"You might say that."

"And how, exactly, do I judge the children's pets?"

"You find something nice to say about each animal. The one with the most spots, or the softest coat, or the waggiest tail, or the prettiest ears . . . something like that. You can make it up as you go along. Just make sure every child leaves with a prize. There'll be only about a dozen or so, all under ten."

"I suppose I could do that, although I don't know if I'm all that good with children. But the person who used to do the judging, is she ill?"

"No, not ill. Not anymore. She's, well, she's dead, actually."

"Oh, I am sorry."

"It's all right; it was natural causes. Nothing suspicious about her death, and no need for you to feel you have to get involved."

Penny ignored the allusion to her amateur sleuthing activities and, after a respectful pause, steered the conversation back to the purpose of Mrs. Lloyd's visit. "You mentioned you wanted to ask me about two things. What was the second thing you were hoping I might be able to help with?"

"Oh, that. It's quite simple. We're short of volunteers for the home-crafts intake on the Friday night, and I hoped that since you live close by, you'd be willing to give us a hand with that. And Victoria, too, if you wouldn't mind asking her. It's really a job for two people. You'll be given the names of registered entrants and all you have to do is check people off when they arrive with their cakes or jam or carrots, or whatever, and put their entries on the table, so everything's all logged in and ready to be judged first thing in the morning."

"That's all? Just log in the competition entries?" Mrs. Lloyd nodded. "Well, that sounds simple enough. I could probably manage that, and I'll ask Victoria if she's available to help. If she's free, I'm sure she will."

"So you'll do it? Wonderful. I knew we could count on you. You should be on-site by four thirty for a briefing. Entries open at five o'clock."

Relieved that Mrs. Lloyd's requests hadn't been nearly as bad as she'd feared, Penny relaxed a little.

"Mrs. Lloyd, how is it that you're involved in the agricultural show? You're not a farmer, and I've never known you to be particularly interested in country pursuits." Until her retirement a few years earlier, Mrs. Lloyd had been the town's postmistress. From her vantage point behind the wooden counter in the post office located on the town square, Mrs. Lloyd had taken a keen interest in the town's comings and goings for decades. She liked to think that nothing much got past her then, or now, come to that.

"No, I'm not all that interested in country pursuits. But my late husband, Arthur, was the town's greengrocer, and he sold all the produce from the farms. Almost everything was local then and available only in season. Oh, you still had oranges from Spain and bananas from wherever, but most of what he sold, especially in summer, was grown on farms right here in the valley. The strawberries back then were delicious. Plump and juicy. Not like the tasteless imported kind you get today. Anyway, Arthur served on the organizing committee of the agricultural show for years, and when he passed away, the other members asked if I would fill his seat. And I said yes. And I'm still doing it. I consider it an honour. One does what one can." She got to her feet. "I'm glad you agreed to help out, Penny. It's always good to give back to the community, even if it's just in a small way. Especially when you're a newcomer."

"Mrs. Lloyd, I've lived here for almost thirty years!"

Now in her early fifties, Penny had discovered the town as a young Canadian backpacking tourist in her twenties and stayed on for an extra night or two, which turned into a week, and then a month, until all these years later, she was still here and had made a good life for herself among the warm, welcoming Welsh people. She'd made friends, started a business, and, except for her accent, had assimilated so completely that she was indistinguishable from anyone born and bred in the town.

"A relative newcomer, then," Mrs. Lloyd said with a teasing smile as she gathered up her handbag. "Well, I'm glad you've agreed to join us. Just go straight to the tent on Friday and ask for Joyce Devlin. She's the president of the show committee and she'll show you what to do. Oh, and as volunteers, you and Victoria would be most welcome to attend our gala awards banquet. Everybody's too tired on the Saturday night of the show, and besides, the farmers have got their animals to get home and see to, so the dinner's held a week later at the hotel. The main prizes, like Best in Show, are awarded then, although most are given out on show day. Everybody'll be at the gala. The tickets are reasonably priced, and you pay for your own drinks."

Two

*B*y Friday afternoon, following three days of intensive work on the part of organizers and volunteers, preparations for the annual Llanelen agricultural show were in the final stages. Sturdy yet portable metal enclosures for the cattle, horse, pig, and sheep competitions had been erected on one side of the site, and the vans, trailers, and horseboxes transporting the animals were beginning to arrive, bumping across the uneven terrain. At the opposite end of the show grounds, cages and lighter pens for the poultry and small-animal events had been set up. Exhibitors were tending to their animals, unpacking displays, ensuring signage was correct, polishing machinery, and seeing to the countless details that would hopefully result in a coveted silver cup or red rosette.

At the centre of the main field, where a few days earlier

Penny had watched Haydn Williams take measurements, stood a massive temporary white fabric structure. To refer to it as a tent would have been akin to calling the *Queen Mary II* a boat. The marquee featured enclosed sides with a row of plastic windows and a distinctive peaked roofline.

"I'm glad you were free and agreed to help out this evening," Penny remarked as she and her friend and business partner, Victoria Hopkirk, picked their way across the field toward the marquee. "I was afraid you weren't going to make it here in time, though."

"I almost didn't," Victoria replied. "The traffic was terrible. The road was positively jammed with exhibitors, and they're all driving slowly because they're towing trailers." She grinned at her friend. "The things we must do to keep Mrs. Lloyd happy. Remember that time she talked us into judging the Christmas decorations in all the shop windows?"

"That was rather fun, actually," said Penny. "I wouldn't mind doing it again. And I know she drives us mad sometimes, but her heart's in the right place. She's lived all her life here in Llanelen, and that's rare these days, when everybody moves around so much. And she cares deeply about this town."

"Well, that's true."

Although the sunny weather had held over the last three days, the uneven ground felt spongy and slightly springy beneath their feet. "We should have worn our boots," Victoria remarked as they approached the marquee. When they reached the entrance, she clutched Penny's arm to steady herself as she slid her shoe along the grass in an attempt to dislodge the clods of dark brown earth that clung to it. "The ground could be even wetter in there"—she indicated the marquee—"because the sun hasn't had a chance to dry it up. That's unless it has a floor, of course, which I doubt."

The door flaps of the marquee had been tied back, leaving a double-wide entry space. As Penny and Victoria were about to enter, a tall woman with a shiny black Labrador retriever bounding along at her heels charged toward them.

From her purple plaid skirt, green wellies, and robust figure, Penny recognized her as the woman she'd seen measuring the field with Haydn Williams on Wednesday morning.

"Hello," said the woman in the purple skirt. "I'm Joyce Devlin, chief cook and bottle washer, and you must be Penny and Victoria. Evelyn Lloyd told me to expect you. You made it, and on time, too, I'm pleased to see. Ready to get to work, are you?" She spoke briskly, in a no-nonsense manner, and without waiting for a reply, she gestured to the open doorway of the marquee. "Let's go in, shall we?"

A dozen or so tables had been placed end to end under the plastic arched windows that ran along alongside of the marquee. Each table had been covered with a white tablecloth, which fell almost to the ground, creating the illusion of one very long table. At the table farthest from the entrance, a faded, tired-looking woman of about sixty smoothed the tablecloth, then took a couple of steps back to check its length. On the other side of the marquee, two men were setting up the tables and chairs for the refreshment service.

"Barbara," Joyce called. Hearing her name, the woman at the end of the long table hurried over with a stack of papers on a clipboard and a roll of white stickers. She handed them to Penny, along with a black marking pen. "Now, you'll see on the entry forms here that each entry has been assigned a number," Joyce explained. "So when someone

13

arrives with her entry, a pie, let's say, you just take her name, find her entry form, check off the 'Received' box, and write the entry number the secretary has assigned on the sticker. Slap it on the bottom of the pie plate so that we'll know whose pie it is. The numbers must match the entry forms so that we'll know who the winners are, because, of course, all entries are blind-judged. Oh, and while we prefer that all entries in the baking competition are on white plates, for exhibiting purposes, if somebody does enter something on a blue willow pattern plate, for example, you may accept it. It won't be disqualified on the grounds that the plate might identify the owner, because all our judges come from out of town. The jams and marmalades will be in glass jars, of course, but we don't mind what kind of lid they have. A lot of them will probably look alike because we all buy our jars and lids from the same shop. One year, polka dots were very popular, as I recall. And gingham tops never go out of style. Anyway, when you've finished checking in all the entries, please put the forms in alphabetical order, keep the no-shows separate, and we'll be back to collect them just after eight, when entries close."

"And what should we do with the entries?" Victoria asked. "The cakes and things."

"Come with me." With her dog at her side, she led the way to the long table. Tent cards spaced a few feet apart indicated what that section of the table was reserved for: baked goods, vegetables, floral arts.

"Everybody will arrive at once, especially at the beginning, so just leave the item in the proper spot, and then, when things ease up a bit and you get a few minutes, you can arrange the entries nicely," Joyce explained. "Group all the pies together, cakes together, and so on. Makes it easier for the horticultural and home-craft judges in the morning." She looked from Penny to Victoria and then checked her watch. "Any questions? No? Right, well then, if there's nothing else, I've got a million things to see to, so I'll leave you to it. The entrants will be arriving with their offerings in about five minutes. Oh, one last thing. No late entries. The cutoff point is eight o'clock and they must be here by then."

Penny gave the dog at Joyce's side a friendly pat. "She looks just like Emyr's dog, Trixxi," she said as she straightened up. "But I guess all black Labs look pretty much the same."

Joyce's dark, heavy eyebrows lifted in surprise. "Oh, you know Emyr, do you?" Emyr Gruffydd was a local landowner who had a magnificent property called Ty Brith Hall just outside town, and another large estate in Cornwall.

Penny nodded. "I've looked after Trixxi several times. She's a lovely girl."

"Well, to the untrained eye, I suppose all Labs might look the same, although to me they certainly do not. But as a matter of fact, you are quite correct. Emyr's dog is from my kennel, and, in fact, Billie here is Trixxi's aunt. I pride myself on breeding the finest Labradors in North Wales. Got a waiting list as long as your arm. Got a litter now, as a matter of fact. The pups are seven weeks old, and all spoken for."

She glanced down at the dog, who returned her gaze with warm brown eyes, and Joyce's face softened with undisguised affection. "Billie here is the best bitch I've ever had. Her breeding days are over now, but I keep her as a pet, and she acts as a bit of a nursemaid to the new litters." She gave Penny an appraising look. "Oh, aren't you the one judging the children's pet competition?"

Penny nodded.

"Like animals, do you?"

"Love them."

"Well, if you'd like to come out to see the pups at our kennels, just give me a ring." She pulled a slightly tattered business card out of her pocket and handed it to Penny. "But as I said, they're all spoken for." Her pale companion, whom Joyce hadn't bothered to introduce, cleared her throat in an attention-getting sort of way. "Yes, you're right, Barbara. We must crack on." She instructed Barbara to give Penny a program, and then added, "Oh, one last thing. If anyone shows up with an entry but hasn't completed a form, there are a couple of blank ones in the stack. Just write on the form 'late entry,' keep that form separate from the rest, and the treasurer will chase up the payment. It costs twice as much to enter once the deadline is past." She let out an exasperated sigh. "You'd think by now people would've worked out that they have to get their entry forms in on time, but there are always the procrastinators. What can you do?"

At the sound of excited voices approaching, their attention turned to the marquee entrance.

"Brace yourselves," Joyce said. "Here come the ladies with their entries. Right, well, we'll leave you to it. You're going to be very busy for the next couple of hours and then things will taper off."

And busy they were. A steady stream of excited, optimistic competitors presented their offerings of baked goods, including breads, biscuits, plain and fancy cakes, and pies; elaborate and simple floral displays; vegetables of every shape, size, and colour; and iridescent jars filled with jam, chutneys, and marmalade. Penny and Victoria fell into an efficient system, which saw Victoria managing the paperwork, including the application of stickers, and, when the entries were processed, Penny toting them to their designated spots and arranging them in groups of like with like.

As the evening wore on, the steady stream of entrants dwindled to a trickle until about thirty minutes before the entry deadline, when Penny and Victoria had the marquee all to themselves. Victoria, standing at the entrance, watching the activity at the livestock pens farther down the field, pointed to a tall, familiar figure striding into view.

"It's Gareth. I wonder what he's doing here."

Penny placed a light hand on her friend's arm and peered around her. "He was brought on board to manage the show's security. Rural crime is on the increase at an alarming rate, apparently. Whole flocks of valuable sheep stolen right out of their fields. With so many expensive animals all in one place, the show organizers want to make sure there's none of that."

Gareth Davies, formerly a detective chief inspector with the North Wales Police, now retired, was an old friend of Penny's. At one time, there'd been the beginning of a romance, but she'd gradually come to realize that although she liked and respected him enormously, as much as she wanted to, she didn't love him, and never would. After that phase of the relationship had run its course, he'd moved on, and the two had remained fond of each other, in a nondemanding, casual kind of way.

Gareth disappeared from view and the two women stepped back into the marquee and surveyed the white-draped tables, groaning with colourful entries. "It must be getting close to eight P.M. How many entries are still to come?" Penny asked.

Victoria tipped the clipboard toward the doorway to catch the light and examined the top documents. "Two are Gaynor Lewis's and—wait, that's strange. Three are Florence Semble's. One cake, one jam, and one marmalade." She looked at Penny. "Did you know Florence was entering?"

"Florence?" Penny shook her head. "No, I didn't. When Mrs. Lloyd asked me if we could help out here this evening, she didn't mention Florence was entering the competition. I'm not surprised, though. Florence's baking is second to none."

"Well, she'd better get her skates on if she wants to get her entries in the competition in time."

Penny did not hesitate. "This is not like her. Florence is the best-organized person I know, and she'd never leave something like this to the last minute. I'm going to ring her and let her know time's almost up. If we know she's on her way, even if she arrives a few minutes late, I'm sure it will be okay to allow her entries."

Penny retrieved her mobile from her pocket, thumbed through the contacts list, and pressed the green call button.

"I'll get it," Mrs. Lloyd called out, rising from the sofa in her sitting room in response to the ringing telephone. She entered the hallway of the comfortable two-storey house on Rosemary Lane that she shared with Florence Semble and lifted the telephone receiver. "Hello?" She listened for a moment, then put down the receiver and walked to the doorway of the kitchen, where Florence was bent over the kitchen worktop, icing a cake.

"It's for you," said Mrs. Lloyd. "It's Penny. She's calling from the agricultural show. Something about your entries."

"Oh, can you take a message or tell her I'll ring her back?" Florence did not look at Mrs. Lloyd, but remained focused on her task. She squeezed the top of a piping bag to force the green icing toward the tip. "I want to finish the decoration on this cake."

Mrs. Lloyd trotted back to the telephone and a moment later, after letting out a loud "Oh my Lord!" dashed back to the kitchen. "Florence!" At the urgency in her friend's voice, Florence's head turned to the doorway. "Penny says the deadline for entries is eight o'clock and she called to see if you're on your way. She's worried if you're late, your entries won't be allowed."

Florence frowned and tilted her head to the side. "The deadline's tonight? Are you sure?"

"Of course I'm sure. That's what Penny just said." She flapped her hands at the cake. "How are you coming along there? Is it almost ready to go? What should I tell Penny?"

"Well, someone's got her wires crossed," said Florence, letting out a long, slow breath of confused disbelief. "What about that telephone call last night telling me I should bring my entries in the morning?"

"Penny was very clear," Mrs. Lloyd responded, her voice rising with impatience. "All entries must be in by eight o'clock."

"Well, in that case, you'd better tell her we're on our way, and then ring for a taxi."

Florence Semble had moved into Mrs. Lloyd's house

several years earlier, ostensibly as her lodger, although Mrs. Lloyd preferred to think of Florence in a rather more genteel term, regarding the woman as her companion. The arrangement suited both of them. They tolerated each other's foibles and, for the most part, were patient and forgiving with each other. The strength of their underlying friendship was obvious, and as Mrs. Lloyd put it, they "rubbed along quite nicely."

And even when Florence had discovered earlier in the year that she was the owner of valuable artwork and could have sold it easily to raise enough money to buy a small property of her own, she had chosen to stay with Mrs. Lloyd.

Never married, Florence had relied on herself her entire life. Straight out of school at the age of seventeen, she'd gone to work at the Liverpool School of Art, and that was the only employment she'd ever had. She'd been eking out a modest retirement when she met Mrs. Lloyd, and had gratefully accepted her offer of accommodation. What Mrs. Lloyd hadn't known when she'd invited Florence into her home was that Florence loved to cook and bake. What a delightful bonus that had turned out to be, although Mrs. Lloyd's waistline had paid a steep price for the indulgence in Florence's light, flaky scones and delicate shell-shaped Aberffraw biscuits.

"There," said Florence a few minutes later. "The cake's ready to go. Have you got the jam and marmalade?"

"I do," replied Mrs. Lloyd, opening the front door. "Let's be having you. The taxi's here."

Three

"Mrs. Lloyd's called a taxi," Penny said when the call ended, "and Florence should be here in about ten minutes." A quizzical expression crossed her face. "For some reason, Florence was told to bring her entries in the morning."

"In the morning? Do you mean tomorrow morning? I wonder why she was told that," mused Victoria. "I'm quite sure I read somewhere . . ." Her voice trailed off as she scanned an entry form. "Yes, here it is. Look," she said, leaning toward Penny and showing her the document. "Right here at the bottom." She underlined the relevant sentence with her finger as she read it out loud. " 'All entries must be delivered to the judging tent by eight P.M. on the Friday evening.' Joyce didn't say anything about entries arriving in the morning. In fact, she was quite clear we couldn't accept late entries. And none of the other entrants we processed to-night mentioned being told to bring their items in the morning. Why would Florence be the only one told that?"

"That *is* strange. Well, in that case, I'm very glad I rang Florence. She'd have been so disappointed not to get her entries in on time. Mrs. Lloyd sounded quite panicked on the phone. She told me that this is the first year Florence got up the courage to enter anything in this show and she's nervous enough about how she's going to do, without this added stress."

Like all the entrants in the Llanelen agricultural show home-craft events, Florence had high hopes that her cake, jam, and marmalade would meet with the judges' approval.

Victoria checked her phone. "Ten minutes to go. Come on, Florence!" Penny and Victoria exchanged anxious glances as the minutes ticked by. And then, at two minutes to eight, Mrs. Lloyd rushed into the tent, arms outstretched, holding two jars of preserves with squares of red-and-white gingham fabric tied over the lids with butcher's twine. Still wearing her full-length chef's apron, Florence followed at a slower pace, carrying a covered cake plate in both hands as gingerly as if it were a basket of baby chicks.

"Set your cake over there on the table with the others and we'll sort it out in a minute," directed Penny as she reached out to take the jars from Mrs. Lloyd. Victoria checked off the jam and marmalade and slapped a sticker on the bottom of each. Penny placed the jars on the table and turned her attention to the cake. Penny held it up so Victoria could apply the sticker to the bottom of the white plate.

"Done and just in time!" Penny said as they set the cake on the table with the others.

"Oh my word," gasped Florence, untying her apron and lifting the neck strap over her head. "I can't thank you enough for ringing to let me know about the deadline. This isn't even the cake I was planning to enter. It's the practise cake, and Evelyn and I were just about to sample it. If you'd called a minute later, there would have been two slices missing out of it! After we'd had a chance to taste it, I was going to set my alarm to get up early in the morning and bake another cake for the competition."

"I'm sure it'll be delicious," said Penny. "What kind is it?"

"Carrot, with a cream cheese icing. You can't see because of the cover, but it's got little orange carrots with green leaves piped around the top. I was going to go for chocolate, because everybody loves chocolate cake, but in the end I went with the carrot."

"The judges are bound to love it. Everything you bake is wonderful," Mrs. Lloyd reassured her.

At that moment, Joyce Devlin entered the tent, accompanied by her pale assistant, towed by Billie the Labrador, this time on a short lead.

"Entries are now closed," Joyce announced, pressing her thin lips into an emphatic line and scrutinizing Mrs. Lloyd and Florence. She acknowledged them, then turned her attention to Victoria. "How did we do?"

"All but two entries submitted," said Victoria, handing the forms and clipboard to Joyce. After scanning the documents, Joyce made a little *hmpf* sound, then passed the completed documents and clipboard to her companion, who frowned as she brushed a straggly lock of brown hair off her face.

"That's all right, Barbara. I'll take care of these two," Joyce said, holding on to the paperwork for the two entries that had not arrived in time to be entered in the competition.

"Now then," said Joyce to Penny. "About judging the children's pet show." Joyce turned to her assistant and said, "Barbara, you'd better give her a program so she'll know where she's supposed to be, and when." Barbara handed Penny a program booklet.

"Right, well, that's everything for now," said Joyce. "Thank you very much, and we'll see you in the morning. Show grounds open at nine A.M. You'll be amazed how many events we get through in just one day. Terrific amount to see and do, and everyone has such great fun." A brisk nod signalled they were dismissed. "Come on, Barbara," she said to the small woman who seemed to accompany her everywhere. "We've got to make sure the tea area's been set up properly. I'm worried they haven't got the cups and saucers laid out, and knowing Dev, we'll have to redo the tablecloths."

"Dev is Joyce's husband," Mrs. Lloyd announced helpfully. "But before you go, Joyce, I want a word with you about a telephone call Florence received. Someone called her last night and told her to bring her entries tomorrow morning."

"I can't imagine who would have done that, or why," Joyce said. She turned to her assistant. "Do you know anything about that, Barbara?"

"No, I don't know anything about that. But I can tell you it wasn't anyone from the show committee, that's for sure," said Barbara. "The entry rules are very strict."

"Well, there's no harm done, really, is there?" said Joyce. "After all, Florence did get her entry in on time, didn't she?"

"Well, yes, but only because Penny here rang to warn us the deadline was fast approaching, and we had to go like the clappers to get here in time."

"Well, there's nothing we can do about that now, and if you'll excuse me, we really must get on. Still lots to see to in order to get everything ready for tomorrow, and the sooner we get it done, the sooner we can all be off home to our beds." As Joyce and Barbara edged away, Penny and Victoria gathered up their handbags and prepared to leave.

"We'll drive you home, of course," said Victoria to Mrs. Lloyd and Florence as they trooped out of the tent. The air was warm, with the lingering gentleness of a late-summer evening. But the days were shorter than they had been a month ago, and long, deep purple shadows were gathering. They walked through the show grounds in the fading light that slanted across the tops of the ancient hills that cradled the town, passing farmers and their families settling their animals for the night, until they reached the well-trodden path that led to the field that had been designated as a car park.

"Here we are," said Victoria, unlocking her car. "Mrs. Lloyd, why don't you jump in the front and Penny and Florence can hop in the back."

"We're both in our sixties," said Florence, "so at our age, I don't know about jumping and hopping, but we'll do our best."

"Speak for yourself, Florence," said Mrs. Lloyd. "I'm as agile as someone half my age. It's all those years stood behind the counter in the post office. Gave me the stamina to last a lifetime."

"Oh!" said Penny as she was about to get in the car. "Sorry, I left the program in the marquee. I'm just going to run back for it."

"We'll pick you up at the exit," said Victoria.

Penny hurried back to the marquee, lifted the entrance flap, and scooped up the program from the table where she'd left it. As she turned to leave, voices drifted on the evening breeze from around the side of the tent, and she inclined her head to listen.

"I don't care who wins," a woman was saying in a low voice, "as long as it's not her."

"I wish you hadn't said that," replied her companion with a distinct note of irritation in her voice. "I really don't feel at all comfortable with this. And who knows. Maybe she won't win anyway." The second speaker's voice trailed off as the women moved away, and Penny was unable to catch any more of the conversation. She replayed the words in her mind as she walked to the field gates, where Victoria waited with the car. Penny opened the door to the backseat and climbed in.

"It's always such fun viewing the animals on show day," Mrs. Lloyd was saying. "They've all been coifed and groomed within an inch of their lives. They look as if they've just stepped out of the beauty parlour."

"Or had a day of pampering at the Llanelen Spa." Victoria grinned. Then, over her shoulder, she asked, "Did you get the program you were after, Penny?"

"Yes, I did, thanks."

Penny fastened her seat belt as the car pulled onto the main road and Victoria drove the short distance to the attractively proportioned two-storey, grey stone house on

Rosemary Lane where Mrs. Lloyd and Florence Semble lived.

"I'm really curious about that telephone call, Florence," Penny said. "The one telling you to bring your show entries in the morning. What can you tell us about it?"

"Well, I sent in the entry forms a few weeks ago and then last night someone rang to tell me I should bring my entries on Saturday morning."

"Can you remember the name of the person who rang you?"

"I don't think she said. If she did give her name, I don't remember it."

"But it was a woman?"

"Oh yes, it was definitely a woman's voice; that much I do know. She just said she was calling on behalf of the show committee to let me know the submission times had changed for some categories and that I should bring my cake to the judging tent by eight o'clock Saturday morning. I told her I was also submitting raspberry jam and marmalade and she said it would be all right to bring those in the morning, too. I didn't think anything of it, really. In fact, I thought they were doing this so everyone's entry would be as fresh as possible. Flowers, for example, would look better for the judging if they'd been picked and arranged that morning. Or maybe they were expecting so many entries that they were setting up two intakes."

In the front seat, Mrs. Lloyd shifted slightly to her right, as if to hear better.

In the dim light of the car's interior, Penny couldn't discern the expression on Florence's face, but her voice sounded thick and wooden.

"Are you all right, Florence?" Penny asked. "What are you thinking?"

They pulled up in front of Mrs. Lloyd's house and Victoria switched off the car engine. Nobody moved.

"Well, you heard what that Barbara person said. It wasn't someone from the show committee who rang me, so I can only think that it must have been somebody else who didn't want me to enter the competition, for some reason."

"What do you think, Penny?" Mrs. Lloyd asked. "What do you think's going on?"

"I'm not sure, but Florence might be right. Victoria and I logged in lots of entries and no one mentioned a phone call about bringing their entries in the morning. Why would Florence be the only one to receive that call?" She thought for a moment. "Unless someone else did, too. Victoria, do you remember the names on the no-show entries? I wonder if they got called, too, telling them to bring their stuff in the morning."

"There were two entries left over," Victoria replied. "The name on both was Gaynor Lewis. She was down for a jam and a marmalade. The name sounds vaguely familiar, but I can't place her."

"Gaynor Lewis!" exclaimed Mrs. Lloyd. "Oh my goodness!"

"Who is she?" Penny asked.

"She's the president of the Llanelen branch of the WG," Mrs. Lloyd said. "You know, the Welsh Women's Guild. Everybody just calls it the WG. You must have heard of it."

Penny and Victoria murmured little noises of assent. Of course they'd heard of the WG. It had been founded in Wales during the Second World War to help with efforts on the home front and now focused on old-fashioned home arts and crafts like sewing, baking, gardening, and knitting, some of which had never gone out of style, and some of which were making a comeback and being taken up by young people.

"And not only that," Mrs. Lloyd added, twisting further in her seat in an attempt to address Florence directly, "Gaynor Lewis is your archrival. On the rare occasion when her raspberry jam or marmalade doesn't take home first prize, everybody hears about it. It's all or nothing with her. She used to always win the cake competition, although she hasn't for the last couple of years, and it looks as though she didn't bother to enter that category this year. If she loses, she complains to anybody who'll listen about how biased the judging is and how the show organizers, led by Joyce Devlin, had it in for her."

"Oh dear," said Victoria. "Like that, is it?"

"It certainly is," said Mrs. Lloyd. "Joyce is Gaynor's sister-in-law, and they don't get on. Never have, never will. All the drama! But besides that, there are rivalries going back years. Like with poor Mari Jones. She's been desperate to take home a first-place rosette for one of her cakes for as long as I can remember, but she never has, poor soul." Mrs. Lloyd sighed. "The competition itself is fierce. I wouldn't go as far as to use the word *backstabbing,* but you'll probably see for yourselves tomorrow."

"That doesn't sound good," said Florence as she opened the car door. "What have I let myself in for? But I'm too tired to think about this anymore tonight. I'm sure we've all had enough excitement for one day, and there's nothing more we can do tonight. Perhaps we'll find out more about what's going on tomorrow. The main thing is, thanks to you two, I got my entries in on time."

"Florence is right," said Mrs. Lloyd. "We'll leave it there for tonight. And thank you so much for giving us the lift home. We'll see you at the marquee tomorrow morning."

"Good luck in the competition, Florence!" Penny called after them as they made their way along the path that led to their front door. Their movement triggered the porch light to come on, and for a brief moment their retreating figures were silhouetted in a beam of bright white light before they disappeared into the house.

Four

As Penny walked to the show the next morning, pausing for a moment to admire the bright pink and purple wildflowers that lined her path, she passed dozens of vehicles parked on the verge of the lane that ran alongside the fields. By nine o'clock, the field that had been designated as a car park was full.

Victoria had left her car at home, as show organizers had urged the hundreds of spectators to do, and together with Mrs. Lloyd and Florence, she'd taken the shuttle bus to the site.

They joined the rest of the eager showgoers who stepped off the bus into a field crowded with mud-spattered heavy vehicles equipped with trailers for transporting livestock. A soft breeze drifting down from the wooded hills carried the occasional lowing of a cow or the bleating of a sheep, intermingled with unmistakable livestock smells. And happily for all, the organizing committee's prayers had been answered; the day promised to be fair and warm.

The aluminium pens set up for the show animals were filled with common and fancy breeds of sheep, goats, horses, pigs, and cows being bathed, brushed, and combed to look their best when they entered the judging rings to compete for a prized red rosette or a coveted silver cup.

Victoria waved to Haydn Williams, who pointed proudly at the Welsh mountain sheep he was grooming, and in response she grinned and gave him an encouraging thumbs-up. Mrs. Lloyd and Florence trailed behind her, stopping to talk to friends and neighbours, as they threaded their way through the crowds. Interested townsfolk mingled with anxious exhibitors—mainly robust farmers, their faces brown from open air and sunshine, wearing baggy trousers, chunky sweaters, and tweedy flat caps. Mrs. Lloyd, dressed in the countrywoman's uniform of pleated skirt, puffy vest over a warm jumper, and sensible shoes, made a few casual remarks about the animals they passed, but Florence remained silent. This wasn't unusual, as she often retreated thoughtfully into herself, but she walked with her head down, shoulders stooped, and, unusually for her, took little interest in the activity going on all around her.

"I'm sure your entries did very well," Victoria assured Florence as they reached the marquee, where Penny, her hands stuffed into the pockets of a warm fleece, waited for them. Florence acknowledged Victoria's remark with a polite but tight smile.

"Quite a few people have already gone in," Penny said, stepping aside to allow Mrs. Lloyd and Florence to enter the marquee ahead of her. Diffused sunlight filtered through the plastic windows, bringing in a little warmth. Having been protected by the tent over the past few days, the uneven grassy ground had not had the opportunity to dry out, and as a result, it was still slightly springy and damp underfoot, as Victoria had predicted.

The four women eased their way into the end of the queue that snaked slowly along in front of the long table laden with entries. Curious show visitors mingled with anxious entrants who took their time examining the displays and pointing out the results to their friends.

The first category was the vegetable group. Entries had been artfully displayed, some on risers covered with white cloths, which added height and interest to a colourful show of leeks, tomatoes, carrots, sweet corn, cabbages, and lettuces. Prizewinning produce had been singled out for recognition with red or blue ribbons, along with a certificate bearing the name of the person who had entered it.

Next came the floral-arts displays. "No prizes for guessing who won most of these," remarked Penny. And she was right. The name *Heather Hughes* appeared on certificates beside several arrangements, ranging from lavish sprays to a single white rose. A well-known and much respected local gardener, Heather served as a judge at various flower shows, including a prestigious one held every spring in London.

The women admired the displays with their intoxicating scents as long as the line behind them allowed, until the pressure to move along propelled them farther down the table.

Florence took a deep, calming breath as they shuffled closer to the baking entries. Her sharp, eager eyes scanned the entries over the shoulders of the women standing in front of the table. After what seemed an eternity, the women ahead of her finally moved on and at last she and Penny were positioned in front of the home-baking categories.

It was a bountiful, mouthwatering display: fruit and savoury pies of every description, their golden brown crusts embellished with cutouts of leaves, acorns, or flowers; traditional Welsh cakes speckled with currants; ginger biscuits; cherry scones; chocolate Swiss rolls; date and walnut loaves; summer puddings; and, of course, cakes. Round and square cakes in two classes: plain and fancy, all set out on white plates. Victoria sponges and lemon drizzles dominated the plain category, while two-layer iced chocolate and walnut cakes shone in the fancy category.

In the centre of the table, on a raised silver cake stand, was a two-layer round cake, decorated in perfectly piped roses in graduated shades of frosting from red to a mid-range pink to a pale pink. A showy red rosette was affixed to the cake stand. Its trailing red ribbon, upon which *Best in Show* was emblazoned in yellow, flowed over a silver cake server.

"Oh," said Mrs. Lloyd. "Look at that! Best in Show. Who made it, I wonder." She picked up the certificate beside the rosette and read it out loud. "Best in Show: Cakes, pies, and biscuits. Elin Spears." As she dropped the certificate back on the table, she added, "I might have known. She's won the cake prizes for the last couple of years. It's always the same people who keep winning everything."

"Elin Spears," murmured Penny. "Name sounds familiar." She turned to Victoria. "Does she come to the Spa? That's probably where I know the name from, although she's not one of my clients."

"Maybe she does," Victoria replied. "I can't remember the name of every client, but the name rings a bell."

Florence tapped Penny on the arm to get her attention, then gestured at the table. "Are my eyes playing tricks on me? I don't see my carrot cake here. Do you?" She pointed to the chocolate and walnut cakes, each with a thin slice removed for judging. "It should be right there, in with that lot. Mine was two layers, as well."

Penny's eyes swept the table. "No, I don't see it, either," she said leaning forward to get a better view of the table. "It's not here. It should be. You submitted it on time, and we know it was officially entered in the competition. We'll have to speak to someone and find out what happened." She gave Florence what she hoped was a reassuring pat on the arm. "It's very strange, but don't worry, we'll find out what happened to it."

As a deep frown creased her forehead, Florence pressed her fingers over her mouth as she scanned the entries one last time.

They shuffled on to the jams, marmalades, and chutneys. "Oh, look, Florence." Mrs. Lloyd pointed to a jar of jam with a piece of red-and-white gingham fabric tied to the top, at the front of the display of preserves. "There's your raspberry jam, and it's come in first!" She rubbed her hands together in glee. "Well done. I'm happy for you but not the least bit surprised. I've eaten a lot of jam in my time, and nothing comes close to yours. It's the perfect combination of sweet and sharp."

Florence rarely allowed herself a full smile, but she couldn't help showing her delight at having come in first in the category. Before she really had time to savour her victory, though, the gentle surge of the crowd behind them encouraged them to move on to the next part of the display.

"Let's see how you did here, Florence," said Mrs. Lloyd, picking up the winning jar of marmalade with its red-and-white check-patterned top.

"That's not mine," said Florence. "Mine had a plain silver lid that I covered with a square of red-and-white gingham, tied on with a bit of butcher's twine."

"Yes, I remember the bit of gingham, but I thought perhaps the judges removed that and you had a red-and-white lid underneath." Mrs. Lloyd leaned over to examine the certificate beside the jar of marmalade and frowned. "No, it isn't yours, Florence. It's Gaynor Lewis's entry. I might have known." She lowered her voice. "You remember I told you about her last night. She's the president of the Women's Guild and sister-in-law of Joyce Devlin, chairperson of the show. Gaynor always wins in the jam and marmalade department, but I thought this year you were in with a chance because yours are just so much better than anyone else's. Well, I was right about the raspberry jam. I wonder what happened here with the marmalade. Yours should have won, not Gaynor's."

"Let me see that," said Florence, taking the jar from Mrs. Lloyd and holding it up to the light. Pretty as it was, with the sun shining through it, sparkling off the jar's cut-glass pattern and transforming the contents into a bright jewel-like colour, Florence was looking for something else.

"The distribution of fruit isn't equal here," she said. "Frankly, I'm surprised the judges would give this top marks. In mine, the distribution of fruit was equal. Let me show you."

A quick search through the dozen or so jars of marmalade revealed none with a red-and-white gingham top.

"Where's mine?" Florence demanded. "It should be here."

Florence and Mrs. Lloyd took a closer look at the jars with silver lids, picking up one after the other, until they had examined every one. Florence shook her head each time. That jar was too big. This jar was the wrong shape. The orange peel in the other one was too finely chopped.

"Now you didn't write your initials on the lid or do anything that would identify you and get you disqualified, did you, Florence?" asked Mrs. Lloyd.

"No, I certainly did not. And I have to say how disappointing this is. It seems terribly unfair. First there was that misleading phone call telling me to bring my entries on Saturday, and now both my cake and marmalade entries are missing. We moved heaven and earth to get them here on time, and they were officially entered. All present and correct. I must say, I'm not impressed by how this competition has been run. I wonder if anybody else has had entries go missing, or am I the only one? There's something very peculiar going on."

Mrs. Lloyd pulled the program book out of her handbag. "Don't you worry, Florence. I'll get to the bottom of this. Who are the judges this year?" she mused. "Might be worth our while to find out. The names will be listed in the program book. I've a good mind to launch a protest over your missing marmalade. And the cake," she added. She began flipping through the program book, but Florence gently closed it.

"No, Evelyn," said Florence. "You mustn't. Not now. I don't want any fuss. Please, just leave it."

"But something's not right," Mrs. Lloyd protested, gesturing at the jars. "Those leftover entry forms last night. They were in the name of Gaynor Lewis. So if she didn't get her entries in on time, how is it that her marmalade is on the table, winning first prize, and yours isn't? I'm going to be speaking to Joyce Devlin about this. There's something very irregular going on here, and I mean to find out how this happened."

"Why don't you let us look into that?" suggested Penny. "Victoria and I were responsible for checking in the entries, so if we were to ask why Gaynor Lewis's marmalade was admitted after the deadline, it might look more official. But we probably won't be able to do that until the show's over. The organizers will be too busy today. So Florence is right. Let's leave it for now. This isn't the right time."

Perhaps because both she and Florence were outsiders, Penny had felt an immediate connection to her. Penny had lived in Llanelen for almost thirty years, Florence for about three, but in many ways they were both still trying to prove that they belonged in the community. That they had earned their right to be there. Both contributed to Llanelen life, making it a better place. Penny, a gifted and skilled artist, often donated her watercolour paintings to charitable causes, and Florence happily catered local special events, such as the opening of a new exhibit at the museum, in addition to teaching a cooking class in the town hall to help young mothers learn how to stretch their food budgets.

Mrs. Lloyd mulled over the suggestion that Penny and Victoria should be the ones to raise the issue of Florence's missing entries. "You might be right," Mrs. Lloyd finally agreed. "Go on, then. And if we're not happy with what you find out, I will use my influence as a member of the show's organizing committee to demand an official inquiry. But one way or another, Joyce will be hearing about this; you can count on that."

Florence sighed, although it was difficult to tell if it was a sigh of resignation, disappointment, or a melancholy mixture of both.

"By the way," said Penny, "I was wondering what happens to all the jams and cakes at the end of the show. Are they donated to the nursing home, say, or some other worthy cause?"

"No," said Mrs. Lloyd. "The food products will remain on display until four-thirty today and then the owners can come and pick them up. If they want them. Anything unclaimed is discarded, because they've all been opened and sampled, although I suppose the person who does the clearing up could take anything left over. Food items can't be raffled or given away, because they were made in home kitchens and may not have been made or stored in accordance with food hygiene regulations."

"Well then," said Florence. "I'll collect my raspberry jam at the end of the day and that'll be the end of it."

"And you'll collect your certificate and rosette, too," said Mrs. Lloyd. "But that won't be the end of it. It'll be the start of it."

When they had finished looking at the food and floral exhibits, the little group wandered over to the other side of the marquee, which had been designated as the tea area. Although the area was pleasantly crowded, Florence and Mrs. Lloyd managed to find an empty table. Victoria joined them, but, after checking her watch, Penny remained standing.

"I've got to get ready for the judging of the children's pets," Penny said.

"There'll be a steward waiting for you at the ring," said Mrs. Lloyd, "and he'll have a box of rosettes and certificates you can use for prizes. First-place winners in each category get rosettes and the rest get consolation prizes."

"I hope I remember to say the right things," said Penny. "I thought of a few last night." She pulled a piece of paper out of her pocket. "Right, well, enjoy your coffee and cake or whatever you're having for your elevenses."

"Let's all meet up at the end of the day," said Victoria. "I'm probably going to go into work for a few hours, but I'll be back with the car later, when the parking situation eases up a bit, and I'll give you a lift home."

Penny strolled through the field, pausing to observe the judging of the horse classes, including the hardy, stocky Welsh mountain ponies and cobs, whose ancestors had worked down the slate mines, and the tall, noble shires with their feathery feet, who for centuries had ploughed fields and pulled heavy wagons.

After a few minutes, Penny tore herself away from the equine judging and walked on until she reached the enclosure where the children's pet competition was to be held. As Mrs. Lloyd had said, a steward was waiting for her, and he turned out to be none other than farmer Haydn Williams. The two greeted each other, and after Haydn had offered a few helpful tips on how she might carry out her role, she asked him to help her line up the dozen or so children with their pets.

She walked up and down the row, pausing to have a word with each child. Haydn had suggested she ask each one a question about the animal's health or how the child cared for the pet. She was touched by the earnest sincerity of their answers, their eagerness to please, and their obvious love for the animals they cradled in their arms or who stood patiently beside them.

"Now, then," she said, "who wants to win a rosette?" Her question was answered by cheers, waving hands, and enthusiastic grins. "Mr. Williams here"—she beckoned to Haydn—"is going to hold the basket for me, and if you win a prize, he'll check your name off on his list. Let's get started. First place in the friendliest-dog class goes to . . . Gypsy!" She pointed to a black cocker spaniel whose tail wagged vigorously and who strained at her lead to get to Penny. Penny laughed as she patted the little dog and handed a rosette to her young owner, whose endearing smile revealed two missing front teeth.

Penny moved down the line, awarding prizes, until she came to a girl wearing a pink net tutu and a glittery top. She held a Yorkshire terrier in her arms, dressed in the same pink net skirt and little top. "And you must be our two-of-a-kind entry," Penny said. "What are your names?"

"I'm Macy," the little girl said, and, indicating her dog, added, "and this is Tinker. Short for Tinker Bell."

"Well, I don't think we'll see any better than you today, so I'm giving you first prize in your class." She pinned a ribbon on the dog's dress and handed one to the girl, but as she started to move on to the next child, the girl burst into tears.

"What's the matter?" Penny asked, crouching to the child's eye level. As she did so, she caught a glimpse out of the corner of her eye of Gareth Davies leaning on the metal rail, watching her. She ignored him to focus on the girl. "Where's your mum? Is your mum or dad here with you?" The girl nodded and pointed to a woman with blond hair the same colour as the girl's who was standing with the parents ringing the enclosure. The woman waved, and the girl thrust her dog into Penny's arms and ran out of the enclosure and into her mother's arms. The child wrapped her arms around her mother's waist and buried her face in the warmth and security of the woman's jacket. Penny hesitated for a moment, then followed the girl, leaving Haydn in charge of the children in the competition.

"I'm not sure what happened," Penny said when she reached the mother, handing her the little dog. "Macy and Tinker won first prize in the two-of-a-kind competition, with their absolutely lovely outfits, but it seemed to upset her."

"Oh, she's just so happy that she won, aren't you, poppet?" the woman said, cradling her daughter's head.

The little girl looked up at her mother, her wide eyes threatening to release more tears. "No, Mummy, that's not why I'm crying. I wanted my *nain* here to see me. She promised me she'd be here, and she isn't . . ." The last sentence trailed off somewhere between a whine and a wail.

"Macy's *nain* made the costumes, and we thought she'd be here to support her in the competition," the woman explained. "We've looked everywhere but haven't seen her yet, have we? I tried ringing her, but she's not answering. We don't know where she is, but I expect she's on her way and she just got held up, that's all."

"Look," said Penny, taking a step backward and glancing at Haydn, who was doing his best to entertain the impatient children until Penny returned, "I've got to get back to the judging, but you're obviously concerned, so here's what I'd do if I were you. I'd have a word with that man over there." She gestured at Gareth. "He's a former police officer, senior rank, and he'll be able to provide some suggestions. I know him, and you might find talking to him reassuring. I shouldn't be too much longer, so if you want to wait, I can go with you when you speak to him. I'd be glad to do that."

"Thanks, but I really don't want to talk to the police, retired or not."

"Oh, I didn't mean any official involvement," Penny replied. "I just thought he could give you some advice."

"No." The woman shook her head. "Mum's probably just delayed somewhere. I'm sure she'll be along soon, with a perfectly reasonable explanation. She's likely in the grounds somewhere, having a natter with a friend, and she's forgotten all about the time. The show grounds are a big place, and she could be anywhere." The woman glanced down at her daughter's blond curls and gave them a reassuring stroke.

"It's all right, Macy love," she said. "You can tell your *nain* all about the show when we see her. We'll go round to hers later and she'll give you something nice for your tea, like she always does. How about that? Now, should we go see the chickens? See if your granddad's won a prize like you did?"

The little girl shook her head. "I want to watch the rest of the pet contest. Then we'll go see Granddad."

Five

When the last pup had been praised, and the last prize presented, Penny scanned the faces of the spectators who had gathered to watch the children's pet competition. At some point, unnoticed by her, Gareth Davies had slipped away. She wasn't surprised. There would have been plenty of demands on his time.

As Penny and Haydn led the young contestants through the opening in the metal enclosure and watched them reunite with their proud parents, Macy's mother approached, with Macy by her side.

The woman's face was set with tense anxiety. Acutely aware of Macy's presence, and not wanting to upset the child further, Penny did not ask if there was any news of Macy's grandmother.

"I'm Michelle Lewis," the woman said, her hands resting lightly on her daughter's shoulders, "and you know Macy."

"I certainly do." Penny smiled at the girl's upturned face. "Did you enjoy the rest of the pet show?"

The girl nodded. "My best friend won the ribbon for the cat the judge would most likely want to take home." Deep frown lines crossed her forehead and she looked up at Penny with intense blue eyes. "You're not going to, though, are you?"

Penny assured her the cat was quite safe and would be going home with its owner, and then she introduced herself to Michelle.

"Oh, I know who you are," said Michelle. "I've just started getting my hair cut at your salon."

Haydn, who had been standing beside Penny, nodded at Michelle and began to edge away. But before Penny could thank him for his help with the pet show, Michelle spoke, and Haydn remained where he was.

"I'm just going to pop round to Mum's," Michelle said, "just to check if she's . . ." She glanced at her daughter. "And I think it best if Macy stays here at the show, with her grandfather. To save me a bit of a time—well, quite a bit, actually, as it'll take me at least twenty minutes to walk over to the fur-and-feather area, drop her off, walk back, and get out of the car park. So I hope it's not too much to ask, but I wondered if you'd mind walking Macy over to her granddad. He'll be with the fur-and-feather people. Carwyn Lewis is his name."

"I know Carwyn," said Haydn. "I saw him about thirty minutes ago. I can take them over."

"Oh, I don't suppose you've seen my mother anywhere on the grounds this morning, have you?" Michelle asked him.

Haydn shook his head. "No, sorry, can't say as I have."

"Well, I'll be as quick as I can," Michelle said. "It's just that Mum might have fallen or something, so . . ."

"Of course," said Penny. "We'll deliver Macy safely to her granddad and she'll stay there until you get back, and you'll pick her up from her grandfather, will you? Is that the plan? Is that what I should tell him?"

Michelle nodded. "Yes, I should be back within the hour, but let me give you my number, just in case you need to reach me, and I'll ring Dad to let him know you're on your way."

"But your father . . ." said Penny after she'd added Michelle's number to her mobile phone contact list. "Perhaps he might know where your mother is?"

Michelle shook her head. "No, he won't know anything. They're separated." She kissed her daughter good-bye and then, after reassuring the little girl that she wouldn't be gone any time at all and would be back before she knew it, Michelle handed the Yorkshire terrier to Penny.

After taking a few steps, Michelle turned around, gave her daughter a reassuring wave, then set off at a brisk pace for the car park. A moment later, she broke into a gentle run.

"Right, then, Macy, let's get you over to your granddad, shall we?" said Penny. "Does your dog like to walk, or should I carry him? And why don't you tell me a little more about his name. I've been wondering this whole time why he's called Tinker Bell."

Macy laughed. "He's not a boy; he's a girl."

With Macy chatting happily between Penny and Haydn, and showing them things of interest along the way, the three walked through the crowded show grounds. They strolled past several canopies where various products, ranging from pet treats to dog-grooming services, were being promoted. The last canopy was the mobile office of Jones the Vet, available in case of injury to any of the animals. Just beyond that, they reached a larger canopy that sheltered hundreds of cages from the sun.

"Here we are," announced Haydn. "Fur and feather." Members of the fur category, including rabbits, gerbils, hamsters, and ferrets, peered out from behind the tiny bars of cages of various sizes, some made of wood, most of metal, and a few, stylish and rustic, fashioned by hand in dark brown wicker. On the other side of the canopied area, facing the fur group, was the feather contingent: pigeons, ducks, geese, chickens, mourning doves, and turkeys. Smaller birds were caged; the larger ones were penned. Fresh bedding in the bottoms of the cages absorbed droppings, and despite the warmth of the space, there was no unpleasant odour. There was, however, plenty of avian noise, as the birds honked, clucked, cooed, and called to one another.

Judges, wearing distinctive armbands to identify them, moved from cage to cage at a measured pace, making notes on clipboards, occasionally pointing to an especially good-looking creature and asking the owner to remove it from its cage so they could examine it more closely.

"*Taid!*" Macy called out, breaking free from Penny and running toward an exhibitor who stood in the rear of the space, hands clasped behind his back, while he waited for the judges to reach him. At the sound of her voice, he turned, and his eyes lit up as a generous grin and a look of undisguised joy spread across his face. He crouched slightly to bring himself down to the girl's level, his arms outstretched, as she ran to him.

"I guess we delivered her to the right person," Penny remarked with a sideways glance at Haydn.

"That's Carwyn Lewis all right."

With Macy safely in the care of her grandfather, Penny and Haydn slowed down to examine the many breeds of birds entered in the competition. Stately, elegant chickens, tall and thin, contrasted with others that were short and plump. They all came in rich colours, some with feathers speckled in cream and brown, others the glossiest of blacks. Hens looked back at them with bright yellow eyes; roosters with extravagant tail feathers, proud of their plumage, took no notice of them.

Haydn and Penny walked on.

"I didn't realize geese were so big," said Penny as they paused in front of several white birds with bright orange beaks in a metal pen. One goose, apparently in a bad mood and tired of being looked at and talked about, hissed and rushed toward her, flapping its wings.

When they reached Carwyn Lewis, he extended his hand to Haydn. "Hello, Haydn." After returning his greeting, Haydn introduced Penny. Carwyn's eyes were the same unusually deep blue as Macy's, and they crinkled at the corners when he smiled at her. His teeth were white and even. Penny estimated him to be in his late forties, possibly early fifties, but he looked trim and he was better dressed than most of the other exhibitors. His beige trousers fit well, and his blue shirt was clean and pressed.

"*Taid*'s not wearing his vest," said Macy. "It's dark green, and it's got buttons and pins on it, and he wears it when he looks after the chickens, but not today."

"Well, I had it on earlier, when I first arrived, but I took it off because it's so warm in here, I don't need it." He smiled at her. But Macy had already lost interest in the vest and wandered over to peer at the chickens.

"Can I show Penny our chickens?" Macy asked her grandfather. Without waiting for an answer, she grasped Penny's hand and pulled her closer to the cages, explaining as she pointed with her other hand, "Here they are. They're called Silkies, and my granddad's ever so proud of them." Penny admired the striking-looking birds; with their furlike white feathers and such fluffy crests on their heads, they looked as if they were wearing adorable little caps.

"They're so soft," said Macy. "I love holding them." She pointed to the bottom of their cage, where a few feathers had fallen. "Sometimes *Taid* gives me the feathers and I put them in my dolls' hats."

"Oh, they're very glamorous birds," Penny said. "They look as if they're all dressed for the red carpet."

Haydn touched Penny gently on the arm. "The judges are coming. We'd best leave Carwyn to it. He'll want a few minutes to prepare himself, without us as a distraction."

"Of course," replied Penny, and after a hurried good-bye to Carwyn, Macy, and her little terrier, they walked to the other side of the exhibit and admired a pen full of brown-and-white lop-eared rabbits.

"Michelle mentioned that her parents are separated," Penny said casually, with a quick glance over her shoulder at Carwyn and Macy. "Do you know if Carwyn's"—she groped for the right words—"seeing anyone?" From the crisp crease in the sleeves of his shirt, unless he was fond of ironing—and to be fair, some men enjoyed it and were good at it—she thought it likely that there was a woman in his life. He had that well-cared-for look about him that suggested he wasn't on his own. The exact opposite of bachelor Haydn, actually, whose clothes were always rumpled and mismatched.

Haydn looked blank, and Penny remembered from a previous time, when he'd been fond of a woman but helpless to do anything about it, that he was a little on the naïve side when it came to relationships and women. No matter. Mrs. Lloyd would probably know all about Carwyn Lewis's personal life.

"I really would have liked to ask him if he knew anything about his ex-wife's whereabouts," Penny said, "but it wouldn't have been right to say anything about that in front of Macy. I'm not good at guessing children's ages, but she's only what, six or seven? You don't want to upset her, and besides, she shouldn't be involved in such a grown-up problem as her grandmother going missing."

"Why would you want to ask Carwyn about that?"

"Well, I'm concerned about her, and just curious, I guess."

"Never mind. We don't know that she's missing. Maybe there'll be news of her when Michelle returns."

"Maybe."

They reached the area that led to the judging rings, and Haydn joined the crowd heading to see the horses. Penny checked her watch. Almost lunchtime. She rang Victoria, who had taken the shuttle bus back to town and returned to work at the Spa. Penny decided that she, too, would go into work for the afternoon. She hoped to bump into Michelle Lewis as she left the show grounds, but when she didn't, she decided to return at the end of the day, in case there was news about Michelle's missing mother.

Six

"Well, Florence," said Mrs. Lloyd at the end of the afternoon, "that's another show almost over, and I don't know about you, but my arches are killing me. It's been a long day and I could do with a sit down, so I suggest we make our way to the tea tent for a little refreshment. It's almost time to pick up your jam, and once we've done that, hopefully Victoria will be here to give us a lift home. We've seen everything there is to see and done everything there is to do. When you've seen one sheep, you've seen them all."

"I wouldn't say that," Florence replied. "There were several really nice varieties I'd never even heard of, and I thought they were all lovely, especially the ones with the black faces."

"Well, yes, they are nice, but when you've lived in Llanelen all your life, as I have, you've seen your fair share of sheep.

Lovely as they are, black faces and all, and much as I do like them."

"I wonder how Penny got on with the prize giving this morning," Florence remarked. "She seemed a bit wound up about it. I thought we would have bumped into her at some point."

"Oh, she'll have been fine. How hard can it be to hand out prizes for cuddly rabbits and friendly dogs? And I doubt Penny was here all day. Victoria said she was going to slip back to the Spa and work for the afternoon, and I expect Penny joined her. There wasn't all that much here to keep them entertained all day, and besides, they've got a business to run."

Mrs. Lloyd checked her watch as she and Florence approached the marquee.

"Now that most of the prizes have been handed out, folk are starting to leave. It's almost four-thirty, so the women who want to pick up their jams and cakes will be along any minute. The farmers will be packing up soon, too, and that'll be it for another year. So much planning and work goes into the show, and then it's all over in one day."

They entered the marquee, to find just two tables in the tea area occupied. When they were seated, a middle-aged woman wearing a flowered apron offered them a choice of fruitcake or a slice of lemon drizzle cake with a cup of tea or coffee.

"Oh, lemon drizzle for me," said Mrs. Lloyd. "Just the thing. How about you, Florence?"

"I'd like the fruitcake, please. With a cup of tea."

The server disappeared and then a few minutes later set

down a slice of fruitcake in front of each woman, along with a cup of tepid tea in a disposable cup.

"Sorry," she said. "The lemon drizzle's off. That's all that's left. No charge." She retreated to the serving area as Mrs. Lloyd looked sadly at the fruitcake, took a sip of tea, and made a little *blech* sound. She started to turn in her seat to see where the server had gone, but Florence put a restraining hand on her arm.

"You can't complain, Evelyn," she said evenly. "It's the end of the day and they're giving away everything that's left because no one wants to take it home. You're not paying for this. If you don't like it, just leave it." Mrs. Lloyd folded her arms, saying nothing, just as Penny entered the tent. Catching sight of Mrs. Lloyd and Florence, she headed over to their table and took a chair facing Mrs. Lloyd.

"Hello, Penny," Florence said. "We'd hoped to see you after the pet show to find out how it went."

"Oh, I left shortly afterward and managed to put in a few hours at work. Saturdays are our busiest day at the Spa, as you can imagine."

"What did I tell you?" Mrs. Lloyd said to Florence, then turned her attention back to Penny. "So, on your way home, are you?"

Penny nodded. "Since I walk right past, I thought I'd pop in and see if you were still here."

"Only for a few more minutes, probably," said Mrs. Lloyd. "We're just waiting to collect Florence's jam. But tell me, how did you get on with the judging of the children's pets? Any problems? Tantrums or the like?"

"All right, I guess," said Penny. "I made up silly categories as I went along, and the children and their parents seemed happy enough. Except for one little girl." She described the winner of the two-of-a-kind class in floods of tears because her grandmother wasn't there to see her and the little Yorkshire terrier dressed in the matching pink tutu netting with sparkles.

"Oh, that sounds adorable," said Florence.

"It does," agreed Mrs. Lloyd. "And what is this little girl's name?"

"Macy she's called."

"Macy," repeated Mrs. Lloyd. "That's not a common name around here. The only Macy I know is Gaynor Lewis's granddaughter."

"That's the one," said Penny. "Gaynor Lewis's daughter was very concerned about her mother. Hadn't heard from her all day. Not answering her phone. So after the children's pet competition, Michelle—that's Gaynor's daughter—decided to pop round to her mum's house to check on her. She asked Haydn Williams and me to walk little Macy over to her grandfather at the fur-and-feather area, and after we'd done that, I went to work. I haven't heard anything more. That's really the reason I dropped in. To see if there was any news. I hope nothing untoward has happened to her."

"Well, that *is* interesting," said Mrs. Lloyd. "Now that you mention it, I didn't see Gaynor today, and that's very strange. A regular fixture here at the show, Gaynor is, checking out how all her Women's Guild friends did in all their classes, but most especially, she's concerned about how her own entries placed. And somehow she managed to win first place in the marmalade competition, although I still think Florence's was better."

Florence leaned forward as if to say something, but before she could speak, a group of chattering women burst into the tent, carrier bags draped over their arms, or carrying small boxes. They headed for the home-craft and floral tables, and as some women congratulated the winners, who graciously wished their rivals better luck next year, they swooped down on the displays like scavenging birds of prey. In moments they'd picked the tables almost clean, gathering up their entries and bagging or boxing them for the journey home. Their entries collected, they departed quickly.

When they had left, Mrs. Lloyd rose from her seat and, followed by Florence, with Penny at her side, the three trooped over to the display tables. Florence picked up her jar of raspberry jam and its first-place certificate and tucked them in her handbag. They scanned the few remaining entries. Gaynor's first-place marmalade had not been claimed.

"Oh for heaven's sake!" exclaimed Mrs. Lloyd, cross and upset all over again. "First your cake—which we took great pains to deliver on time—apparently doesn't make it into the competition and neither does your marmalade. And now Gaynor Lewis can't be bothered to claim her so-called winning entry with its unequal distribution of fruit. What on earth is going on?"

"I hope you're not going to kick off, Evelyn," said Florence. "We agreed earlier that we'd leave it for now. Let's give Penny and Victoria a chance to find out what happened to my cake and marmalade."

"Well, I hope they get some answers soon," bristled Mrs. Lloyd.

As she finished speaking, Joyce Devlin's black Labrador, Billie, bounded into the tent, followed by Joyce herself, with

Barbara, the woman who'd been assisting her the evening before, trailing along behind, clutching her clipboard to her chest. Mrs. Lloyd nodded a vague greeting in their direction and then commented to Florence, "Well, here comes Joyce, probably making her final rounds, so I guess you could say the fair's officially over. And I'm sorry, Florence, I know I said I'd let it be, but I really must have a word with her about your missing cake and marmalade. And now's as good a time as any."

Florence laid an imploring hand on her friend's arm. "Oh, please don't. This just isn't the time. We agreed that Penny and Victoria would look into it." Mrs. Lloyd, now bent on her mission, lightly shook off Florence's hand. Bustling toward the new arrivals, she called out, "Joyce! I need a word with you."

Florence sighed. "When she gets a bee in her bonnet, there's just no holding her back. I know she means well, but honestly, I wish she'd just leave it. Joyce'll have had a long, stressful day and this just isn't the right time."

While Joyce and her companion turned their attention to Mrs. Lloyd, Billie made her getaway and struck out across the marquee to the area where the tea had been served. Nose to the ground and tail wagging, she took careful stock of the area, and finding nothing edible of interest, she veered back toward the display tables. The dog hesitated in front of the table where the jams, marmalades, and chutneys had been displayed, ignored what remained on the flower tables, and stopped in front of the crumbs of the cakes, pies, breads, and biscuits just as Mrs. Lloyd and Joyce wrapped up their conversation. Joyce and her assistant set off for the tea area.

Mrs. Lloyd glared after them, let out a frustrated sigh, and rejoined Florence and Penny.

"It didn't go well, I take it," said Penny. "What did Joyce say?"

"She said she's too busy right now to even think about it, and that if we want to lodge a protest, we can." Mrs. Lloyd made a little noise that signalled her exasperation. "She's not telling me anything I didn't already know, and besides, a right lot of good a protest would do. Florence already came in first with her jam, and her cake and marmalade never made it into the competition, so what's to protest? The protest rules cover if you disagree with a judging result, but how can we do that when two of Florence's entries weren't judged? They weren't *there* to be judged. I'm certainly going to bring this up at the next committee meeting. What's needed is a proper investigation and perhaps an overhaul of how items are accepted for entry." She turned her full attention to Florence. "Seems to me someone's got it in for you."

Penny thought back to the snatch of conversation carried on the evening breeze the previous night when she'd returned to the marquee looking for her program booklet. "I don't care who wins as long as it's not her," the woman had said. As long as *who* didn't win? Had she been referring to Florence? With two of Florence's entries somehow missing, that seemed possible. And if she had meant Florence, who didn't want her to win, and why not? Although Florence was a relative newcomer to Llanelen, she had a growing reputation for her baking and catering skills. The refreshments she'd provided for a recent exhibit opening at the museum had garnered high praise from the mayor herself. It was certainly possible that someone with much deeper roots in the community than Florence, used to winning rosettes year after year, and feeling she deserved to win, did not welcome this threat to her dominance of a specific category.

Penny wished she'd recognized the voices. People always describe small towns as being places where "everybody knows everybody," but Llanelen had a population of more than three thousand, and nobody could possibly know everyone.

"Well, I think you've done all you can for today, and then some," Florence said to Mrs. Lloyd. "Please, let's leave it for now. We're all tired and it's time we were off home. We can think about this later. I'll just check the table where we had our tea to make sure we've got all our bits and pieces, and then as soon as Victoria gets here, we can be on our way."

"I suppose you're right." Mrs. Lloyd gave in, adding, "I'll wait here for you." As Florence returned to the tea area, Mrs. Lloyd and Penny idly perused the baked goods table, where only a few plates remained unclaimed.

Something brushed against Penny's leg and she looked down and saw Billie tucking her nose under the white tablecloth and the front half of her sleek black body disappearing under the table. "Off, Billie!" Joyce's voice boomed across the tent from the tea-service area, where she was speaking to the woman loading the last of the cups and saucers into the caterer's red plastic boxes. "Leave it! Come here!" In response to her voice, Billie's tail began wagging and she backed out from under the table, leaving the tablecloth swaying gently behind her. Licking her lips, she charged past Penny, a white blob clinging to the top of her black nose. Curious, Penny raised the tablecloth and, lowering her head, peered under the table. Then, she lifted the cloth higher and steadying herself with one hand on the table, sank to her knees.

"I think we've found Florence's carrot cake," she said, looking over her shoulder at Mrs. Lloyd. "And that's not all."

Seven

As Mrs. Lloyd instinctively took a step closer to the table, Penny rose to her feet and held up a warning hand. "Best stay where you are, although there's been so much foot traffic through and around here today, I suppose it really won't matter. Still, for the sake of appearances, don't come any closer."

"But what is it?" demanded Mrs. Lloyd, her wide blue eyes expressing concern and puzzlement in equal measure. "What have you found?"

"Let's go and sit down," Penny said, steering a protesting Mrs. Lloyd in the direction of the empty tables in the refreshment area. They reached a table and Penny pulled out a chair for Mrs. Lloyd. Florence joined them and Penny gestured to the chair beside Mrs. Lloyd, indicating that Florence should sit with her. When the two bewildered women were seated, Penny stepped away and placed a call on her mobile. When she had finished, she rejoined Florence and Mrs. Lloyd, sinking into a chair and resting her chin on her hands.

"What is it?" Mrs. Lloyd asked again, a small tremor in her voice. "Will you please tell us what's going on?"

Penny's mind raced over what she had just seen, trying to find the right words to describe it. Should she mention the blue-veined dead hand, with a gold wedding ring, resting lightly on top of a smashed cake, its white icing smeared with splotches of orange and green that had once been decorative carrots? And what about the ashen, blood-drained face with the parted lips and staring, sightless eyes?

"There's no way to soften this, so I'm just going to tell you," Penny said. "It's a body. A woman's body. I didn't recognize her. I don't know who she is. I just rang Gareth, and he's on his way here now to take charge."

"A body!" Mrs. Lloyd gasped. "Here, in the marquee? Are you saying there's a dead body under the cakes and biscuits table? Oh my Lord. How long has it been there?"

"Since people have been coming in and out all day, it was probably placed there sometime after we left last night and before the tent opened for the judging this morning," said Penny. "I can't see anyone being able to put something like that under the table while the show was going on, can you? I mean, think about it."

"No, I suppose not," said Mrs. Lloyd. "I wonder who it is, though." She mulled that over. "Could be one of the judges, I suppose. There's a lot of rivalry that goes on behind the scenes, I understand, and some of the judges aren't too popular with the losers." She glanced at Florence and then

64

let out a little gasp. "What about the authorities! We've been serving food in this marquee all day, and just over there"—she tipped her head in the direction of the table that hid the body—"well, I mean there must be a food hygiene regulation against that sort of thing. You know what those health and safety people are like. Oh, when word of this gets out, we could be in big trouble."

"I don't think the show committee will be in any kind of trouble for violation of health and safety standards," said Florence. "It's an unsavoury thought, yes, but no one was to know."

"Well, someone knew!" retorted Mrs. Lloyd. "Whoever left that body there knew. And they must have known it would be found at the end of the day, when everything was taken down." She made a little *tsk*ing noise. "Disgusting, that, really, when you think about it. Leaving a body for some other poor soul to find. It was a good thing Penny here was the one to find it. It's not the first body she's found. But it could have been found by someone of a more nervous disposition, someone like . . ."

"You?" suggested Florence.

As they were speaking, Penny's eyes followed Joyce Devlin, who had emerged from a blocked-off area at the rear of the marquee and, with Billie at her heels and Barbara by her side, was heading toward the exit. Penny stood up.

"Oh Lord. Now what?" Mrs. Lloyd asked.

"They're leaving." Penny sighed and sat down. "I was about to suggest that they stay, because I'm sure Gareth will want to speak to them, but then I thought I don't really have the authority to ask them to do anything. If the police want to talk to them, and I'm sure they will, they'll find them."

The issue was resolved when Gareth Davies entered the tent just as Joyce approached the exit. Tall, with an air of calm authority about him that inspired trust, he spoke to her for a few moments. She looked at her watch and then raised an arm in a wild gesture.

"She doesn't have time for this," muttered Florence, interpreting the body language of the unfolding scenario. "She's a busy woman. The show's closing and, body or no body, she's got things to attend to."

A moment later, Florence's take on the situation was revealed to be correct. Gareth stood to one side, making room for Joyce, her companion, and her dog to leave.

"He's not a police officer anymore," commented Penny. "He can't actually force them to stay. If Joyce wants to leave, she's perfectly free to do so. Although I wonder what he said to her. If he told her that a body had been discovered, wouldn't you think she'd want to stick around and find out more? Seems like a very odd reaction."

"And that woman with her," commented Mrs. Lloyd. "Barbara. She's such a little mouse, you hardly take any notice of her."

Gareth paused for a moment, as if gathering himself together, and then made his way to the table where the women were seated. He greeted each one by name, then pulled out a chair and sat down. "So," he said to Penny, "the police are on their way. Tell me how you happened to find the body."

"It's under the table," she replied, pointing. "Over there. Joyce's black Lab, Billie, was sniffing around under the table and came out with cake icing on her nose. You know what

Labs are like. Always looking for crumbs and things to eat. So I thought in case she got into something that could hurt her—chocolate, maybe—I'd better see what she was up to, and when I lifted up the tablecloth, that's when I saw it. A woman's body."

"Not to mention Florence's carrot cake is there, too," said Mrs. Lloyd, her voice prickling with indignation. "All the trouble she went to, and her cake didn't even make it into the judging. And now we know why."

"We do?" asked Florence.

Mrs. Lloyd turned to her. "Well, we don't really know how it got there, but at least we know where it is. That's a start, I suppose."

"Well, the cake definitely helps us with the 'When?' question," said Penny. "You brought the cake here last night at eight o'clock and it was on the table when we left last night, about eight-fifteen. And it must have been under the table, along with the body, when the judges arrived this morning."

"That would make sense," said Gareth. He then asked Penny if she'd been able to get a look at the person's face and, if so, whether she'd recognized it.

"No, I didn't recognize the person, but it's a woman, and I have an idea who it might be." He waited, tracing tiny circles on the white tablecloth with his index finger. "While I was judging the children's pets entries, one little girl became upset that her grandmother wasn't there. I spoke to the child's mother, and she said that they hadn't been able to get in touch with her mother—that's the child's grandmother—and I suggested she speak to you. I pointed you out to her." She frowned. "Did she speak to you?"

It was Gareth's turn to frown. "No, she didn't."

"Well, I'm not surprised. She said she didn't want to get the police involved, even a retired officer."

"And what's her name?"

"The woman I spoke to?" Gareth nodded. "The little girl's mother is called Michelle Lewis, but her mother—the one she was concerned hadn't turned up—is called Gaynor Lewis. So it could be her. She's the president of the WG."

"The WG. Oh, right. The Women's Guild. My grandmother belonged to that. It's been around for a long time."

Gareth patted the pockets of his jacket and Florence, sensing what he was looking for, pulled her little notebook out of her handbag, wrote down the name *Gaynor Lewis,* tore out the page, and handed it to him with a tight-lipped smile.

"To save you some time," said Penny, opening up the contact list in her mobile, "here's Michelle Lewis's phone number." She held out her phone, and Gareth copied down the number. "And there's something else," Penny continued. "I don't know if this is important or not, but Gaynor's marmalade wasn't officially entered in the competition by the time entries closed at eight P.M."

"And yet it won first place!" exclaimed Mrs. Lloyd. "And Florence's marmalade, which *was* entered on time, is nowhere to be found. How can that be? Believe me, I intend to get to the bottom of that."

"Erm, well." Gareth frowned slightly and rubbed his chin. "I'm not sure I quite grasp the significance of the marmalade, but the police will be here in a minute, so . . ." His voice trailed off as he folded his hands and rested them on the table, his arms outstretched. The little group sat in silence.

Penny looked more closely at him, as if she were seeing him for the first time in a long while. There was something different about him, but at first she couldn't place it. And then she realized he was wearing new glasses and had a slightly different haircut. He exuded that same cared-for look that she'd recognized earlier in Carwyn Lewis. Gareth was spoken for, Penny realized. She knew he'd been seeing a woman from Edinburgh, but she hadn't realized the relationship had reached the point where his new flame was sprucing him up.

How different our lives are now, she thought. A year ago, Gareth would have been the lead detective on this case, and I would have been eagerly offering suggestions and helping in any way I could, whether he wanted that help or not. And now he's sitting here in a marquee at the end of the day, waiting for the police to arrive. She wondered how he felt about that.

The arrival of Victoria, accompanied by her friend Heather Hughes, the area's most celebrated gardener, interrupted her thoughts. Before Gareth could prevent them from approaching the display tables, Heather and Victoria scooped up all Heather's award-winning floral entries and carried them to the table where Penny and her companions were seated.

"I wondered if you'd like to take these home with you," Heather said to Mrs. Lloyd. "They're a little past their best, having sat in the tent all day, but there might be a day or two left in them."

"Well, that's very thoughtful of you, but—" Mrs. Lloyd began.

"Lovely. We'd be delighted to have them. Thank you," Florence interjected, reaching for the flowers.

"Well, good," said Heather. She paused, taking in their

serious, unsmiling faces before adding awkwardly, "I'll be off, then. See you all at the dinner next week, I hope." The group at the table murmured polite good-byes as Heather walked away. She stopped for a moment about halfway to the exit and looked back at them.

"What's happened?" Victoria asked with a puzzled look. "You're all looking very glum." She fixed her eyes on Penny, who shook her head slightly, then settled them on Gareth. "Something's happened. I can tell. And we noticed a couple of police cars driving up the road, so please tell me what's going on."

"I'll leave Penny to tell you," he replied. "If the police are here, I'd better go and meet them." He stood up, then said to the group, "Best if you go home now. The patholo-gist is probably on his way, and the marquee's going to be cordoned off. The police will need to take statements from everybody, but that can wait. They know where to find you. And anyway, they'll want to talk to you separately."

"What happened?" Victoria repeated, her voice rising with impatience. "What is it?"

"Come on," said Penny. "We'll tell you all about it on the way home." She picked up a single white rose in its simple bud vase and handed it to Florence. Mrs. Lloyd cradled a large bouquet of mixed flowers in her arms, Victoria grabbed a couple of potted plants, and Penny took a spray of red and pink roses. As the four of them walked to the exit, their arms filled with flowers, a uniformed police officer entered the tent and held the flap open for a woman in her mid-thirties, dressed in a smart navy blue pantsuit.

"Hello, Penny," said Inspector Bethan Morgan, adding

with an air of mild resignation tempered by affection, "Now why do you suppose I just knew I'd find you here?"

"Sorry. I guess I just have a knack for being in the wrong place at the wrong time."

"Oh no," gasped Victoria. "You haven't! You've only gone and found a body."

Eight

"And so you see, it was actually Joyce Devlin's Labrador, Billie, who found the body," Penny concluded as Victoria slowed her car to a stop in front of Mrs. Lloyd's house on Rosemary Lane. "I just happened to be there."

"And not only that, but Billie found Florence's missing carrot cake," added Mrs. Lloyd.

Victoria switched off the car's engine, and before anyone could move, Florence spoke. "It's been a long, eventful day, and I know we're all tired, but it would mean a lot to us if both of you would join us for a drink or a cup of tea. You don't have to stay long, but when something awful happens, you just feel you need to talk it over, don't you? We'd rather not be on our own at the minute."

Not keen on the idea of being on her own, either, with no one but Harrison, her handsome grey cat, for company,

Penny readily agreed, and Victoria did, too. They all piled out of the car and, arms once again laden with Heather's flower arrangements, made their way up the path. Florence unlocked the door and led the way inside.

"Go through," Florence instructed, gesturing toward the sitting room. "I'll just take the flowers to the kitchen and see to them. Won't be a minute."

As Penny and Victoria sank into the comfortable sofa, Mrs. Lloyd adjusted the curtains, then asked Penny and Victoria what they'd like to drink. "Florence will no doubt prepare tea, but if you'd like a glass of wine or sherry, you may certainly have one."

"Tea will suit me just fine, thanks," said Victoria. "I'm trying not to have any alcohol at all in my system now when I drive."

"What about you, Penny?" asked Mrs. Lloyd.

"I'd love a glass of white wine, please."

Mrs. Lloyd left the room, then returned with a glass of chilled white wine, which she handed to Penny. She lifted the lid off the glass sherry decanter, poured herself a drink, and everyone sat down. By unspoken agreement, no one said anything while Florence remained out of the room. Penny took a sip of wine while Mrs. Lloyd sat poised on her chair, holding her sherry glass by the stem. Every few minutes her eyes wandered in the direction of the doorway, where Florence finally appeared, carrying a tea tray.

"As we haven't had supper yet, I cut a few sandwiches, and there're scones I made yesterday," she said, setting the tray on the table. Florence poured a cup of tea, handed it to Victoria, and then held out the plate of sandwiches.

When everyone had helped themselves to a salmon-and-cucumber sandwich, expertly cut into neat quarters, Mrs. Lloyd took an appreciative sip of her sherry. She licked her top lip, leaned forward, and said, "Now then, Penny, what about this body? You think it might be Gaynor Lewis?"

"Yes, I think it very well could be," said Penny. "We know Gaynor wasn't at the show, which you said wasn't like her. And if it does turn out to be her, what do you know about her, Mrs. Lloyd?"

"She's the president of the Women's Guild, as I think I mentioned earlier, and she likes all the homemaking arts, like sewing and baking and cooking. She used to live with her husband, Carwyn, on a farm not too far from Haydn Williams's. He still lives there, Carwyn does, and raises fancy chickens. Hens. Every now and then, we get eggs from him."

"Lovely, those eggs are," added Florence.

"Yes, I met him and his chickens this morning," said Penny. "He seemed rather charming."

"Anyway, they separated years ago, Gaynor and Carwyn. I don't know if they ever got properly divorced. The breakup wasn't amicable, by all accounts. There were rumours that he was seeing someone else, and sure enough, it wasn't long after Gaynor moved out that his new lady friend moved in."

Ah, thought Penny. The other woman. So there is someone.

"And is he still with this woman?" Penny asked.

"As far as I know." And then, anticipating Penny's next question, Mrs. Lloyd added, "Elin Spears is her name."

"Elin Spears," repeated Victoria. "I just heard that name somewhere recently, but I can't place it."

"She won the grand prize at the show for her cake," Florence reminded everyone.

"Oh, right," said Victoria.

"The thing is," continued Mrs. Lloyd, "I don't really know much more than what I've just told you about Gaynor. Our paths rarely crossed, so I just know what I heard through the grapevine. Of course people talked about the marriage breakup at the time, but I haven't heard that much about her since."

Penny smiled. The grapevine, she thought. Well, that's one way to describe it. Mrs. Lloyd had an insatiable appetite for what many people would call gossip. "If you want to know more about Gaynor Lewis, the person you should be speaking to is her sister-in-law, Joyce Devlin. Although, you might take what she says with a grain of salt. The two positively loathe each other, or so I've been told, so whatever she tells you is bound to be biased."

"Yes," said Penny, "I remember you mentioned that last night. Sister-in-law. So Gaynor is married to . . ."

"No, it's the other way around. Joyce is married to Gaynor's older brother, Daffydd Devlin. Are you with me?"

"I think so. Joyce Devlin is married to Gaynor Lewis's older brother."

"That's right," said Mrs. Lloyd.

"And why don't they like each other?" Victoria asked.

"I'm not sure. If I ever did know the reason, I've forgotten it. As long as I've known them, they've been on poor terms. Barely on speaking terms, really. Avoid each other as much as they can, but of course living fairly close, they can't help running into each other now and then."

"Christmas must be a barrel of laughs in that family," remarked Victoria.

"Quite often whatever it is that starts off a row in a family is something small and trivial," mused Florence. "I know of two sisters who didn't speak for years because of an argument over a Bath bun. One sister grabbed the last one, the other wanted it, and all hell broke loose. It ended with one sister throwing the bun at the other, and neither got to eat it. Of course it wasn't the bun they were fighting over; the bun just represented some long-standing issue that had never been resolved. And sometimes these rows go on for so long that nobody can even remember what started it."

Mrs. Lloyd gave her a sharp look. "My, Florence, listen to you. Aren't you the family counsellor."

Florence shrugged off the comment and calmly sipped her tea, while Penny and Victoria exchanged amused looks.

"But Mrs. Lloyd, when you say Joyce and Gaynor avoid each other, they must have to work together on the agricultural show, if Joyce is the president of the show committee and Gaynor is president of the Women's Guild. I know the Guild isn't directly involved in the running of the show, but there seems to be a fairly heavy WG involvement in it."

"Not really. Certainly not officially. A lot of WG members enter their baking and jams in the home-craft classes, because there's no other real competition around here for that sort of thing, but that's it. They enter the competitions and that's all."

Penny contemplated Florence, who was buttering half of a light, flaky scone before slathering it with some of her homemade raspberry jam.

"Are you a member of the WG, Florence?" Penny asked.

Florence looked up from her task, knife poised. "Me? Good heavens, no."

"Have you ever thought about joining? I'd have thought with your domestic skills, they'd be lucky to have you."

Mrs. Lloyd's eyes narrowed slightly, and as Florence caught a glimpse of her, a sly smile formed at the corners of her lips. Before she could reply to Penny's question, though, a pinging in Penny's pocket indicated an incoming text. She pulled it out, glanced at it, and then said, "It's Gareth. Maybe he's got news."

"You'd better read it to us, then," said Mrs. Lloyd eagerly.

Penny's eyes flickered over the small screen. "He says the body has been identified and it is indeed Gaynor Lewis's."

They reflected on this, and then Mrs. Lloyd said, "Well, we're not surprised. We'd got that far ourselves. We were almost sure that's who it was, weren't we?"

Penny nodded. "He says she was stabbed with a long blade."

"A long blade," mused Victoria. "What's that supposed to mean?"

"I think that refers to something like a bread knife," said Florence, holding her hands about a foot apart, "compared to, say"—she brought her hands close together—"a paring knife, which I guess would be considered a short blade. At least that's how I would interpret it."

"Yes, that makes sense," said Penny, leaning forward as she placed her empty glass on the coffee table. She caught Victoria's eye and added, "Well, as Florence said, it's been a long, eventful day, and it certainly didn't end the way we expected it to. But it's time Victoria and I were on our way, so we'll leave you to your supper."

"We're just going to have a bit of cold ham and salad,"

78

said Florence. "There's plenty, and you'd be more than welcome to stay and share it with it us."

"Yes," said Mrs. Lloyd enthusiastically, "indeed you would."

"That's a kind invitation, and another time I'd love to," said Penny, "but I really must get home to feed Harrison. When I'm late with his dinner, I hear about it."

"Of course," said Florence. "When you don't have a pet, you don't think about things like that.

"What you were saying before," said Florence as they all got to their feet, "about the Women's Guild. Besides the jam, which they made to help with the food supplies during the war, I'm not sure exactly what the WG does nowadays. I was thinking when I saw all the wonderful baked goods and preserves at the show that I might like to attend a WG meeting, just to learn a little more about it."

"I think that would be an excellent idea," said Penny. "I'd go myself, but I have to work, so perhaps you could let me know what you find out." She placed a slight emphasis on the last four words, and Florence gave a slight nod.

"I'll go, too," said Mrs. Lloyd. "I used to belong to the WG—although many years ago that was—and for some reason I stopped going. Can't think why now."

As Penny and Victoria were leaving, Florence ducked into the kitchen and returned with a jar in each hand. She held up a jar of marmalade in her right hand, and in her left, a jar of raspberry.

"You choose," she said to her delighted guests. After a quick, consolidating glance at each other, Penny reached for the jam and Victoria went home happy with the marmalade.

When their guests had left, Florence set about preparing supper while Mrs. Lloyd watched the evening news on television.

Over their evening meal, Florence and Mrs. Lloyd discussed the events of the day until they'd squeezed the topic dry and had reached no conclusions.

"We must have Penny and Victoria over for supper one of these evenings," said Mrs. Lloyd. "That would be fun."

"I agree," said Florence. "I'd like that." She passed Mrs. Lloyd the basket of bread rolls. "You know, Evelyn, what Penny said about having to get home to feed her cat got me thinking. I've never had a pet. Never been in a position where I could keep one, but now I'd rather like to have a cat myself. What do you think?"

"Well, we could get a cat, I suppose. After all, the prime minister has one. But it would have to be the right kind of cat, mind. Not some awful creature keeping me awake all night with its yowling because it wants to go outside. Or the kind that sharpens its claws on the furniture and hangs off the curtains."

"No, of course we wouldn't want a cat like that. We'll find a nice genteel cat. A well-behaved kind of cat. I believe Penny got hers from Emyr Gruffydd."

"Oh, well then," said Mrs. Lloyd. "That would be the right sort of cat. We won't do better than that."

Nine

Shortly after ten the next morning, Penny went downstairs, opened her front door, picked up the Sunday newspaper, and then retreated inside to make her breakfast. She glanced at the headlines while she made coffee. As she waited for a frozen croissant to warm, she put a pat of butter in a small white dipping bowl, and a generous dollop of Florence's raspberry jam in another. She loaded a tray with her breakfast and carried it to the table.

She poured a cup of coffee, then tore off a piece of flaky croissant and spread it with a little butter and a lot of Florence's jam.

It was just as Mrs. Lloyd had described it: sharp and sweet. No wonder it had won first place in the competition. She picked up the little bowl and contemplated the jam as unanswered questions danced around in her head. How had

Gaynor Lewis's jar of marmalade made it into the competition? And what had happened to Florence's marmalade?

And even more important, what had happened to Gaynor Lewis?

She opened the newspaper to the arts section, and after reading the same paragraph three times, she gave up and folded up the newspaper. She took a sip of coffee while she thought about what Mrs. Lloyd had said last night. "If you want to know more about Gaynor Lewis, the person you should be speaking to is her sister-in-law, Joyce Devlin." Penny got up from the table and walked to the cupboard. She pulled a business card out of the jacket she'd worn to the agricultural show and reached for her phone, and when she'd completed her first call, she rang Victoria.

"How would you like to go and see some Labrador puppies after lunch?"

The drive to the Devlins' farm took them down winding roads, past endless lush pastures and vibrant green fields in a lovely configuration of timeless landscape. It was a beautiful afternoon and the late-summer sun warmed the hedgerows and stone walls that flanked the narrow road.

"This is it," said Penny, pointing to a newly painted sign that announced DEVLIN LABRADORS AND BOARDING KENNELS in bold letters under a picture of a black Labrador's friendly face. They turned off at the gate and drove up the rutted lane until they reached a grey stone farmhouse. The door had once been a proud, dark green, but weather had taken its toll and it was now a faded, lacklustre grey-green. Victoria grasped the black ring door knocker and struck it twice on the matching plate. A banging noise resonated within the house, and a few minutes later, with Billie at her side, Joyce appeared, wearing a faded pinafore over a shapeless navy blue dress. It took a moment for her to recognize her callers, and then a wary but resigned look flashed across her face.

"Hello, Joyce," said Penny. "Thank you so much for seeing us today. We know you're busy, and, well, after the way the show ended, I'm sure you had a long night."

"I'm a bit tired, yes. The police were here this morning asking questions, and there're always dogs in the kennel that need attending to. I can't give you very long, but come in."

She stepped aside to allow Penny and Victoria to enter. Jackets and waterproof overcoats lined each side of the whitewashed entryway. Beneath the coats, several pairs of Wellingtons were neatly arranged, and above them hung four faded *Cries of London* prints in dusty frames.

"Go on through," said Joyce, gesturing toward the rear of the house. They entered a large room, with the whitewashed walls, exposed wooden ceiling beams, and slate floors typical of Welsh farmhouse kitchens. An Aga cooker stood against one wall, beside an inglenook fireplace.

A tall, sturdy man who appeared to be in his early fifties—about the same age as Joyce—wearing a plaid shirt and a rough pair of trousers held up by ancient braces, set an empty mug on the table and stood up as the women entered. He looked blankly at Penny and Victoria, then his eyes settled on Joyce.

"My husband's just going out to the kennels to check on the dogs," Joyce explained to Penny and Victoria. "I won't be long, Dev," she said to her departing husband's back. "You get started, and I'll be out to help you soon as I can." She turned her attention back to her visitors. "Have a seat," she said, gesturing to the table. "Now, you wanted to discuss the marmalade, and that's fine with me, because I want to get this business cleared up, so we can put it behind us and all move on."

"Well, first, we want to say we're very sorry for your loss," said Victoria. "We understand Gaynor Lewis was your sister-in-law."

Joyce acknowledged her condolences with a tiny nod but did not reply.

"Yes, we did want to talk to you about the marmalade," Penny began. "As we see it, there are two issues: Florence Semble's marmalade, which was entered properly in the show, never made it to the judging stage."

"And Gaynor Lewis's entry," Victoria added, "which we hadn't checked in by the deadline, somehow not only made it into the show but won the category. That seems very unfair to Florence."

Joyce massaged her forehead with a work-roughened hand dappled with sunspots. The skin was loose, and her nails looked brittle and uncared for.

"If you remember, there were two entry sheets left over when entries closed at eight o'clock, both Gaynor's," said Penny. "You were very clear in your instructions that we were not to accept entries after the deadline. But the thing is, Gaynor hadn't arrived by the time we left, so maybe the best place to start would be to ask you if you know why Gaynor's entries were allowed."

Joyce let out a small sigh heavily laced with exasperation of long standing. "Bloody woman. Even though she's dead, she's still causing problems." She stood up. "I need a coffee. Would you like one?"

"Well, if you're making it anyway, yes, please," said Penny.

Joyce picked up a teaspoon off the worktop, added measures of instant coffee to three mugs, poured in previously boiled water from the kettle, added a splash of milk, gave them all a good stir, and plunked the mugs on the table. Victoria, who normally took sugar, said nothing. Joyce sat down and took a deep breath. She cupped her hands around her mug and leaned forward slightly.

"Right. Let's get to it. Here's what happened on the Friday night," said Joyce. "Gaynor rang me just before eight o'clock, just as Barbara and I were on our way to the marquee to see you, actually." Her eyes tracked from Penny to Victoria, then to a spot somewhere near the ceiling. "Gaynor said she wasn't far away but was caught in slow traffic. She knew I was still on-site, and she asked if I could just give her a few minutes' grace until she got there with her entries. Because she'd called to let me know she was almost at the show grounds, I agreed, albeit with some reluctance. I told her she'd have to look sharp, as I still had a lot to do and I couldn't hang about waiting for her to turn up. And then Barbara and I arrived at the marquee and met up with you. And you know what happened then. We wrapped things up, and you left. Shortly after that, Gaynor came rushing into the marquee, I accepted her entries, and I set them down at the end of the table, ready for the judging in the morning.

"Then I got called away to an incident in the livestock area. There was something going on with the horse people." She made a vague palm-up hand gesture. "Many exhibitors

85

choose to spend the Friday night before the show camping on the grounds because they don't want to leave their livestock unattended, see. And of course, there's always something happening in the run-up to the show. A crisis every five minutes, it seems like. Barbara and I practically spent the whole time running from one disaster to the next, putting out fires." She took a sip of coffee. "Not literally, of course. And not with you two. Everything went quite smoothly there. For the most part. Unless, of course, you count what happened to Gaynor, but that wasn't anything to do with you. I meant the logistics."

"So you left the marquee. Did Barbara leave with you?" Penny asked.

"She did."

"And Gaynor was still there when you left?" asked Penny.

"She was. But since her jam and marmalade had been accepted, I reckoned she'd be leaving, too. It was getting late. And besides, what reason would she have had for sticking around?"

"Well, that's a very good question," said Penny. "And it could be key to solving her murder, because she must have met up with someone after you left, and therefore you could be the second-to-last person to see her alive."

The only sound in the room was Joyce's sharp intake of breath.

"I hadn't thought of it that way."

"Did you see anyone when you left the tent?" Penny asked.

"I saw lots of people. There were lots of folk about, and all sorts of things going on," said Joyce. "It was still light, so people were setting things up, working on exhibits, moving their animals in, ready for the judging in the morning. All the last-minute things. The police officer who was in charge of security was there, keeping an eye on things." Joyce's eyes narrowed. "You're asking a lot of questions. I went over all this with the police, but I must say, I'm not sure they were quite as probing as you."

"Sorry," said Penny. "It's just that when we were talking about Gaynor, I was interested in what happened after we left."

"My friend here gets carried away sometimes," said Victoria, throwing Penny an affectionate grin. And then, turning her attention back to Joyce, Victoria asked, "But Gaynor is, or was, I should say, your husband's sister?"

"That's right. She's the younger sister of my husband, Daffydd. Everybody just calls him Dev. You met him. Well, sort of met him. I should have introduced you, I suppose, but he was just on his way out. Anyway, yes, she was his sister and she's been nothing but a right cow since the day we got married. Or before, truth be told."

"What do you mean?" asked Penny.

"She didn't want Dev to marry me. Said he was marrying beneath him. He could do better. You know the sort of thing. And it just got worse after we were married. She criticized everything Dev and I did." She paused for a moment, and when she continued, her voice was slightly shrill, with an exaggerated, mimicking tone. "She didn't like the way we were bringing up our children. We were spending too much money on our dogs. My housekeeping was terrible. I didn't bake cakes from scratch."

"That must have been hard to live with," remarked Penny.

"Oh, it was. And besides the constant criticism, she was

87

always on at me or Dev about some perceived slight. There was no pleasing her. We used to invite her to family dinners, and she always found some excuse not to come, and then when we gave up and stopped inviting her, she complained we never invited her to dinner! But gradually, I learned to tune out her negativity, if you know what I mean. I took no notice of her, in my personal life, and tried to be civil to her in public, or when I had to be. I reached the point where she just wasn't worth one more minute of my time. I was done with her."

"I can certainly understand that," said Penny. "But I'm curious as to why you allowed her late entries in the show? Doesn't sound as if you owed her any favours, or had any particular reason to be nice to her."

"Well, that's the thing, isn't it? If she'd been a reasonable sort of person, I would have been able to say, 'No, sorry, Gaynor, rules are rules and you missed the deadline, you daft mare, and maybe next year you'll show up on time with your jam and marmalade like everybody else.' And that would have been the end of it. Lesson learned. But I let her jam and marmalade in because if I hadn't, she'd have kicked off, and her nastiness would have started up all over again, and I'd never have heard the end of it. And I really didn't want her turning on Dev and having a go at him. He's not well, and he doesn't need her kind of stress in his life."

"So anything for a quiet life," commented Victoria.

"Yes, I suppose you could say that." Joyce took a moment for her breathing to slow, then continued. "So yes, I did let her bally marmalade into the competition. But I didn't judge it, and I had nothing to do with it winning."

"But what about Florence's marmalade?" asked Penny. "Do you know why that didn't make it into the competition?"

Joyce, who had been taking slow sips of the now-tepid coffee after she finished her diatribe, shook her head and set down her cup. "That I do not know. But really, Gaynor is dead, and why can't that be the end of it? Let her have her little posthumous bit of marmalade glory. What does it matter now?"

"Well, Florence isn't dead, and it matters to her," said Penny, her voice rising slightly. She paused to take a calming breath, then continued. "She feels that for some reason, someone didn't want her marmalade in the competition, and we"—she tipped her head in Victoria's direction—"have to agree with her. It certainly looks that way. It's important to Florence that we get to the bottom of this. And besides being completely unfair to her, the integrity and reputation of the show are at stake. If people think the judging is unfair, or, and I hate to use the word *fixed,* but to put it bluntly, if people think the competition is fixed, then next year no one will want to enter."

"And Mrs. Lloyd isn't happy, either," said Victoria. "You serve on the show's organizing committee with her, so you must know what she's like. In fact, she's already tried to confront you herself about this, and her next step would probably be to bring the matter to the attention of the whole committee. We told her to leave it with us. To keep things, well, unofficial and contained, you might say, before it gets out of hand."

"And to try to keep it out of the newspaper," said Penny.

"If the *Post* got wind of it, which they could do very easily, since Mrs. Lloyd's niece is the star reporter, and if she started asking questions—"

"All right, all right," said Joyce with a flash of temper, interrupting Penny. "You've made your point. I'll ask around and see what I can find out, although it does seem a bit petty to me. I can't think of any reason why someone would not want Florence's ruddy marmalade in the competition. Let's put things in perspective here. It's just a rural agricultural show, and not a very large or important one at that. In the grand scheme of things, it's not a big deal."

"Well, apparently it was a big deal to somebody," said Penny. "Somebody, perhaps, who thought Florence was a threat to them? Somebody who wanted to win very badly? You see, Florence received a telephone call telling her that she should bring her entries to the tent for judging in the morning. Saturday morning, that is, long past the deadline. So when the entry deadline approached on Friday night and we hadn't received her entries, I called her, and Florence and Mrs. Lloyd hurried over with Florence's preserves and cake, and made it just in time."

"But perhaps it wouldn't have mattered too much if they'd been a few minutes late," said Victoria, "as apparently there's some flexibility. If you know the right people, that is."

Joyce shot her a thunderous look.

"Look, I've already said I'll see what I can find out." She tapped her fingers lightly on the table. "And to be fair, that phone call does put a different slant on things. That almost makes it look like sabotage. And now that I think about it, I did hear that there was talk at the Women's Guild about Florence being a threat. Some of the long-standing members,

90

who were used to coming in first or second every year, felt threatened by her. Word had got round that she was just that good."

"Are you a member of the WG?" Penny asked.

"Oh God, no. Gaynor was the president of the WG, in case you didn't know, so there's no way I'd be going to those meetings. Not with her there, lording it over everybody. But I know women who are members, like Barbara, and I heard the talk about Florence and her baking and cooking skills."

She drained the last of her coffee and adjusted her position in her chair as a signal that she was getting ready for the conversation to come to an end.

"And you're right about the perception about the integrity and impartiality of our show. We do have high standards, and we must be seen by everybody as being fair and impartial. I'll ask Barbara if she heard anything."

"Who's Barbara when she's at home?" Victoria asked. "We saw her with you, and wondered about her."

"The woman who was with you in the tent on the Friday evening and again on Saturday," Penny said. "Small, timid-looking. Holding on to the files and things?"

Joyce nodded. "Barbara Vickers. She's the show secretary. Keeps all the paperwork in order. Deals with suppliers. Makes everything run smoothly. Honestly, I don't know what we'd do without her."

She stood up. "I must say, it feels rather good to get all that Gaynor business off my chest. I've probably been waiting years to unburden myself. I know what they say about not speaking ill of the dead, but I feel a lot better for it." Her tone softened. "And now I expect you're ready to see some puppies?"

"Yes, we certainly are!" and "Yes, please!" Penny and Victoria said at the same time.

"Right, well, just give me a minute or two to get changed, and then we'll have a quick tour of the kennels. But don't go getting any ideas about the puppies. They're all spoken for, and there's a waiting list, besides. You mustn't get your hopes up."

"Before you go, Joyce, have you got a photo of Gaynor?" asked Penny. "I'm curious to see what she looked like when she was alive."

Joyce walked over to a substantial Welsh dresser that took up almost half of one wall. A beautifully crafted, solid piece of oak furniture, with cupboards and drawers similar to a sideboard making up the lower part, and utilitarian shelves with plate racks on top, the Devlins' dresser had the well-worn, polished patina of an heirloom that had been lovingly cared for down through generations. Commemorative plates, souvenirs of events in the life of the nation—like the late Queen Mother's hundredth birthday—and decorative plates with patterns of songbirds, Christmas scenes, autumn landscapes, and black Labrador retrievers filled the display shelves. Two dusty brown-and-white ironstone platters, one large and one small, were interspersed among the plates. Joyce combed through a pile of papers on the flat surface of the sideboard part of the dresser and pulled out a framed photograph. "It was taken quite a few years ago," Joyce said as she handed the photo to Penny. "That's the three of them. Gaynor and her brothers. That's Dev on the left, and Andy on the right, before he . . ." She then shuffled out of the room, her tattered brown sheepskin slippers making light scuffing noises on the slate floor. Billie followed her.

92

Before he what? thought Penny. Died? Committed suicide? Moved to Australia?

Victoria picked up the used mugs and took them to the sink. As she tipped the untouched coffee out of hers and rinsed all three, Penny took the photograph to the window and, angling it to catch the light, examined the subjects. Two men stood on each side of a woman wearing a flowered dress and a bright blue fascinator over curly brown hair swept back from her face. Penny recognized the Llanelen church behind them. Probably taken at a summer wedding, she thought. The woman squinted slightly into the sun, and her smile seemed forced and insincere. The men posed as if unwillingly, looking awkward and stiff in their suits and ties, and the distance between all three seemed uncomfortable and strained.

The photographer had not been close enough to capture details of the woman's face, but in this image she looked unremarkable and ordinary. Penny thought she could have bumped into her in a shop or passed her on the street without noticing her, and in all likelihood, she probably had. She showed the photograph to Victoria, who glanced at it, gave a dismissive little shrug, and said nothing.

Penny took one last look at the photograph, then walked over to the dresser to put it back. The flat surface of the dresser had become a catchall for paper clutter. As Penny's eyes flicked across farm equipment catalogues, church newsletters, programs from the agricultural show, and magazine cuttings, several unopened envelopes with FINAL NOTICE printed on them in red letters caught her attention. At that moment, the clicking of Billie's toenails on the slate floor announced she and Joyce were on their way, and Penny scuttled across the kitchen to join Victoria beside the sink just as Billie and Joyce, now wearing a shapeless pair of grey worsted trousers and a black cardigan, entered the kitchen. Penny handed her the photograph.

"Right. Boots on, and we'll be off," Joyce ordered as she lightly dropped the photo on the kitchen table.

Ten

Billie led the way down a rutted path to a weathered wooden farm outbuilding. It didn't look like much from the outside, but when Joyce opened the door, they stepped into a clean, warm space with the distinctive smell of a new building emanating from fresh paint and recently installed flooring.

Spacious individual dog kennels flanked each side of an aisle that ran down the centre of the building. Some were fenced off to about waist height; others were self-contained, with high walls and a door. "These are quiet spaces reserved for nervous, anxious dogs who might be upset by the barking of other dogs," explained Joyce.

Each kennel was furnished with a soft bed raised off the floor. Several dogs, including a beagle and a boxer, were already in residence and barked friendly hellos. "Those are our guest boarders," said Joyce. "We take care of them whilst their owners are away. The humans can go on holiday knowing their dogs are perfectly safe and well cared for with us. We used to do that for no charge, if you can believe it, but now we've turned dog boarding into a proper business. We charge, and people are more than willing to pay."

They continued on to the end of the building and Joyce indicated a door. "That leads to a safe, fenced-in area where they can have a proper run." She opened another door. "And here's the kitchen." It was a small but well-equipped area with a sink, storage space, refrigerator, and microwave. Her husband, Dev, stood at the worktop with his back to them and did not turn around. "This is where we store and prepare all the food, including any kind of special diet. We also keep medications and supplements in here.

"And best of all," she announced, unable to hide her enthusiasm, "next door is the nursery." She joyfully threw back the door to reveal six roly-poly black Lab puppies, safely enclosed in a large, well-padded play area, tussling and climbing over one another under their proud mother's watchful eye.

"Oh!" exclaimed Penny and Victoria at the same time.

"I suppose you'd like to give them a cuddle," said Joyce, scooping up a couple of sturdy pups. "That's fine. It does them good to be handled and played with. Helps with the socializing." Supporting the puppies under their bottoms with one arm and wrapping the other arm around them, Victoria and Penny hugged the puppies to their chests, gently nuzzling the tops of their soft heads with their chins and cheeks. "Oooh." They breathed in the warm, sweet puppy smell and grinned as the squirming puppies licked their faces, their tongues pretty splashes of pink against their round black faces. Penny and Victoria admired the tiny paws with their pink pads and tried to avoid the puppies' playful nips with their sharp milk teeth. They stroked and snuggled the delightful little creatures, laughing as they passed them back and forth and took photos of each other holding them.

"I don't want to give her back!" Penny exclaimed when Joyce reached out for the puppy, indicating visiting hours were over. After returning the pups to their mother and littermates, they left the nursery, passing Joyce's husband, who was still working in the kitchen, as they made their way out of the building.

"Since you got me thinking about our family history," said Joyce as she walked with them across the front of the farmyard to Victoria's car, "something occurred to me when I went upstairs to change."

"What's that?" replied Penny.

"Well, Gaynor had been separated from her husband, Carwyn, for quite a few years, and he's been living with Elin Spears for almost as long. So I wondered if now, with Gaynor out of the way, those two will finally get married. Elin's been after him to marry her for years, or so Gaynor always said. And why shouldn't Elin have him? Now that Gaynor's gone, Elin will be taking over as president of the Women's Guild, so she might as well have it all."

"What!" Penny's eyes widened.

"Oh, yes," said Joyce, slowing down as they approached Victoria's car. "Gaynor was president of the WG, and Elin was vice president. They didn't like it, but that's what the membership voted. How the two of them managed to work together, I have no idea, but Elin will take over the role of president now. They've got a meeting coming up this week, and it should be interesting."

"Will you go?" Penny asked.

"No, it's not for me. And anyway, the meeting's on Wednesday, and Dev and I've got an appointment."

"Well, you've certainly given us a lot to think about," said Penny as she opened the car's passenger door and Victoria walked around to the driver's side. "I'm sorry that we took up much more of your time than we intended. And thank you for the kennel tour. The puppies are wonderful, and the dogs who get to stay there are very lucky indeed."

Joyce nodded good-bye and took a step back as Penny closed the car door and rolled down the window. Leaning out a little, she said to Joyce, "But you will have a word with Barbara about that phone call Florence received, asking her to bring her entries Saturday morning, won't you?"

"Yes, I said I would, and I will. As soon as I get around to it. We've got two dogs booked in tomorrow, and the gala dinner coming up on Saturday, so it's going to be a busy week."

Penny rolled up the window, and as Victoria's car pulled out of the farmyard, she looked back and waved at Joyce, who was standing there with Billie at her side.

When the car had disappeared through the gate, Joyce started for the house, then, changing her mind, returned to the kennels, where her husband was washing the floor. The swirling cotton fibres made a light swishing noise as he moved the mop rhythmically back and forth. He did not look up from his work.

"Dev!" she said. "Finish that up quick as you like and then come to the house. I've got to ring Barbara, and then you and I need to talk about your doctor's appointment."

Eleven

"The puppies are adorable, aren't they?" Victoria commented as they drove down the lane that led from the Devlin farmhouse. "I wish I could have one."

"I bet you do. They're not puppies for long, though. Pretty soon you've got a big dog that needs a lot of training and exercise, and your time is no longer your own. And it won't be for the next ten years or longer."

"Thanks for the reality check. I needed that. No puppy for me, then." She turned onto the narrow road that would take them into Llanelen. "I wasn't sure what Joyce was going to be like, but she was much nicer, really, than I thought she would be. I guess we got the wrong impression of her at the show."

"Yes, she was," agreed Penny. "She seemed so curt at the

agricultural show, but that was probably because she had a lot on her mind and so many things to see to."

"Probably. It's a lot of responsibility running a big show like that, with so many moving parts and so many people depending on you. And she's a completely different person when she's with her dogs. She's probably one of those people who prefers dogs to people."

"True." Penny gazed out the window at the fleeting scenery. Patches of purple heather mingled with streaks of yellow gorse blanketed the hillsides, alive and shimmering in the golden light of midafternoon.

"I wonder about those dog kennels," Penny said. "State-of-the-art."

"Yes, they are," agreed Victoria.

"Must have cost a bundle. I wonder where they got the money to build them."

"Bank loan?"

"Maybe. Could have used the farm property as collateral, I suppose," Penny mused.

"What's up with you? Why would you be thinking about the Devlins' sources of income? I thought you'd want to talk about the puppies all the way home."

"Because the dresser is covered in bills marked 'Reminder' and 'Final Notice.' If they can't afford to pay their electric and gas bills, how could they afford to build a new kennel? And one as elaborate as that?" She glanced at Victoria's profile as her friend concentrated on the road ahead.

"Maybe they can afford to pay the bills but are just careless or slow," said Victoria. "Some people, when a bill arrives, instead of paying it right away, they toss it aside, telling themselves they'll pay it later. And then they forget about it, and payment notices start arriving."

"Hmm, maybe," said Penny, "but in this case, I don't think so. It seems unlikely that Joyce could manage to pull off a big project like the agricultural show if she can't even manage to pay her own bills on time."

"She could pull off an event like that," replied Victoria, "if Barbara took care of all the little details, as she seemed to do, and Joyce just had to tell her what to do."

"Maybe," said Penny again, "but something about those unpaid bills doesn't feel right." A few minutes later, they arrived at Penny's cottage. "Are you coming in?" Penny asked. "I hope so. Joyce gave us lots of things to talk about."

"I'm coming in only if you promise to make me a proper cup of coffee. Joyce's was pretty bad."

Penny laughed. "I can do that. And what about something to eat? Are you hungry? I could probably find some cheese and crackers."

"No, you're all right, but I wouldn't say no to a biscuit or something sweet. I won't stay long, and I'll have supper when I get home."

Penny unlocked the front door of her cottage. It had been built in the nineteenth century as accommodation for successive families of local slate-quarry workers, but as the slate mines closed in the twentieth century, the cottages had been sold off. This one had been bought by a schoolteacher who had befriended Penny when she first arrived in Llanelen. The teacher had died a few years ago, leaving the cottage to Penny, who had modernized and decorated it to suit her tastes, while retaining much of the building's original charm, including a working fireplace, slate floors, low ceilings with beams, woodwork, and a Rayburn cooker. It was the first property Penny had owned, and she loved it, as well as the security and independence it represented. She acknowledged that the cottage was one of the reasons her relationship with Gareth Davies had not progressed. Penny simply could not bear to leave her snug, comfortable home to move in with anyone else, and she didn't want someone moving in with her. The cottage was just right for one person but too small for two. Penny recognized the irony of her thinking, knowing that the cottage's previous inhabitants would have included large families with several children.

"Why don't you put the kettle on while I look for . . ." Her voice trailed off as she looked around the tidy sitting room with its wing chairs and sofa in a bright floral pattern set against the palest yellow of the walls. "Where did I put it?" she muttered.

"Put what? What are you looking for?" Victoria called from the kitchen over the sound of running water.

"The program from the agricultural show. I just want to check . . ." Penny entered the kitchen and pulled a drawer open. "Joyce had a stack of them on her Welsh dresser. I can't think what I did with mine."

"Did you look at the program Friday evening after you got home?" Victoria asked. "Did you take it to the show with you on Saturday? If not, look in the handbag you had with you on Friday night." Penny closed the drawer and handed Victoria a beige canister marked *Coffi*.

"Yes, I did look at it Friday night. Thanks. I know where it is now." Penny left the kitchen and ran lightly upstairs. A few minutes later she skipped back down the stairs waving the blue program guide as Victoria entered the sitting room carrying a coffee tray.

"I just want to check to see if that friend of Joyce's, Barbara Vickers, is listed as a member of the organizing committee, or even as a judge," Penny said. "I think Joyce referred to her as the show secretary, but I wondered if that's an official role or if she's an unofficial helper, like a volunteer."

"Any particular reason you're interested in her?"

"No, not really. It's just that we know so little about her, and yet she was everywhere with Joyce before and during the show, so I'm curious about her."

While Victoria poured the coffee and added a teaspoon of sugar to her mug, Penny leafed through the booklet, examining all the categories. "Barbara Vickers is not listed as a judge, but I didn't really think she would be," Penny said. "If she had been, I'm sure someone would have mentioned that, and anyway, she was too close to the organizing end of it to serve as a judge. But oh, wait a minute, here we are."

Penny pointed to the inside back cover. "The executive committee. Barbara Vickers is listed as the general secretary. According to this, other secretaries look after various events—there's a trophy secretary, for example—but Barbara seems to be the one in charge." She ran her finger down the list of names. "Hmm, this is interesting."

"What is?"

"Joyce's husband, Daffydd Devlin, is the treasurer."

Victoria's eyes met Penny's over the rim of her coffee mug. She leaned forward and set it on the table between them.

"Why do you find that interesting?"

"Well, we were talking on the drive home about how the Devlins don't seem to be paying their bills on time, and yet

103

Dev is the show treasurer. If he's not managing his own money well at home, why is he managing the show's money? I wonder if the show's bills are being paid on time." Penny sat back in her chair and crossed her legs. "You know, Dev being the treasurer raises a possibility about where the money might have come from for the new kennel."

Victoria thought about that for a moment.

"Are you suggesting that Dev stole from the show funds to pay for the kennel?"

"No, no. *Suggesting* is much too strong a word. I'm just . . . musing . . . indulging in a bit of 'what if.' "

"Okay. Well, we're not suggesting he did, but we're saying let's suppose for a moment . . . what if he did . . . and if he did . . . then Joyce must have known about it," said Victoria, "because, well, she's the committee chairman, so she knows how much money the show has on hand. . . ."

"Or she should know," said Penny, emphasizing the word *should*. "You're in charge of business operations at the Spa, and you know all about our financial situation, but I don't. Maybe I should, but I don't. I just don't pay attention to that. I trust you, and I just let you get on with the job. So if Dev was stealing from the show, it doesn't necessarily follow that Joyce would know."

"You're right," agreed Victoria. "But I think she would know about the money from the kennel end. She took great interest in the design of those kennels, so surely she'd know where the money to build them came from."

Penny nodded. "Yes, I think she would. So, let's say Dev stole the money and Joyce knew about it. And what if Gaynor somehow found out and threatened to go to the authorities? She and Joyce didn't get on. There was no love lost between them, according to Joyce. And we know that Joyce met up with Gaynor in the tent after we'd left, so she might have had the opportunity to kill her."

"So Joyce, and possibly Dev, too, killed Gaynor to keep her quiet." Victoria mulled that over. "It's possible, I suppose. They'd be worried about the kennels and the dogs, and Joyce would want to protect her standing in the community."

"Not to mention that one or both of them—Joyce and her husband—could be charged with embezzlement, or whatever it's called, and the consequences of that would be serious. People have killed for less, that's for sure."

Victoria nodded. "Much less."

"I suppose we could ask Mrs. Lloyd if the show's books have been audited recently or if anyone's noticed any unusual financial activity," said Penny.

Victoria winced. "We have to be really careful here. We have no proof of anything, and to even suggest that the Devlins could have been stealing from the show committee's accounts, especially to Mrs. Lloyd, could be risky. The slightest hint that something might be amiss, and she'd be all over it. We don't want to say anything that could affect the Devlins' reputations. That could land us in big trouble, and even affect our business."

"Yes, of course, you're right. I knew as soon as I said it that it was a terrible idea. Just forget I said anything. But speaking of our business, you take care of our accounts. If someone wanted to steal from a company, how would they do it?"

"There are a few ways. But first, people who steal from a company or charity usually don't think of it as stealing, and that's one of the reasons why smaller organizations, like the rural show, are so vulnerable to theft. The people who steal from organizations like that think of it as borrowing. Just a temporary loan, to tide them over until they get back on their feet, sort of thing, and then they'll pay it all back before anybody finds out. I'm pretty sure if the Devlins are involved in something like this, that's how they'd see it." Victoria paused, taking a breath before continuing.

"Anyway, if Dev was stealing from the agricultural show, he could have set up a fake set of books that seem legitimate. There'd be payments to nonexistent suppliers. Companies that don't exist. So for example, it would look like the show paid four hundred pounds to the Best Lighting in the World Company, when in fact there is no such company, there was no such payment, and the four hundred pounds went straight to the Devlins."

"I see. And could there be pretend payments to real companies?"

"There could. And they'd look legitimate, and probably wouldn't be questioned. Say there's a recorded payment of, oh, I don't know, one hundred pounds to the Women's Guild for catering, when in reality the good ladies of the WG donated all the pies and scones that were served in the refreshment tent. So the WG actually gets nothing, and the Devlins take the one hundred pounds for themselves."

"You're making it sound very attractive, and not all that difficult."

"It isn't difficult, really, and that's another reason why a lot of small charities do become victims to this kind of fraud." Victoria took a sip of coffee. "And there's another way. They could inflate the bills and skim some off the top. So let's say they're invoiced five hundred pounds for something. Dev pays the invoice, but he enters it in the books as a six-hundred-pound expense."

"And he pockets the one-hundred-pound difference."

"Correct. But to be honest, I'm feeling a bit uncomfortable even talking about this, and using their names, as if they're actually doing it. We have no proof that any of this has been going on."

"No, we don't," Penny replied. She sighed. "Do you think we should do anything?"

Victoria considered her answer carefully before she spoke. "I'm not sure we should do anything. We need much more to go on—this is really only vague speculation. And I'm not sure if I should even suggest we poke around and see what we can find out."

"All right, then. Let's set that aside for a moment and think about this. What kind of expenses would a show like this normally have?"

"The usual. Advertising, printing. Are the judges compensated? Do they rent the fields?"

"Rent! They do rent the marquee," said Penny, a trace of excitement in her voice. "Mrs. Lloyd said something about that. She said the marquee rental cost—oh what was it? Six thousand? Six thousand pounds for one day? Does that seem like a lot to you?"

"I don't know. I've never rented a marquee. I imagine the cost would depend on what size you want."

"If we could find out what the company charged for the marquee, and what the show paid, that would be a good start."

"Start to what?"

"To seeing if the Devlins were fiddling the show's finances.

And like we just said, if they were, and if Gaynor Lewis found out about that, or even suspected them of it, that could be motive enough for murder."

"I don't see how we can find out how much a marquee would normally cost when we don't have the exact measurements." Victoria finished her coffee and set the mug down. "What about this Barbara Vickers?" she suggested. "She seems close to Joyce. She was always making the rounds with her at the show, and she seemed in charge of the paperwork. What about trying to talk to her?"

"We could try. She shouldn't be too hard to find."

"The thing is," said Victoria, "if you do approach her, you don't want to scare her off. She doesn't look the chatty type. So just ringing her up out of the blue and launching into a lot of questions probably won't get you very far. 'How big is the marquee? How much did you pay for it?' You need to be subtle and start off slowly. It might be best if you do it in a casual situation, if you can. She'd be more likely to talk to you if she's relaxed."

"True, although she didn't look like the sort who relaxes very much."

"But there's another woman of interest here, and that's Elin Spears," said Victoria. "Don't forget about her."

"Oh, right. The other woman."

"Joyce said Elin's been after Carwyn to marry her, and now that Gaynor's out of the way, maybe now he and Elin will tie the knot. I wonder just how badly Elin wants to marry Carwyn, and what lengths she'd go to in order to make that possible."

"Bumping off an inconvenient spouse has certainly happened before," Penny agreed, "although I wouldn't say that's

108

a solid foundation on which to build a marriage. Still, I'd like to know more about her."

"Then I'm sure you'll find a way to do just that."

Victoria stood up. "Well, thanks for the decent coffee. I'd best be off. Want to get the week off to a good start with some laundry and cleaning out of the way. And all that talk about invoices reminded me I've got a few to pay tomorrow. I don't like to keep suppliers waiting."

Penny reached for her keys. "Let me just grab a bag and I'll go out with you. Time for a little walk before an early supper."

"Litter picking?"

Penny locked her door and they walked together to Victoria's car. And then, with a cheery flap of her hand out the car window, Victoria drove off, leaving Penny to follow on foot along the lane that led into town. She didn't plan on walking that far, though. She intended to walk only as far as the site of the agricultural show, picking up litter and recyclables from the roadside.

She took her time, picking up a crushed beer can here and an empty crisp packet there that had been thoughtlessly tossed onto the verge or into a hedgerow. Bloody hell, she thought as she tossed one more empty plastic water bottle into the bag. What is wrong with people? They have the good fortune to live in one of the most beautiful places on earth, and they have to spoil it by throwing rubbish all over the place.

Her carrier bag was almost overflowing by the time she reached the site of the agricultural show. The fields that just yesterday had been filled with the sights, sounds, and smells of show animals and spectators now lay silent and almost empty in the soft, slanting light of late afternoon. Only the marquee remained. She could make out a uniformed police officer silhouetted against its whiteness, with blue-and-white crime-scene barricade tape behind him, cordoning off the entrance. Two police cars and a forensic services van with their distinctive blue-and-yellow checkerboard livery were parked nearby.

As Penny gazed at the scene, an investigator dressed in white overalls emerged from the marquee. The uniformed officer lifted the tape and the white-clad figure ducked under it, then walked purposefully toward the van. Penny watched for a few more minutes, her mind churning, and then she set off at a comfortable pace for home.

She could think of two people who might gain from Gaynor's death: Joyce Devlin, if she and her husband had stolen from the agricultural show funds to pay for their new kennels, and Elin Spears, who would now be in a legal position to marry Gaynor's widower.

After a few minutes of allowing her mind to flit back and forth between the two women, she realized she was mentally spinning her wheels. She didn't even know Elin Spears, so how could she possibly speculate about her? And as for Joyce, she had no evidence of financial wrongdoing. Penny forced herself to stop thinking about the murder and allowed her mind to wander in rhythm with her steps.

Walking is so much better with a dog, she mused. She loved when Emyr Gruffydd left his black Lab, Trixxi, with her when he had to be away from home. The long rambles, the companionship of a lovely dog, the emotional satisfaction she got from the simple act of giving Trixxi a drink of cool water at the end of their walk. Seeing Joyce's puppies this morning had filled her with longing for a dog of her own. Not a puppy, though, an older dog. Possibly a retired breeding dog, like Billie, or more likely, a shelter dog in need of a loving home.

Feeling a slight twinge of guilt at the thought of how her grey cat, Harrison, would adjust to a dog in the house, she sped up just a little.

And just as she made her way up the stone pathway flanked by lavender bushes that led to her candy-apple-red front door, surrounded by climbing white roses, Penny thought of an easy way to meet Elin Spears. She let herself into her cottage, then pulled her phone out of her pocket and rang Victoria, who had just arrived home.

"It's so obvious, I'm surprised we didn't think of it," Penny said, gazing out her sitting room window at the lightly moving branches of her apple tree. "We go to the Women's Guild meeting on Wednesday. I expect everyone can manage without us for a couple of hours." She listened for a moment, then laughed. "Oh, I'm sure Mrs. Lloyd will be there. Probably wouldn't miss it for the world."

Twelve

Three days later, Florence locked the front door and she and Mrs. Lloyd set off for the Women's Guild meeting, held at the community centre on the last Wednesday afternoon of every month. "There was really no need for you to come with me," grumbled Florence. "Sometimes I like doing things on my own, you know."

"Yes, I do know that. But as I told you, I used to be a member of the WG, although that was many years ago. It wasn't really right for me at that time, but I thought I'd come along today to see if things have changed. I'm sure they must have. Nothing stays the same, does it? You have to move with the times if you want to stay relevant."

"What a load of tosh," said Florence with a light laugh. "You just want to go to the meeting today because of what you might hear about Gaynor Lewis. Whereas I have a genuine interest in the Guild's activities."

The Welsh Women's Guild was loosely modelled on the Women's Institute, a British institution since 1915. The WI movement spread from Canada, where it had begun eighteen years earlier, and was taken up by British women eager to contribute to the World War I home-front efforts by helping with food production. The WI flourished in rural areas, towns, and villages, providing women with an opportunity to share and celebrate skills such as baking, sewing, and gardening. As the twentieth century passed, the organization also took on social causes, campaigning and fund-raising for serious global issues as wide ranging as protecting honeybees, preventing and rescuing victims of human trafficking, and improving access to prenatal care.

Florence opened the door to the community centre and they passed through the vestibule, pausing to read the notices pinned to the bulletin board, then entered the meeting hall.

Light poured in through tall windows, casting rectangular shapes across dark blue carpeting. Straight-backed chairs with seats and backs upholstered in a gold fabric had been neatly arranged in two rows, facing a wooden table covered in a forest green felt cloth with yellow letters spelling out *Llanelen WG* sewn on in a curved pattern. Under the lettering was an appliquéd version of the organization's logo.

Seated at a small table just inside the door was Bronwyn Evans, the rector's wife.

"How nice to see you both," she said to Florence and Mrs. Lloyd. A small woman with faded blond hair worn in the same pageboy style she'd had since she was a girl and dressed in a plaid pleated skirt with a powder blue twinset and pearls, Bronwyn greeted each of them with a warm smile. "Quite a turnout today," she remarked. "We don't usually get this many at our meetings. Most of the members are already here, plus several visitors, like yourselves."

"That'll be the murder," Mrs. Lloyd said easily. "Murder always draws a crowd, don't you find?"

"Well, I'm not sure. . . ." As a flummoxed Bronwyn found herself lost for words at how to respond to that, Mrs. Lloyd continued. "Penny and Victoria are hoping to come today, too. I knew they'd want to be here. When I rang Penny to remind her about the meeting, she said Victoria was juggling their schedules to give them enough time to get away from the Spa for a few hours this afternoon. I'm sure they'll find a way."

"Yes, it's often a challenge for working women to get to our meetings," said Bronwyn. "And mothers with young children." She turned an official-looking legal-size ledger toward them. "If you would just write your names under the heading where it says 'Visitors,'" she said, pointing to the place, "under the names of these other ladies. And visitors pay a small fee of two pounds." She held up a small brown basket, and when Mrs. Lloyd and Florence had finished signing in, they each dropped their coins in the basket. Bronwyn frowned as she set the basket on the table.

"What's the matter?" asked Florence. "You look a bit worried."

"I am, a little. We may have to put out more chairs. And although I'm not on the tea rota, I do hope there'll be enough cake. If not, I suppose we could always nip round to the bakery, although here at the WG, it's traditional to serve only what we ourselves bake. Ties in with who we are, you see, and what we expect of ourselves."

"I thought as much," said Florence, keeping a round cake tin level as she withdrew it from the depths of her carrier bag. "Perhaps you could use this. It's a Victoria sponge with a raspberry jam filling. I made it just this morning. You can't have too much cake, I always say."

Bronwyn's eyes lit up. "Oh, bless you, Florence, that's brilliant! I'll give it to Mari right now and you can have your tin back." As she spoke, a woman entered the room carrying a cut-glass serving dish on which slices of chocolate cake protected by cling film had been arranged in careful rows. Bronwyn waited until she had set the plate on the refreshment table, then handed the cake tin to her, with an explanation and a brief introduction to Florence and Mrs. Lloyd. By now, three or four women had gathered in line behind Mrs. Lloyd and Florence, so Bronwyn handed them song sheets and then gently suggested that they move on into the room and find places to sit. "Just introduce yourselves, although I'm sure you know almost everybody anyway, Mrs. Lloyd."

Mrs. Lloyd greeted a few women and then, happening to turn her gaze to the door, murmured to Florence, "Here they are!"

Penny and Victoria, standing in front of Bronwyn, signed in, then took a few hesitant steps onto the blue carpet.

"I knew you'd find a way to make it," Mrs. Lloyd said, greeting them. She turned to Florence and added, "Wasn't I just saying as much?"

"Indeed you were," agreed Florence. "Quite a turnout, isn't there, Penny?"

Penny scanned the room. The meeting had attracted about

thirty women, including several she didn't know, and quite a few she did. She recognized a few from the Spa, who, although not her manicure clients, availed themselves of other services, such as hair, massages, or skin treatments. She smiled at a couple of women across the room and nodded and raised a polite hand in greeting at another. And then she caught sight of a small solitary figure standing alone off to one side, head lowered, writing in a pocket notebook.

Barbara Vickers.

Before Penny could cross the room to speak to Barbara, Florence remarked that the meeting was about to begin. "We'd better find our seats," she said. The two rows of chairs had filled up quickly with middle-aged and elderly women, leaving only a couple of empty single seats. "If we can find any, that is."

Mrs. Lloyd had a word with a white-haired woman in the second row, everyone obligingly shifted along, and Florence and Mrs. Lloyd settled into the two empty chairs at the end of the row. Victoria and Penny remained standing at one end of the tea table, their backs brushing the wall.

Bronwyn, Barbara, and a woman Penny didn't know but assumed to be Elin Spears took their places at the table at the front of the room. When the last of the chatter died down and she had their full attention, the woman called the meeting to order.

"Right then, ladies, we'll begin as usual with the singing of 'Jerusalem.' Please stand." She nodded at a woman seated at the upright piano, who, on cue, swung around to face her instrument, and as the opening chord filled the room, accompanied by a rustling of song sheets, the women rose to their feet. Their strong feminine voices rose purely and

117

confidently, and when they reached the last two lines of the hymn, "Till we have built Jerusalem / In England's green and pleasant land," Penny found herself moved, suddenly and deeply, as her heart flooded with love for her adopted homeland, with its rich cultural past, beautiful architectural heritage, stunning country views, and the occasionally quirky eccentricities of its people. Her eyes threatened to prick with tears, but the moment passed as the hymn finished and those in the audience took their seats.

The woman leading the meeting remained standing, her hands resting lightly on a document on the table in front of her. "I'd like to begin by welcoming everyone," she said, making eye contact with members of her audience, "and as we have several visitors with us today, I should introduce myself. My name is Elin Spears and I'm the vice president of the Llanelen branch of the WG."

She spoke in a clear, practised voice with no trace of nervousness, as if she was used to public speaking. She wore a pale pink jacket over a white blouse and black trousers. Penny and Victoria had speculated on the way to the meeting how Elin Spears would address the death of Gaynor Lewis, and now they were about to find out.

"We are meeting today under difficult and shocking circumstances," Elin continued. "I don't need to go into details. You know what I'm talking about. So before we get to the reading of the minutes and the meeting proper, I'm sure you would wish to acknowledge the sad and untimely death of our president, Gaynor Lewis." She paused as a murmur rippled throughout the room. "And since apparently it's standing room only today, it seems other people are taking an interest in what happened, too." With a lot of effort, Penny resisted glancing at Victoria, and the two kept their eyes focused on the speaker.

"Although we had our personal differences, I want to pay tribute to Gaynor. She brought a tremendous amount of energy to her role with the WG, and worked tirelessly to help the organization achieve its goals. She was never too busy to donate a cake to a worthy cause or sew a blanket for a new baby, and she threw herself into our campaigns with everything she had. I would ask you now to rise and we'll observe a moment's silence in her memory." The audience rose again, a couple of the younger members helping the older, less steady ones to their feet, and everyone stood, with their hands clasped in front of them, heads slightly bowed. Penny peered around the room from under her lowered eyes and sensed a slightly embarrassed awkwardness. Perhaps it had to do with the nature of the long-standing rivalry between the deceased and the woman in front of them leading a tribute in her memory.

To signal the observance was over, Elin Spears cleared her throat, and after a general shuffling as everyone sat down again but before the business part of the meeting got under way, Penny whispered to Victoria, "Does she come to the Spa?" Victoria shook her head and raised her shoulders slightly.

Elin Spears glanced in their direction. "Now, before we begin the meeting properly, would someone please see if we can find a couple of chairs for our guests who are standing." A woman in the front row jumped up and scurried into the corridor, returning with a man carrying two chairs, which he set down beside the tea table. Penny and Victoria nodded their thanks and sat. Bronwyn read the minutes of the last meeting, and after signing them, Elin Spears called for the treasurer's report.

Barbara Vickers, Joyce Devlin's agricultural show assistant, got to her feet and, referring to the notebook she had been writing in before the meeting started, announced, "We have a balance of one thousand five hundred and thirty-six pounds, fifty-two pence."

"Thank you, Barbara," said Elin. She made a few announcements about upcoming events and then asked if there was any new business. A woman in the second row raised her hand, and when Elin acknowledged her, she stood up.

"I'm wondering what's going to happen with the executive now that Gaynor's gone. I mean, she was our president, so will you . . ."

"As your vice president, I'll assume the role of acting president until a new president is chosen at the next regularly scheduled election," replied Elin. "That's what the role of vice president is for, and that's the process that's laid out in our rules." A little ripple of agreement spread through the audience.

"And what about Gaynor?" another woman asked. "Will we do anything in her memory?"

"We'll discuss that at a later date, but now isn't the right time. It's too soon." Elin's eyes narrowed slightly as she surveyed the room. "Now, before I introduce our guest speaker, there is one more piece of business I've been asked to mention.

"A very important part of our Llanelen WG heritage has been misplaced. As you know, many years ago, we were presented with a beautiful silver cake stand, engraved server, and knife by the late Mrs. Gruffydd, and part of the set seems to have gone missing during the agricultural show. We always display the set on the table with the Best in Show award, and when it came time to do that, the stand was there, and the server, but not the knife. I can't think why someone might have taken it, but if you did, or you know what happened to it, please make arrangements with me or Bronwyn to return it. It's part of a valuable set, and we want it all back together. I'm sure you all know what it looks like, but just to remind you, the knife and server have mother-of-pearl handles." Mrs. Lloyd frowned, leaned forward slightly, and seemed about to say something, when Florence put a gentle restraining hand on her arm and gave her head a little shake, as if to say, *Not now.* Mrs. Lloyd relaxed back into her chair. Elin scanned the small audience, but her expectant expression was met with blank looks. A small sigh escaped her bright red lips.

"Well, if there's nothing else, I would now like to introduce our guest speaker." After a few remarks from Elin, a somewhat bewildered-looking woman wearing a navy blue-and-white-striped pullover and a white yachting-style peaked cap that was no doubt meant to be jaunty but came across as silly, gave a brief talk on the pleasures of canal boating.

When the speaker had finished, Elin thanked her, advised everyone that next month's meeting would feature an informative talk by a volunteer from a local owl rescue group, reminded the group that there was still time to sign up for the upcoming trip to Speke Hall, just outside Liverpool, and closed the meeting by inviting everyone to enjoy a cup of tea and slice of homemade cake.

An enthusiastic din of light conversation broke out as the women made their way to the tea table. Cups and saucers in pretty floral patterns of snowdrops, roses, and daffodils had been arranged in neat rows on one side of the table, where a smiling woman in a grey suit poured tea from a catering-size aluminium teapot that held sixteen cups. It had the usual handle on the side for pouring but also had a second handle affixed to the top over the lid so that the pourer could use both hands to support and steady the heavy pot. The Guild members accepted cups of tea, helped themselves to slices of cake, then stepped away from the table to make room for others. Their conversation provided a low background hum as Elin Spears, accompanied by Bronwyn Evans, circulated.

They reached Penny and Victoria just as Penny was about to try to make her way over to speak to Barbara Vickers, who was deeply engrossed in what looked like a serious conversation with a fellow member. As Bronwyn said, "And I'd like to introduce you to Penny Brannigan and Victoria Hopkirk," Penny turned her attention to Elin Spears. "They own the local Spa," Bronwyn continued, "but Victoria is also a musician—plays the harp—and Penny is a watercolour artist of some note."

"Oh, yes, I know the Spa. Many of us get our hair done there, including me, occasionally. And surely it's Victoria whose talents are of some note," Elin said, a little twinkle in her grey-blue eyes punctuating the pun. Slightly shorter than Penny, she held out a small hand as she ran an appraising eye over her. "Perhaps one or both of you would be willing to give us a little talk one day." Her eyes shifted to meet Victoria's. "We're always looking for interesting speakers."

"Yes, I would enjoy that," said Penny, who had previously spoken at various groups. Elin turned her attention to Victoria, who confirmed that she, too, would be happy to speak to the group.

"Perhaps you're even thinking of joining the WG?" Elin continued. "We love to welcome new members."

"I've been after them for years to join," said Bronwyn, "although I know it's difficult when they've got a business to run, but I do hope now that they've been to a meeting, they'll think about it." She reached out to Mrs. Lloyd and Florence, who were hovering nearby. "But these two ladies might very well be interested."

"Interested in what, Bronwyn?" asked Mrs. Lloyd as she was pulled into the little group.

"Becoming a WG member."

"Oh, we are interested, aren't we, Florence? I was just saying the other day how foolish I was to let my membership lapse. Can't think why that happened."

"That's wonderful," said Elin as she shifted slightly away and scanned the room. "Our membership secretary is right over there"—she indicated a tall woman in a black skirt and a bright yellow jacket—"and she'd be more than happy to sign you up. Join today and you'll be able to go along with us on our day trip to Speke Hall next week. And what a treat that promises to be."

"Oh, Speke Hall," said Mrs. Lloyd. "That sounds wonderful. I love any building with 'Hall' in its name."

"And Florence here very kindly brought the Victoria sponge we're all enjoying so much," Brownyn said with a nod in the direction of the tea table. "She's a wonderful baker."

"Is she?" Elin, who had won Best in Show in the baking category at the agricultural show with her two-layered cake covered in graduated shades of pink icing roses, tilted her head to one side as she sized up a potential rival through slightly narrowed eyes. "How thoughtful of her to bring a cake. I must try some, if there's any left."

"Congratulations on winning Best in Show for your cake," Penny said. "It was absolutely stunning. A real showstopper." Elin seemed genuinely pleased by the compliment and thanked Penny with a broad smile that created tiny wrinkles around her eyes.

"Elin won that award for the second straight year," said Bronwyn.

The conversation ended, Elin and Bronwyn glided away to speak to others.

"I'll be right back," Penny said to Victoria as she set off in search of search of Barbara Vickers. She scanned the room, but Barbara was nowhere to be seen. Damn, thought Penny. She'd hoped to speak to Barbara at the meeting today, and she was annoyed to have missed her.

The women began placing empty cups on the table, gathering up their handbags and jackets, and saying their goodbyes until either the Speke Hall outing or next month's meeting. With the crowd thinned, two women began piling empty cups and plates on trays and carrying them to the kitchen across the corridor.

Florence turned to Penny. "I'd just like to pop along to the loo before we go, and I wonder if you'd mind asking the women in the kitchen who looked after the tea for my cake tin. If I leave it here, I'm sure it will be misplaced by the next meeting. My name's written on a piece of tape on the bottom."

"Of course."

Penny crossed the hall and was about to enter the kitchen

when a woman leaning against the worktop said to the woman loading cups and saucers into the dishwasher, "That was quite the speech Elin made about Gaynor, wasn't it?"

The other woman let out a light laugh. "You'd almost think she meant it, pet, wouldn't you?" Sensing someone in the doorway, the women turned around. Both carried more than a few extra pounds, as evidenced by the cardigans that stretched to cover their ample bosoms. With their white hair styled in the same one-length bob that reached just below their ears, and their almost identical eyeglasses, they could easily have passed for sisters.

"Oh, hello. Sorry to bother you," said Penny. "Only, I've just come to pick up Florence Semble's cake tin. She brought a Victoria sponge in it, but I'm not sure what it looks like."

"Oh, right," said Mari Jones, the woman who had been leaning on the worktop. She wiped her hands on her apron and pointed to a table where a cake tin sat with several plastic storage containers. "It's just over there." Penny picked up the tin, checked for Florence's name on the bottom, and, after thanking them, left the room and turned into the corridor, but she remained just outside the door, her back pressed against the wall.

"Do you think she heard?" one woman asked the other.

"Nah."

Cake tin in hand, Penny returned to the meeting room and approached the tall woman in the black skirt and yellow jacket, who was placing a couple of file folders into a worn brown leather briefcase.

"I'd like an application form to join the WG, please," Penny said as Victoria, raising her arms to adjust the blue velvet ribbon holding her short blond ponytail, caught her eye and threw her a conspiratorial nod and smile. "On second thought," added Penny, "better make that two."

On the short walk from the community centre back to the Spa, Victoria commented, "The missing Women's Guild cake knife that Elin talked about sounds as if it could be the one used to kill Gaynor Lewis. Gareth said the weapon had a long blade, remember? We should tell the police about it."

"We probably don't have to," Penny responded. "Didn't Elin say it's engraved with the WG logo or something? And if it is, the inscription will lead the police to the Women's Guild. The police are smart enough to figure that out."

"I'm not sure that's what Elin said," Victoria replied. "I think she said the server was engraved."

They stopped outside the little supermarket on the town square to wait for the traffic lights to change.

"The server, the cake knife. It doesn't matter which one has the engraving, because of course, you're right," Penny said. "We should tell the police. I don't know what I was thinking. I guess it just seemed to me that Bethan doesn't need me telling her the obvious. But the police always remind us not to withhold anything. To give them the information and let them decide if it's important or not."

The lights changed and they crossed the street.

"And if the WG's missing cake knife does turn out to be the knife the police have, at least that would clear up a little mystery for the Women's Guild," said Victoria. "They'd know what happened to their cake knife."

"I'll let Bethan know," said Penny.

Thirteen

I'm really glad you rang me," said Inspector Bethan Morgan that evening as Penny showed her through to her sitting room and waved her into a chair. "You've been on our list of persons to speak to in the Gaynor Lewis investigation and I'm sorry I haven't got round to you before now. I still need to take your statement, but you know how stretched our resources are. With so many people coming and going at the agricultural show on the Friday night, the night that Gaynor Lewis was killed, we've got a lot of interviews to conduct, as you can imagine. And most people aren't as reliable a witness as you, so I reckoned you'd keep."

Bethan and Penny had known each other for several years. When they'd met, Bethan had been an ambitious, dedicated sergeant assisting DCI Gareth Davies. On his recent retirement, Bethan had been promoted to inspector and was now a senior investigating officer with the Major Crimes Unit of the North Wales Police. Penny had supported both police officers through several cases, suggesting leads and passing along insights, information, and observations. Her opinions had always been seen as helpful and had been well received, and, occasionally, even sought out. Until a recent case, the first one Bethan had led on her own, when she had responded coolly when Penny stepped forward with information. Penny had been confused and hurt by Bethan's dismissiveness and apparent change in attitude toward her, but she had put it down to a young police officer's determination to succeed on her own, combined with a little overconfident stubbornness. But when the case stalled, Bethan had realized that she needed Penny's help, and had accepted it, at first grudgingly, and then gratefully.

And Penny had learned to choose her words carefully so Bethan wouldn't mistake her trying to help for her telling the police officer how to do her job.

"So," said Bethan running a hand through her dark curls and stretching out her legs. "You mentioned you had something for me. I'm all ears."

"It may be something you already know, but I thought I should tell you that Victoria and I attended the Women's Guild meeting today, and it seems they're missing a special knife. It's part of a silver set consisting of a cake stand, server, and knife that was presented to the Guild many years ago. The Best in Show cake at the agricultural show is always displayed on the stand, apparently, along with the knife and server. On Saturday, the server was on display beside the cake stand, but there was no knife. When we heard about the missing knife, it occurred to us that the missing Women's Guild cake knife could be your murder weapon."

"Why would you think that?" Bethan asked in a measured tone.

Penny realized that she could be sailing into choppy water by revealing operational information, given to her by Gareth Davies, Bethan's former boss, that Bethan wanted withheld from the public. Penny struggled with how best to respond, then decided that being up-front was the best way forward to keep her relationship with Bethan on an even keel.

"You know I found the body," Penny said. Bethan nodded. "Well, Gareth texted me Saturday night to tell me that the body had been identified as that of Gaynor Lewis and that the murder weapon was a knife with a long blade."

Bethan exhaled slowly. "Okay. I just wondered how you knew."

Penny heaved an inward sigh of relief. "I think it just slipped out. I hope you're not upset that he told me."

"No, I'm not upset. He shouldn't have mentioned it to you, but to be fair, technically, I shouldn't have allowed him to remain in the tent when the tablecloth was removed and the body was exposed. But since he was there, and with all his years of experience and expertise"—she gave a little shrug—"I figured, Why not let him have a little look? I'll take all the help I can get."

You've changed your tune! thought Penny, relieved that Bethan's more open attitude gave her permission to continue helping the police with their inquiries.

"Oh," said Penny, "about the knife. I almost forgot. There's something else that might help you." Bethan leaned forward. "The missing Women's Guild knife has a mother-of-pearl handle."

"The Women's Guild," Bethan said slowly. She steepled her hands and touched her lips with her fingertips as she weighed that information.

"Yes, and Gaynor Lewis was the president."

Bethan sat back in her chair and the tension drained out of her face. "Now that *is* interesting. We've been focused on the agricultural show people, but the information you've given me opens up another line of inquiry."

"The thing is, though," said Penny, "I've come to realize that the agricultural show committee and the Women's Guild are closely linked, both through what they do and the people involved."

"That's true," said Bethan. "We've discovered that the members of the Guild are heavily into the competitions, and the members of one family, the Devlins, seem to be running both organizations—Gaynor Lewis as president of the Women's Guild, and her sister-in-law, Joyce Devlin, as chair of the agricultural show committee."

Penny nodded.

"Anything else you can tell me?" Bethan asked.

"Yes, there is something. About the Devlins. Victoria and I visited Joyce Devlin's farm on Sunday. They've just had new dog kennels put in. All state-of-the-art. But I noticed some unpaid bills in the Devlins' kitchen, so I wondered where the money for the kennels came from. With Daffydd Devlin being treasurer of the show committee—"

"Farm financing is always complicated," said Bethan before Penny could finish her sentence. "There's probably a really simple explanation where they got the money, but we'll look into it." Was there a faint whiff of the old dismissiveness in Bethan's response? Penny wondered. She mentally shrugged it off. She'd done her bit and passed on the information to Bethan, and what Bethan chose to do with it was entirely up to her.

"Well, thank you for this. We'll talk again soon, I'm sure."

Penny opened her front door and stood to one side to allow Bethan to exit first. "I'm going to the agricultural show gala on Saturday night. I'll keep my ears open, if you like," Penny said as they walked together to Bethan's car.

"Please do," said Bethan. "Gareth will be there, too, I understand."

"There is something I'd like to know. If you can tell me, that is," Penny said.

A light smile crossed Bethan's face as she unlocked her vehicle, then turned to face Penny. "Now what would that be? I ask myself."

"The murder weapon. Did the knife have a mother-of-pearl handle?"

Bethan teased out the moment before replying. "Yes."

Fourteen

"Morning, Penny." Rhian looked up from her receptionist's desk and smiled a warm greeting as Penny entered the Spa on Saturday morning. "Looks like you've got a busy day ahead of you. Everybody's fully booked today, with the agricultural show gala dinner tonight, but Mrs. Lloyd just called, and apparently she forgot to make an appointment to get her hair done for the event. She asked if we could squeeze her in sometime today. Alberto said to tell her to come in as soon as she could, before he gets too busy, so I did. She should be here any minute."

Penny touched the ends of her blunt-cut bob and said, "I wonder if Alberto can squeeze me in, too."

"You're pushing your luck. He's only got one pair of hands, Penny."

"Right. Well, I'd better crack on, then."

Eirlys, Penny's assistant, was preparing for the day's work when Penny entered the manicure studio opposite the hair salon at the end of the corridor. Bright sunshine filtered in through the east-facing window, lighting up the wall display of nail varnishes in graduated colours from pale pinks through robust reds. Shades of brown, purple, and burgundy filled a row, and lively, bright shades of blue, green, and yellow for younger clients completed the selection.

A custom-built wall cabinet with fitted cupboards above a worktop and drawers below it took up the whole of one wall. Beside a small rumpled stack of clean white towels piled on the worktop waiting to be folded, Eirlys had placed the list of that day's clients. Penny rested her arms on the worktop and, leaning over, read out the first name on the list.

"Andrea Devlin." She turned to Eirlys. "She must be new. I don't think she's been here before."

"No, she hasn't," said a robust voice from the doorway. A tall, sturdy woman stepped into the room, her glossy chestnut brown hair framing a thin face and just reaching her broad shoulders. Her makeup had been expertly applied; the foundation was the perfect match for her skin tone, the eye shadow and mascara defined her eyes, and the effect was finished off with a bright slash of red lipstick. She wore tailored navy blue trousers with a pale blue long-sleeved blouse rolled back at the cuffs. "And it's pronounced *On-dray-ah.*"

Penny apologized for mispronouncing her client's name, then invited her to sit at the manicure table nearest the door. Eirlys set a basin of warm lavender-scented water in front of her. As Andrea tentatively dipped her fingertips in the soaking bowl, a puzzled look flashed across Eirlys's face, but she said nothing and went about her work, folding the pile of towels.

"Your last name is Devlin," said Penny to her client as she took the seat opposite her. "I know a Joyce Devlin. Any relation?"

"She's my sister-in-law."

Sister-in-law, thought Penny. The relationships in that family are already hard to keep straight, and now here's another relative.

Eirlys finished folding the towels and stacked them neatly in their basket. "Right, Penny, that's the towels done, so I'll be off now to the cash-and-carry to pick up that special order, and then I'm filling in for Rhian on the front desk for an hour. I'll be back in time for my afternoon appointments."

"Very good, Eirlys, but be back as soon as you can. We're going to be busy today, so it's all hands to the pumps. We may even have to try to fit in a walk-in client or two, like Alberto did."

"I'm happy to work through lunch today, if you need me to," said Eirlys. "I shouldn't be long." Just as she stepped into the corridor, she bumped into Mrs. Lloyd, who was on her way to the hair salon across the hall.

"Oh, Eirlys, dear, you almost bowled me over! Just wanted to pop my head in and have a quick word with Penny," said Mrs. Lloyd. At the sound of her voice, and the little flurry of activity in the corridor, Penny and her client turned their faces to the doorway.

Mrs. Lloyd smiled at Penny, and then, as her curious gaze moved to the woman getting her nails done, Mrs. Lloyd frowned slightly and her head tipped forward. Her eyes narrowed and as she gave a little start, her smile melted into a little *o* of puzzled surprise. She seemed about to say something, but as she struggled to shape the right words, Alberto emerged from the salon and crossed the corridor holding a zebra-striped hairdresser's cape. He reminded Mrs. Lloyd they were short of time and made an impatient gesture to encourage her to move into the salon. Mrs. Lloyd's attention snapped back to Penny.

"I just wanted to let you know that I've saved two places for you and Victoria at my table tonight at the agricultural show dinner. The secretary who looks after the seating placed some women from the Women's Guild at my table, too." Mrs. Lloyd raised her hand in a brief good-bye gesture and then, after another quick sideways glance at Andrea, hurried across the hall to get her hair done.

Andrea lowered her eyes and exhaled a long, soft breath.

"Are you all right?" Penny asked.

"Yes, I'm fine."

But Penny didn't think she was fine. Something had sparked instantly and rapidly between Andrea and Mrs. Lloyd, creating an arc of confused recognition. Perhaps Mrs. Lloyd had seen something in Andrea's appearance that was slightly different or unexpected, and had realized, as Penny had known when she'd turned around after reading Andrea's name on the day's client list, seen her standing in the doorway, and heard her pronounce her name in a practised, modulated tone, that Andrea was a transgender woman.

After a few more minutes of quiet soaking time, Penny lifted one of Andrea's hands out of the water and dried it gently, as she had done with countless other women. But this hand was different. Bigger, certainly, and the ring finger was slightly longer than the index finger.

As she began shaping the nails, she asked, "You're not from around here, are you?"

Andrea gave her a sharp look, then settled back into the chair as a small, tired laugh escaped her. "No, not anymore. I grew up here but left as a teenager, and I've been gone for years. Been living abroad. Started working in Berlin after the wall came down. I'm a painter and decorator, and there was a lot of work to be had in Germany in the early nineties after reunification."

"Oh, that's interesting," Penny said as she did a quick calculation. That would put Andrea in her mid-forties.

"So I lived there for a few years, and then I moved to Holland, where I've been living until recently." She gave Penny a sly smile. "But going by your accent, you're not from here, either, are you?"

"No, I'm originally from Canada, but I've lived here in Llanelen, gosh, almost thirty years. So this is my home now."

"No desire to move back?"

Penny shook her head. "I have no close family there, and I've been gone so long that there's nothing for me to go back to." She was silent for a moment and then decided to risk asking some questions of her own.

"What brings you back here now after all that time away?"

"A family matter."

That vague answer could mean just about anything, so Penny kept her response just as noncommittal. "Oh, I see. Yes, well, families . . ."

"Believe me," said Andrea, "I was really surprised to find

myself back here. But then, when I thought about it, I decided I should come, and I discovered I really wanted to."

Penny had finished applying the base coat and asked Andrea what colour nail varnish she would like.

"Well, she hated brown, so I'd like the brownest brown you've got." She rose from her chair, scanned the display of nail varnish bottles, and selected one. She set it emphatically on the table in front of Penny and took her seat. "That one." She held out her hands and Penny picked up the bottle and shook it.

Andrea let out a little laugh. "Oh, this is delicious. She hated this colour and I'm wearing it to her funeral!"

Penny blinked, holding the nail varnish applicator suspended above her client's fingernail. "You're here for a funeral?"

"Oh, yes. I don't know yet when it will be. My sister died. You probably heard about it. Gaynor Lewis. She was murdered, actually. It's too bad about the way she died, of course, but I can't say I'm sorry she's dead." She leaned forward as her body tensed. "She was a vicious, controlling bully and I hated the very bones of her." Saying those words, Andrea's previously well-modulated feminine voice lowered and the words dripped with bitterness just as the tiny drop of nail varnish that had formed on the tip of the little brush Penny was holding dropped onto the white towel, staining it the colour of dried blood.

Gaynor was her sister, thought Penny. And then everything fell into place when she remembered the photo Joyce Devlin had shown her in the kitchen. "That's the three of them," Joyce had said, "Gaynor and her two brothers. That's

Dev on the left, and Andy on the right, before he . . ." And now Penny could complete the sentence: "before he transitioned to a woman."

"Yes, everyone in town knows what happened to Gaynor," Penny said. "And I'm sorry for your loss. But under the circumstances, are you sure you want this colour?"

"Why? Does my reasoning sound petty to you?"

"*Petty*'s not the word I was thinking of." Penny replaced the applicator in the bottle. "It's you I'm thinking about. Your sister isn't here to see you wearing brown nail varnish, so this isn't about making a point with her. It's about you, and the only person you're hurting is yourself. Your wearing that colour because she hated it seems self-destructive. It locks you into negative feelings toward your sister. It perpetuates something negative, and that isn't good for you." Andrea's eyes met Penny's briefly, then flickered away. "Rather than choosing a colour someone else wouldn't like, why don't you choose a colour that you would like?" Penny suggested gently. "Something that you would enjoy wearing and would make you happy?"

After a moment's hesitation, Andrea returned to the display case and, hands behind her back while she swayed gently back and forth, examined the shelves. She selected two bottles of slightly different shades of a brilliant reddish orange hue and returned to the table with them.

The manicure completed, Penny walked Andrea down the corridor to the front desk, where she paid. Mrs. Lloyd, seated in the reception area, followed them with intensely watchful eyes, then stood up as Penny said good-bye to Andrea and closed the door behind her.

"If you've got a minute, Penny, I'd like a quick word, please," she said with a glance at Rhian. "Better make it in private," she added in a hushed tone.

Penny led the way to the quiet room, and when they were seated, Mrs. Lloyd blurted out, "Now you know me, Penny. I speak as I find. I was that shocked to see him here, in Llanelen of all places, looking like that."

"She's a transgender woman, Mrs. Lloyd," said Penny. "We have to respect that, and we must refer to her as 'she.'"

"But he isn't a she! He worked here in Llanelen as a painter and decorator. He did up my house after Arthur's aunt died, for pity's sake. And then he disappeared and we heard he was working on the Continent."

"Berlin."

Mrs. Lloyd let out a little snort of disgust. "Well, that explains it, then. It'll be all those German nightclubs. Decent folk can't begin to imagine what goes on there." She stood up. "His poor family. What they must be going through. First Gaynor, and now Andy's back, looking like that."

"No," replied Penny firmly. "Her name is Andrea." She pronounced it *On-dray-ah*.

Mrs. Lloyd repeated the pronunciation a couple of times, as if trying it out.

"Tell me something," said Penny. "You've lived here a long time and know just about everybody." And their business, she added silently. "Did you not hear that Andy Devlin had become Andrea?"

"No, I didn't. I expect the family didn't know what to make of it, so they just kept it quiet."

"Yes, I guess they did," Penny replied.

"And besides, I expect they were afraid of what folk would

say. People will talk, you know, Penny. Still, we've got to move with the times, I expect."

"It's true that times have changed," said Penny, "but even so, it took a lot of courage on her part to come back to this small town, unsure of what kind of reception she would get."

"True. Well, I must let you get on. I'll see you tonight at the dinner."

Fifteen

Joyce Devlin, wearing the same olive green dress with ruching and cap sleeves that she wore every year to the Llanelen agricultural show's gala dinner, greeted Penny and Victoria with a friendly hello as they entered the function room of the Red Dragon Hotel. At her side stood her ruddy-faced husband, Dev, looking out of place and uncomfortable in a navy blue suit that fit him as if it had been borrowed for the evening from a bigger brother.

"So pleased you could make it," Joyce said, extending a tanned, freckled hand. "Do go in"—she waved a hand toward the centre of the room—"and I hope you enjoy the evening. I'm sure you'll see lots of people you know."

Silver trophies and plates, returned by last year's winners and polished in readiness to be presented to those who had earned them this year, were arranged on a draped table along one wall. Although ribbons and rosettes had been handed out on the day of the show, the top awards, including Best in Show, were presented at the banquet. Because the winners were named at the show, there were no surprises, but the organizers felt that handing out awards at the banquet gave the top winners a little extra recognition, added purpose and focus to the evening, and ended the event on a high note.

Penny and Victoria paused to admire the prizes, then moved deeper into the room.

Round tables seating eight, covered with dark green cloths, were grouped in front of a small portable riser stage. A centrepiece of yellow roses, complemented by bright yellow cloth napkins at each of the eight place settings, graced each table.

The tables were filling up quickly as Penny and Victoria scanned the room, searching for Mrs. Lloyd. They recognized Gareth Davies, seated at a table with a RESERVED sign in the centre of it, near the stage. He was facing away from them, one arm draped lightly along the back of the chair of the blond woman seated next to him. Gareth said something to the woman and she turned to him, then smiled broadly and leaned into him with a familiar, easy manner. Gareth raised his hand from the back of her chair and placed it lightly on her shoulder for a moment, then dropped it back onto the chair.

"I wouldn't mind speaking to him later, if we get the chance," said Penny. "He might be able to tell us something about how the Gaynor Lewis investigation is going."

Victoria smiled. "He might."

As they were about to move on, Mrs. Lloyd stood up to get their attention and waved them over to her table.

"Oh, there she is," said Penny. They threaded their way between the almost-full tables to join her.

Florence, sitting on Mrs. Lloyd's left, acknowledged their arrival with a friendly nod and a warm smile.

"You can sit here beside me, Penny," Mrs. Lloyd said, indicating the empty chair on her right. "And Victoria, let's have you over there on the other side of Florence." Satisfied with her seating arrangements, Mrs. Lloyd sat down. "Now, as I mentioned to Penny at the Spa this morning, several members of the Women's Guild were assigned to our table, so let me try to introduce you to Mari and Delyth." The size of the table, combined with the volume of the background din, made conversation across the table difficult, and Mrs. Lloyd had to raise her voice to be heard. "Mari and Delyth were helping out with refreshments at the meeting, so we didn't see too much of them." Penny recognized them as the two white-haired women performing the washing-up after the tea service, when she entered the kitchen to retrieve Florence's cake tin. She smiled at them as Mrs. Lloyd moved on to the attractive woman sitting next to Mari. "And of course you remember Elin Spears, vice president of the WG. She chaired the meeting we attended."

"Of course." Penny offered an all-encompassing smile across the table. She thought back to the exchange she'd overheard, when either Mari or Delyth had said something along the lines that Elin had spoken her kind words about Gaynor Lewis almost as if she meant them. She wondered whose side Mari and Delyth were on. Were they friends of

145

Elin's, or had they been friends of Gaynor's? Or both? Or neither?

Having managed the introductions the best she could against the background noise, Mrs. Lloyd took a sip of water and turned slightly in her chair to contemplate her fellow diners. She always made an effort with her appearance, and she was looking particularly smart this evening in a cranberry brocade evening suit shot with metallic gold thread. Penny was about to compliment her on her outfit when the conversation level dropped as the guests realized the event was about to begin. Joyce Devlin and her husband, followed by a couple Penny didn't recognize, Barbara Vickers, and Michelle Lewis, made their way to the table where Gareth and his companion were seated. Michelle's blond hair, piled on top of her head and held loosely in place with a red plastic clip, sprouted loose strands that bobbed in time with her steps.

When the little procession reached the table reserved for show officials, Joyce's entourage took their seats, while Joyce herself continued walking to the small stage. As she stepped onto the riser, the room quieted further and all eyes turned expectantly toward her.

"Good evening, everyone," she said. "My name is Joyce Devlin, and it's my pleasure to welcome you tonight to the Llanelen agricultural show's gala dinner. Dinner service will begin in a few minutes, and following the dinner, we will have the presentation of this year's Best in Show awards. Bottles of wine are available for purchase, along with individual drinks, at the bar. So please enjoy your dinner, and I'll be back to speak to you later."

Was it strange that she didn't mention Gaynor Lewis in

146

her opening remarks? Penny wondered. Probably not. There'd be time for that later.

"I suppose we should get some wine," Mrs. Lloyd said.

"I'll go," said Penny. "Would we like red or white?"

"There're enough of us at the table to do justice to both. How about a bottle of each?"

Penny made her way to the bar as the diners tucked into the salads that had been set out at each place. A small queue had formed by the time she reached the bar, and she had to wait a few minutes to be served. Just as she finished asking for two bottles of wine, a familiar figure came to stand beside her.

"Hello again," said Andrea Devlin.

"Well, hi. You're looking very smart this evening," Penny replied, taking in the cut of Andrea's wide-legged black trousers and the smooth, shiny fabric of her floral-patterned jacket.

"Always nice to have a reason to dress up a bit," Andrea replied.

"And get your nails done."

Andrea laughed and held out her arms to display her nails. "You were right about the colour. This suits me much better."

"Good. And now here you are with nothing better to do on a Saturday night than attend the agricultural show dinner." Penny grinned.

"I might say the same for you." Andrea grinned back. "But yes, my niece Michelle mentioned the dinner, and as you've just pointed out, I didn't have anything better to do, and there were a few extra tickets available, so I thought I'd come along. Haven't found a place to sit yet, though. Where are you?"

"Oh, there's room at Mrs. Lloyd's table for you." Penny pointed out the table just as the barman brought the bottles of wine she'd ordered. "You'll find us right over there. You'd be welcome to join us, if you like."

"Okay, great, thanks. I'll just get my drink and see you in a few minutes."

Penny returned to her seat, and after sending both bottles of wine on their way around the table, she leaned over to Mrs. Lloyd and said, "I bumped into Andrea Devlin at the bar. The tables are full, so I invited her to join us. We've got an extra place." She looked toward the bar, and before Mrs. Lloyd could reply, Penny added, "Here she comes now."

Carrying a glass of beer, Andrea Devlin approached the table, nodded a reserved greeting to everyone, and then slid into the seat beside Penny. With Mrs. Lloyd's help, Penny tried above the din of conversation to introduce her to the rest of the table, and when she'd finished, Mrs. Lloyd leaned forward and spoke over Penny. "Hello. I remember when you"—at this, Penny leaned emphatically on Mrs. Lloyd's arm with her own—"when you painted the sitting room in my house on Rosemary Lane. Wonderful job you did, even though you were just, erm, young. It was one of your first jobs, I believe. In fact, I don't think it's been painted since. Are you still in the decorating business?"

"Yes, I am," said Andrea.

"And where are you living now?" Mrs. Lloyd continued.

"Oh, you know. Here and there. I'm not sure, really. I'm at one of those stages in life when a change of scenery seemed like a good idea. Pastures new, and all that." She took a sip of beer and picked up her fork, ready to make a start on the salad. "I'm toying with the idea of coming back to Llanelen to live. Maybe buying an old property and doing it up. I've seen a couple of places I quite like."

"Really?" said Mrs. Lloyd. "Well in that case, it would be pastures old rather than new, wouldn't it?" She buttered a piece of bread. "You know, Andrea," she enunciated the name deliberately, with just the slightest hesitation, as if she'd just been introduced to her, which in a way, she had. "You might be experiencing what we Welsh call *hiraeth*." She pronounced it *here-eyeth,* rolling the *r* a little, in a breathy sort of way. "Are you familiar with that?"

Andrea stabbed a couple of lettuce leaves. "I don't know what that word means."

"There's no real equivalent in English, but loosely translated, it means an acute longing for a home place. A place that you yearn to return to, and when you are away from it, you feel incomplete. Not homesick. It's deeper than that." She offered Penny a conspiratorial smile. "We know that you don't experience that for Canada."

"No, I can't say I do. But I might if I were away from Llanelen for too long. I'm happy here. This is my home, and it has been for a long time. It's where I belong," Penny said. "Funny you should mention this. Andrea and I were talking about it just this morning."

They continued eating for a few minutes in silence, and then, against the backdrop of scraping cutlery, Penny asked Andrea, "How long have you been back?"

"Oh, not very long," she said with a vague, airy wave. "I'm not stopping here in town, though. An old mate in Betws is kindly putting me up while I weigh my options. I'm doing a little decorating for him in return."

149

"I expect he's glad of that. I know I would be," Penny replied.

"Why? Do you have some painting or decorating work that needs doing?"

"Well, no."

"Didn't think so. Your spa looks beautiful. Lovely colours, if I may say."

"Oh, well, thank you. I just meant that if I did need work doing, I'd be glad to have you do it. My cottage was done up a few years ago, and the Spa was renovated even more recently. So even though I'm not in the market right now for painting and decorating services, I'm sure there's no shortage of work in the area."

"That's true. I get my jobs through word of mouth and usually have two or three lined up. But that's not my real area of interest."

"No?"

"Not really. You see, when I was in Berlin, we worked on beautiful centuries-old properties that had been neglected or altered during the Communist years, and it was a real thrill seeing them restored. So what I really enjoy is working on older buildings. I love the paint colours, and I like working with heritage paints. And don't get me started on vintage wallpapers."

"But is there much of that kind of work to be had around here?" asked Mrs. Lloyd. "On old buildings, and such like."

"There are quite a few National Trust properties in the area, if you include Liverpool and Manchester, and a few private homes, too, in need of that kind of restoration and maintenance work," said Andrea. "But it's not just painters and decorators. There's a great demand for all the traditional building trades, such as carpentry, joinery, stone masonry, brickwork, and plasterwork. If you're good at what you do, word gets around, and there's always work available. More work than you can handle, really."

"So with your sister Gaynor's death, do you think you'll stay in Llanelen, then, or had you been thinking about stopping here anyway?" Mrs. Lloyd asked. "What I'm wondering, I guess, is did that change things for you?"

"Well, I'm not sure what I'm going to do, to be honest, but obviously when Michelle—that's my niece—called to tell me about Gaynor, well . . ." Andrea raised an elegant shoulder in a little shrug, leaving the rest of the sentence unspoken, and open to whatever interpretation Mrs. Lloyd chose to put on it.

"And Michelle. I've been thinking about her," said Penny. "How's she coping?"

"I'm not sure, really. She's got a lot on. She'd been planning a move before all this happened, and, well, with her daughter to worry about, it's an emotional and stressful time. Her partner left a little while ago, so Gaynor had been helping out with the child minding. If nothing else, Michelle will miss that." Andrea's tone was neutral, and she spoke without a trace of the bitterness in her voice that Penny had heard when Andrea had discussed Gaynor during her manicure that morning.

Before Penny could respond, servers moved around the table, removing the salad plates and setting the entrées in front of them. She had chosen the vegetarian option, stuffed portobello mushrooms with rice and maple-glazed carrots.

"Not having the lamb, Penny?" Mrs. Lloyd asked.

"I couldn't possibly. I like them in their fields but not on my plate."

"Well, that certainly sets you apart around here, surrounded as we are by hardworking farmers raising the finest Welsh lamb for the nation's dinner tables."

Penny laughed lightly. "True, but I just can't eat lamb."

When dinner was over, plates cleared, coffee and tea poured, and chairs pushed back from the table as the diners made themselves comfortable, preparations for the prize giving began.

Joyce Devlin returned to the stage and Barbara Vickers positioned herself beside the trophy table. Just as Joyce unfolded a piece of paper, Elin Spears excused herself and headed for the exit. Joyce glanced down at her from the stage as she passed below her. Penny sensed a sudden change in the atmosphere, although she couldn't tell if it was because the prize giving was about to start or because the audience anticipated that Joyce might be about to tackle the elephant in the room and say something about the death of Gaynor Lewis. Reading from the paper, Joyce opened her remarks with a brief but somewhat impersonal tribute to Gaynor Lewis. She concluded by saying, "And a fierce competitor she was, until the last. She would have been so proud to know that her splendid marmalade won the last competition she ever entered."

"And how did that happen, I'd like to know," muttered Mrs. Lloyd. Florence shot her the stern, hushing look often used by mothers in church.

As Joyce wrapped up her comments about Gaynor's untimely death and prepared to present the awards, Elin returned to the table.

Interesting, thought Penny. I wonder if she really had to go to the loo or if she ducked out so she wouldn't have to listen to Joyce say nice things about Gaynor in death, when neither one of them had liked her in life. Still, that happens when someone dies. A dark curtain of politeness descends to hide misdeeds, misunderstandings, and transgressions once thought unforgivable. And there are certain polite conventions to be observed. After all, Joyce had to say something about Gaynor, and it had to be positive.

Penny refocused her attention on the presentation of awards. "And the winner of the Bodnant Silver Salver for Best in Show, floral exhibits, once again is Heather Hughes." Heather was given a hearty round of applause, as she was every year, when she stepped forward to accept the trophy. Mrs. Lloyd had been right when she'd remarked that the same people won year after year.

"Moving on now to the animal husbandry awards," Joyce continued. "The show committee is delighted to present the highly coveted Countryside Cup to our very own Haydn Williams, in recognition of his outstanding contributions to the breeding and rearing of Welsh mountain sheep right here in Llanelen."

Haydn made his way from the back of the room and accepted the cup, an elaborate creation with a silver sheep on top. He hoisted it in front of the crowd, who acknowledged it with good-natured clapping and shouting, then returned to his seat.

"The award for Best in Show in the poultry category, and this includes ducks, chickens, turkeys, and pigeons, goes to Carwyn Lewis for his Silkies," Joyce announced.

Elin rose from the table and stepped onto the stage, where she shook hands with Joyce and accepted a silver trophy.

"Why is Elin Spears up there accepting his award?" Penny asked.

"Because she's his partner, and Carwyn couldn't make it tonight," replied Mrs. Lloyd. "That's why we had an empty place at our table. It was meant for him. I'm not sure why he's not here, though." She adjusted her handbag in her lap. "Perhaps he thought Joyce would have to say something about Gaynor, and he just didn't want to be here for that, so he offered to mind little Macy so that Michelle could be here."

Elin returned to the table, carrying the silver cup by its two handles. She set it down at her place and threw everyone at the table a satisfied smile on Carwyn's behalf. A few minutes later, she herself was called back to the stage to accept the Best in Show award for her prizewinning rosette cake.

When the remaining awards had been presented and everyone congratulated, a last rush of conversation broke out as the event wound down and people prepared to depart.

"I meant to ask you earlier why Carwyn isn't here to accept the award himself this evening," Mrs. Lloyd said to Elin Spears across the table. "I've never known him to miss the dinner, so I wondered if he might have been looking after Macy so that Michelle could be here tonight."

"Oh, no, nothing like that. He's working tonight. Told me not to expect him back until late, but he wasn't sure what time."

"Working?" Mrs. Lloyd looked puzzled. "On a Saturday night? Working where?"

"Oh, you haven't heard?" Elin said, a hint of smugness enlivening her smile. "Well, I'm sure you would have heard all about it in a day or two. Carwyn's bought Maggie's

Coaches. You know, the coach company that does the day trips around the area? of course, he's fully qualified, got all the proper operating licences and permits. So he's been out and about all week, driving. Today he took a group to Manchester for a fancy lunch someplace, then an afternoon concert, then high tea. The trips are really popular, and when we bought the company, of course we agreed to run all the outings already scheduled, so as not to disappoint those who'd already booked. They're mostly seniors and they count on Maggie's Coaches for their day trips. And overnights, too. We've a lovely four-day excursion to Dorset coming up in March. You and Florence might want to get in on that. There's a few seats left. I'll be handling all the bookings, so if you want to go, just let me know."

"Oh, I see," said Mrs. Lloyd. "Well, we'll certainly think about it."

"And I hope you've all signed up for our Women's Guild trip to Speke Hall on Wednesday. Maggie's Coaches will be providing the transport services for that, naturally."

"Naturally."

"Did she just say Speke Hall?" Andrea asked Penny. "What we were talking about earlier. I'm going to be doing some work there."

"Oh, really? Maybe we'll see you there. I've never been to Speke Hall, so Victoria and I decided to go along on the outing. We're both looking forward to it."

Mrs. Lloyd stood up, signalling that as far as she was concerned, both the conversation and the evening were at an end. The rest of the table followed suit, and with polite good nights exchanged, everyone began filing out of the room. The procession was slow as people stopped to exchange a quick word with those they hadn't had a chance to speak to during the course of the evening.

At the exit, Victoria and Penny caught up to Gareth Davies and his dinner companion.

"Hello Penny, Victoria," he said. "You remember Fiona Barton, of course." He gave the woman beside him an appreciative, reassuring glance.

Gareth had been introduced to Fiona a few months earlier when she visited Llanelen with two friends of Penny's. Fiona and Gareth had hit it off over the course of several rounds of golf, and after the visit ended, they had continued seeing each other in Edinburgh, where Fiona lived. A few weeks later, Gareth had told Penny during an awkward and halting conversation that he was developing strong feelings for Fiona. Rather than being upset or hurt, as he had feared, Penny had been relieved. She liked Gareth, and wanted him to be happy, but they had both realized that the kind of deep, romantic happiness he craved was not hers to give.

"Yes, of course I remember Fiona. Nice to see you again. How are you?" Penny said with a sincere smile as Fiona slipped just a little bit closer to Gareth. He placed his arm around her trim waist and she rested her fingertips possessively on his chest. "I was wondering if there's any news on the Gaynor Lewis investigation," Penny asked Gareth.

"Oh, I'm sure there is," he replied smoothly. "But I'm afraid I can't tell you what that is. Bethan hasn't asked for my help, and I'm no longer in the loop."

"And that's a good thing, too," said Fiona in a light, educated Scottish accent. "He's got more than enough on his plate right now while we're getting his house ready to sell.

You have no idea how much work is involved. There's simply masses of stuff to be cleared out."

"Oh," said Penny, "you're selling your house? Finally getting around to downsizing, are you?" A widower with two grown children who had long since moved away, Gareth had spoken occasionally of selling the family home and moving to a smaller house or apartment. But he was attached to his garden, in the same way Penny was attached to her cottage, and could never quite bring himself to commit to moving. But now, apparently, in Fiona, he'd found the motivation he needed. Gareth gave an embarrassed little shrug. "Sorry, I meant to tell you."

"He's moving to Scotland," said Fiona, tucking her arm into his and beaming up at him.

"Oh, right, well . . ." Penny's voice trailed off. She hesitated, unable to find the right words. If she seemed too enthusiastic about Gareth leaving, he might think she was glad to see him go. On the other hand, if she seemed distressed or upset that he was leaving, he might misinterpret that to mean there was still hope of a deeper emotional relationship with her. And she had to be especially tactful with her response in front of Fiona. Penny's initial reaction, however, bordered on relief that Gareth's leaving meant a clean break, and neutrality. As she and Gareth had been growing steadily apart and were not spending nearly as much time together as they used to, it really wouldn't make too much difference in her life if he did move away. But she would need more time, she realized, to sort out her feelings and determine how she felt. Fortunately, Florence and Mrs. Lloyd had joined them just in time to catch Fiona's last sentence and saved her the necessity of replying.

"Moving to Scotland!" Mrs. Lloyd exclaimed. "Whatever for? Don't tell me you're moving there for the golf! We've got perfectly good golf courses right here in . . ." Her words trailed off as she read the meaning behind Fiona's triumphant look and took in the possessive grasp on Gareth's arm. "Oh, I see. Well, that's lovely, and I hope you'll . . ." She glanced at Florence, who stood behind her, head tipped slightly to one side as a soft smile played at the corner of her lips. "Well, we'd best be off home," said Mrs. Lloyd, attempting to recover from her little Scottish gaffe. "Florence doesn't like a late night."

When Mrs. Lloyd and Florence were safely out of earshot, Penny, Gareth, and Victoria burst out laughing. Fiona, who didn't share a history with Mrs. Lloyd as Penny, Victoria, and Gareth did, smiled awkwardly and shot Gareth a questioning look.

" 'Florence doesn't like a late night,' " Gareth repeated. "That's one way to extricate yourself from a conversation."

As Gareth and Fiona said good night and left, Heather Hughes approached Penny and Victoria, carrying the Best in Show trophy for her floral entries. Victoria congratulated her, and then stifled a yawn.

"Look," said Heather to Victoria, "you're tired. Why don't I drive Penny home? It's practically on my way."

"That would be wonderful," said Penny. "Victoria doesn't like a late night!"

"I'm parked just over this way, Penny." Heather pointed with her car keys to the last row of vehicles in the Red Dragon Hotel's car park.

"It's good of you to give me a lift home."

"Oh, it's no trouble. As I said, you're practically on my way," Heather replied as she unlocked the doors. "Jump in." She laid the silver salver she'd been awarded for her gardening efforts on the backseat, started the car, and they soon joined the orderly queue of vehicles exiting the car park. A white coach with *Maggie's Coaches* splashed across the side in purple script idled across from the hotel.

"There was a lot of interest at our table in your dinner companion," Heather said as she pulled out onto the main road that ran through Llanelen.

"My dinner companion? Oh, Andrea, you mean."

"Oh, is that what she's called?"

"Yes. And I can imagine her presence would cause a stir. It must take some courage to return to the town that knew you as someone else after you've undergone such a major transformation."

"I'm not sure of the correct language," said Heather, "but that's something we're all going to have to learn."

"You're not the only one. Mrs. Lloyd is also trying to find her way around that," said Penny.

"I don't want to say the people around here are cruel, because they're not, but I'm quite sure for everyone in Llanelen this will be the first time they've encountered a transgender person. You might see that in more cosmopolitan places like Manchester, but we're not that sophisticated." She laughed lightly. "We're just a small, rural farming community. What do we know? And when confronted with things they don't quite understand, the people here can be, oh, I don't know, unsure what to do or say. As I said, I don't think they intend to be cruel. So they come across as insensitive.

They might lash out. And of course, the gossip! That can be devastating. When my daughter's marriage didn't work out, the things people said and the questions they asked! The poor girl was afraid to show her face in town."

"I'm sorry to hear that," said Penny.

"Anyway, I saw Andrea Devlin in Betws over a week ago. Wasn't sure at first who it was, and it took me a few minutes to work it out. Something about her looked familiar, and when I realized it was Andy Devlin, as was, I was a bit shocked. I had no idea that he'd undergone something like that."

"I don't think anybody knew. The family seems to have kept it all very quiet. So you knew her of old, then?"

"Oh, yes. We went to school together. She's been gone for a long time, though, and a lot of water under the bridge since then. In all our lives."

"And you say you saw her in Betws. I'm curious about that. She mentioned she'd been stopping with a mate who lives there. What day was it, do you remember?"

"Let me see. Thursday or Friday, it must have been. Toward the end of the week." She thought for a moment, then added, "It was definitely Friday, yes, because first I dropped off my entries to the agricultural show. You and Victoria took them in, actually, but you were really busy at the time. And after that I delivered bunches of fresh herbs to the hotel in Betws. I decided to stop in at the café for a coffee before heading home. I was a bit tired, and thought the coffee would perk me up a bit. And that's where I saw her. In the café." And then, almost as an afterthought, Heather added, "She was with Gaynor Lewis."

"What? Wait!" exclaimed Penny. "Are you saying you saw Andrea in the café in Betws with Gaynor Lewis?"

"That's right. They were seated in one of those booths at the front. I ordered my coffee at the counter and then I took a table toward the rear, so I walked past them. Andrea looked up at me, and as I said, her face seemed familiar, but it took me a while to place her. To realize who she was. It puzzled me the whole time I was drinking my latte, actually. Anyway, I had a good view of them from where I was sat, but they took no notice of me. They seemed to be arguing, or at least engaged in a lively discussion."

"And you're quite sure it was Gaynor that Andrea was with? Couldn't have been someone else?"

"No, it was definitely Gaynor. I've been a guest speaker at the WG meetings a couple of times, talking about getting your garden ready for winter, and she introduced me once. The other time I was introduced by Elin Spears, I think it was."

"Could you hear what they were saying? Gaynor and Andrea?"

"No, I was too far back, but you could tell from the look of them—the hand gestures and the tension in the shoulders and so on."

"Oh, right. And what time would this have been?"

Heather hesitated. "Oh, it must have been about sixish, maybe a bit later. Anyway, the café was just about to close and the place was almost empty. Why? Is it important, do you think?"

"I think it's terribly important," said Penny. "You do realize that Gaynor died sometime Friday night, or early Saturday morning. The police will be very interested in tracing her movements on the day she died. Have you called them?"

"No. But you think I should?"

"Definitely. You have to call them in the morning. Ask to speak to Inspector Bethan Morgan. She's the detective in charge of the case, and she'll be glad to hear from you."

"Tomorrow's Sunday."

"That's okay. Call them anyway. A murder investigation doesn't stop because it's Sunday." Heather pulled up in front of Penny's cottage, and after thanking her for the lift home, Penny let herself in to a cool greeting from Harrison, who didn't really approve of her going out of an evening. He much preferred that she stay home and have an early night with him.

Sixteen

Candy floss clouds drifted across a brilliant blue Llanelen sky as Penny entered the town square on the morning of the day trip to Speke Hall. She and Victoria had arranged with their staff to take the day off and both were looking forward to a pleasant outing to a beautiful historic building. And Penny had confided to Victoria that she was hoping the trip would give her the chance to get to know Elin Spears a little better.

Penny waved to Victoria as she waited for the traffic lights to change, and when they did, she crossed the main road and the two friends joined the group of Women's Guild members eager to board the white coach with *Maggie's Coaches* emblazoned across the side in bright purple script.

Short and compact, with a fit, wiry physique hidden under a loose-fitting purple fleece, Carwyn Lewis, owner of the coach, stood to one side of the door, glancing at a seating plan, then telling each passenger her assigned seat number and offering a steady, friendly hand to everyone as they placed a tentative foot on the little wooden step that bridged the gap between the cobbles and the bottom step of the coach.

His dark eyes scanned the square as he checked the list on his clipboard. After running a hand through his short salt-and-pepper hair, he climbed the steps of the coach and addressed the passengers on board.

"We're just short the one passenger. We'll give her a minute or two, and hope she turns up."

"Oh, is it Barbara?" called out a woman from the rear of the coach. "I've just seen her out the window. Here she comes now."

Penny, who was seated beside the window in the first row, peered out and frowned as Barbara Vickers slouched toward the coach. "She's taking her time," she said to Victoria.

Carwyn Lewis leapt out of his seat and descended the stairs to help Barbara board the coach.

"There you are," he said when she reached the top of the stairs. "Saved you a seat right at the front beside Bronwyn." When Barbara was seated, Carwyn started the motor and the coach pulled away.

The coach filled with quiet chatter as the highly anticipated late-summer outing to Speke Hall rolled along. Soon they had left behind the narrow streets of Llanelen and were speeding through timeless landscapes with a strong sense of place on the road to Liverpool.

Carwyn had announced they'd be stopping in about an hour for morning coffee at a garden centre, and everyone was looking forward to that, along with the chance to stretch their legs.

The seats were comfortable, although their dark blue fabric covering was worn and faded. Tired after a sleepless night and an early start, Penny sank back into her seat. Lulled by the steady sound of the vehicle's motor, she closed her eyes and was soon asleep. Some time later, the slowing of the coach awakened her, and she opened her eyes as the coach pulled into the garden centre.

"Right, ladies," said Carwyn. "I need to see everyone back here in forty-five minutes." Penny and Victoria, nearest the door, stepped off the coach and waited for Bronwyn Evans, the rector's wife, who was seated in the window seat across the aisle from them. Several women emerged before her.

"Sorry, I had to climb over Barbara," Bronwyn said as she joined Penny and Victoria. "She's sleeping quite soundly. I don't think she's feeling well."

"I fell asleep myself," said Penny. "Right. Let's go find a cup of coffee. It's just what I need."

"Shall we wait for Mrs. Lloyd and Florence?" asked Bronwyn. "They might think it rather strange if we don't."

Mrs. Lloyd, Florence, and Elin Spears, the WG president, were the last off the coach. As Elin stayed behind to speak to Carwyn, Penny and her friends ambled off in search of coffee.

A massive retail operation, the garden centre featured everything from outdoor furniture to home accessories, stationery, books, a food hall with gourmet specialty jams, confectionery, teas, and coffees, and a busy café. Mrs. Lloyd paused to examine various items as they made their way through the displays, and most of the women from the coach were already seated with their cups of tea and coffee by the time Penny led her group into the café.

When they were settled with their drinks, Mrs. Lloyd remarked that she had been in touch with Andrea Devlin about giving her a quote on some decorating.

"She's going to try to fit us in as soon as she can," Mrs. Lloyd said. "But she's got several projects ahead of us. And she's working at Speke Hall, would you believe! Anyway, I'm thinking about getting the dining room painted."

"Oh, nice," said Penny. "What colour?"

"We haven't decided. You're an artist. You know paint. Do you have any suggestions?"

Penny thought for a moment. "Well, I understand that warm neutrals or bright jewel tones are the in thing right now. And you'll want a colour that works with your sitting room. Or you might want to get the sitting room done in the same colour, so there's what designers call 'flow.'"

"Oh, here we go," muttered Florence. "I told her that the minute Andrea picks up her paint roller, there'll be no end to it, but does she listen? Does she, heck as like."

"You could discuss it with Andrea. She would probably have some good ideas," said Penny. "At the very least, she'll know what colours are popular."

As the conversation continued in a light and pleasant vein, Penny's thoughts drifted away. But when Florence stiffened suddenly and glanced over her shoulder at the group of women seated at a table behind them, Penny's attention snapped back.

"What is it, Florence?" she asked.

"I just heard something that reminded me," she said in a low voice. Everyone leaned forward to hear better.

"What? What did you hear?" asked Mrs. Lloyd.

"Somebody at a table behind us just said 'pet.' She said something like 'The same thing happened to me, pet.'"

"Sorry, I don't understand what you're getting at," said Penny.

"When I heard those words, I remembered. The woman who rang the Thursday night before the agricultural show and told me to bring my entries on the Saturday morning, she used the word *pet*." Florence raised a hand to her forehead, as if the gesture would help her recall exactly what was said. "'You can just bring them in the morning, pet.' Those were her words. That's what the caller said."

Penny's eyes shifted to the left, past Florence. Seated at the table directly behind them were Elin Spears and her friends from the WG, Mari Jones and Delyth, whose surname Penny did not know. Mari and Delyth had sat across from her at Mrs. Lloyd's table on Saturday night at the agricultural show banquet, but because of the size of the table, and the difficulty hearing and conversing against the background din, she had not had a chance to speak to them. Now she hoped she'd get a chance to speak with them during the course of the day.

Mari, apparently sensing a pair of eyes upon her, looked up from the slice of cake she was attacking, and with a fork poised in her right hand, she asked with a smile, "All right? Enjoying yourself?"

Penny returned the smile and nodded as Florence frowned and turned her head slightly. At that moment, Carwyn Lewis, the coach driver, passed by their table and stopped at the next one to speak to Elin. A moment later Elin got up, said something to her companions, and she and Carwyn left.

"Bronwyn, who is that woman with Mari Jones?" Penny asked. Bronwyn didn't have to look to know whom Penny meant. "Oh, that'll be Delyth Powell. They look like sisters, but they're not. They've been best friends, though, for a very long time. Both retired teachers. You don't often see one without the other." She checked her watch. "Our forty-five minutes are almost up. If Carwyn and Elin are going back to unlock the coach, I think I'll go with them and see how Barbara's doing. I hope a little sleep did her good and that she's feeling better. I'm a bit worried about her, to be honest. She looked very peaky. I wonder if I should take her anything."

"Maybe a bottle of water," suggested Florence. "Here, I'll get one and go with you."

"That's probably a good idea," agreed Bronwyn. "As much as I hate those plastic bottles, I guess we really don't have a choice."

Seventeen

*B*arbara had perked up a little by the time the last of the women, many laden with shopping bags filled with items they had bought at the garden centre, returned to the coach and climbed on board. Sitting up straight, both hands wrapped around the water bottle Bronwyn had brought her, Barbara, who had moved into the window seat, acknowledged her friends as they passed her and headed down the aisle to their seats.

Once the coach was under way, it wasn't long before the rugged terrain of North Wales flattened into the level fields of England. On the coach rolled, as countryside gave way to an urban, built-up environment, through Runcorn across the Mersey River on the Silver Jubilee Bridge, and then entered the industrial suburbs of Liverpool. They passed a sprawling car-manufacturing plant, the sun glinting off the roofs and windows of thousands of freshly minted vehicles parked in neat rows, signalling they were almost there, and finally they turned onto a long avenue flanked by old-growth trees, their lush green tops forming a leafy canopy, that brought them to their destination: Speke Hall.

The coach slowed to a stop in the car park. Carwyn switched off the engine, then stood in the aisle, facing the passengers, to remind them that there was no formal tour or program, so they were free to explore the house and grounds as they wished, and to be back on the coach by three-thirty for the journey home. He wished them a pleasant day, then opened the door. He stepped nimbly down the stairs, retrieved the little wooden stool from the coach's luggage compartment, and placed it at the bottom of the steps.

As the women gathered up their belongings, ready to leave, Penny turned to Victoria. "Why don't you go on ahead with Bronwyn," she said. "I'd like to see if I can have a quiet word with Barbara about Florence's marmalade. I haven't given up on that, and I haven't heard back from Joyce. I just want to see if Joyce had a chance to speak to her about it, now that the show and banquet are over."

"Right. I'll wander around in the garden for a bit and see you in, what, twenty minutes at the entrance and we can explore the house together?"

"Sounds good. I can't wait to see that William Morris wallpaper."

Victoria leaned across the aisle to explain Penny's plan to Bronwyn, and as the women filed off the bus, Penny slid into Bronwyn's now-empty aisle seat. Penny introduced herself to Barbara Vickers, explaining their paths had crossed on the

Friday night of the agricultural show when Penny and Victoria had checked in the entries to the home-crafts categories.

"Oh, yes," said Barbara, "I remember you. I'm sorry I wasn't able to really speak to you properly. That was a busy time and we had a million things to do, but still, I should have introduced myself." Or Joyce should have introduced us, thought Penny, but never mind that now.

Penny explained the telephone call Florence had received, asking her to bring in her entries on the Saturday morning, that she had, in fact, entered them on time, and that her jar of marmalade was missing from the competition, and then asked if Barbara could shed any light on what might have happened.

Barbara glanced past Penny. The aisle was now almost clear, with just Elin Spears, Dyleth Powell, and Mari Jones left to disembark.

"Come along now, ladies," Elin said to Penny and Barbara. "Carwyn needs to lock up the coach, and he can't do that until everybody's off." She stood in the aisle, one hand on the headrest of the seat behind Penny and the other hand on the top of the corresponding seat across the aisle, until Barbara and Penny were off the bus.

The group made their way out of the car park and walked toward Speke Hall, with Mari and Delyth in front and Penny and Barbara following. Elin had remained behind to speak to Carwyn, telling Mari and Delyth that she'd catch up with them.

"Well, now that you mention it," said Barbara, "I did notice something. Not on the Friday night or Saturday, but

Sunday morning. It seemed odd," she said. "So I checked, and it does have something to do with your friend's missing marmalade."

Penny's heart beat a little faster, with that same kind of excited anticipation you experience when you've been to three shops looking for an item and then finally, when you've just about given up hope, you spot it in the fourth shop, as if it were waiting just for you to find it. "What is it? What did you see?"

They had reached the cluster of renovated home-farm buildings that housed the shop, restaurant, and reception. Penny and Barbara showed their entry cards to the attendant and accepted a map of the site.

"Actually," said Barbara, shifting her handbag from one shoulder to the other and glancing at Mari and Delyth, who were browsing a selection of pamphlets and books about the property, "I have to go the loo in the worst way. I've not been feeling all that well these past few days. You know how it is. So I'm afraid you're just going to have to excuse me, while I . . ."

Penny pointed to an overhead sign. "It's through there. But before you go, could you just tell me what . . ."

"Sorry," said Barbara, her small dark eyes darting in the direction Penny had indicated and her body shifting slightly in that direction. "It'll take too long to explain." She turned to go, then offered over her shoulder, "Perhaps I'll bump into you later or see you in the café at lunchtime." With that, she darted away, leaving Penny frustrated and burning with curiosity. Damn, she thought. I was so close. What was it that Barbara had seen? She considered following Barbara, but when she checked her watch, she realized it was time to meet Victoria. Torn, she hesitated, then returned to the main path that led to Speke Hall. A few minutes later, Victoria sauntered in from the garden with a small group of people.

"I've just heard that there's a tour about to start," Victoria said. "I thought we could join it. You learn so much more from someone who really knows the place."

"All right. We can do that."

"How'd you get on with Barbara? Learn anything?" Victoria asked.

Penny shook her head. "She wanted to tell me something, but she had to dash off to the loo. At least that's what she said. Mari Jones and Delyth Powell were lurking nearby, and I thought maybe Barbara didn't want to say anything in front of them. Barbara said she'd look for me in the café at lunchtime."

"Well, at least you didn't try to follow her to the loo."

"Oh, believe me, it flashed through my mind, but I thought it best to give the poor woman some privacy, and anyway, it was time to meet up with you."

"Let's just put all that aside for the moment and enjoy this beautiful building," said Victoria. "Look at that!" She pointed to the half-timbered façade with its distinctive black-and-white geometric pattern. "It's stunning."

"You're right," said a stout man in a windproof jacket, who introduced himself as an outdoor tour guide. "It is beautiful. That's the typical wattle-and-daub construction of a Tudor house."

Other visitors joined the group, and the guide continued. "Speke Hall is one of the most important surviving timber-framed buildings in Britain. It was built in stages, and reached its present form in 1598. And it's been sold only once in its five-hundred-year history, and that was back in 1795, to a wealthy merchant who had made a fortune in the West Indies."

The guide provided more interesting details on the building, from its Tudor origins through an extensive Victorian makeover and refurbishment. He reminded them that when the house was built, England was in the turbulent aftermath of Henry VIII's break with the Roman Catholic Church, and because the house had been built by the Catholic Norris family, it included a priest hole, where Catholic priests could be hidden from persecution.

He led the group through a small door and into an open courtyard. Another door, flanked by two magnificent yew trees, lay ahead of them. "That door," explained the guide, "is the original entrance to the house. And just to the right of it, if you look up"—and all eyes were dutifully raised— "you'll see a hole. This is called an 'eavesdrop.' This is where servants could listen to the conversations of the people waiting outside before admitting them to the house. Particularly useful if the people asking for admission were soldiers. Give you a bit of time to hide the priest. So be sure to look for the priest hole on the first floor, in the Green Bedroom."

"What's a priest hole?" asked a boy. Penny judged him to be about ten years old.

"Well, this house was built by a great Catholic family," explained the guide, "and in the sixteenth century, when King Henry the Eighth separated from the Catholic Church, Catholics weren't allowed to practise their religion. Everybody was supposed to follow the new religion that we know

now as the Church of England, with Henry as its head. But some people liked the old religion and wanted to stay with it. And then, during the reign of his daughter, Queen Elizabeth the First, it was a very dangerous time, so big old houses like this became safe havens for Catholic priests, and when the queen's soldiers came riding up the drive, looking for the priest, the family would hide him in the priest hole, for as long as it took. So the priest hole is a secret hiding place. And as far as we know, this house has only one. Some properties have as many as fifteen!"

"Wow!" exclaimed the boy. He seemed satisfied with the explanation, and the guide wrapped up his presentation.

"A docent will be stationed in most of the main rooms of the house, and he or she will be happy to explain everything to you in as much detail as you like." He gave a little farewell nod. "Well, this is where I leave you. I hope you'll take your time and enjoy your tour of the property."

"What's a docent?" the boy asked as the crowd moved forward, leaving the guide to explain.

Penny and Victoria crossed the threshold and stepped back five hundred years in time, into the home of a once-great family. Pleasant domestic smells—old papers and textiles, candle smoke, polished wood, scrubbed floors—that had accumulated across centuries greeted them.

They wandered off down the corridor, exploring from room to room. They admired the carved sixteenth-century panelling of the Great Hall, examined the ornate plaster ceiling of the Great Parlour, and lingered in the library, where Penny was thrilled to see the original green William Morris wallpaper from the Victorian renovation.

After working their way through the treasures on the

ground floor, they climbed the stairs, carpeted with a well-worn burgundy runner, to the first floor, where an elderly man wearing the blue jacket of a volunteer guide rose from a modern folding chair to greet them.

"Please explore at your leisure," he said, adding, "You'll find all the main bedrooms open, but some painting's been scheduled for a couple of the side rooms, and they've been blocked off. I suggest you start here," he added, gesturing to the nearest open door, "at the Blue Bedroom, and you can work your way down to the end of the corridor and around the corner and you'll finish up at the bathroom. You'll find placards in all the rooms explaining the furnishings and the many interesting features. Take your time."

Unusual for its period, the bedroom floor featured a long, dark-panelled corridor with rooms branching off it, rather than the Tudor style of interconnecting rooms. Leaded windows set into the corridor wall opposite the bedroom doors let in diffused light through their diamond-shaped panes, casting weak patterns onto the carpet. Under the windows stood several heavy chests, which appeared to be made of the same dark wood as the panelling—so dark, it was almost black.

The blue woollen damask hangings around the half-tester Victorian bed gave the first room Penny and Victoria entered its name. Two large eighteenth-century tapestries graced the walls, one hung above an ornately carved chest of drawers. The soft, muted light from the window provided just enough atmospheric late-morning illumination to see by.

"That'll be to protect the fabrics," Penny said. "They don't want sunlight on them, especially the tapestries, and besides, it gives you a better idea of what the room would have looked and felt like hundreds of years ago, when there was no electric light. It must have been very peaceful to wake up here." She peered out the window at the garden below, and after one last glance around the room, they stepped back into the corridor.

Except for the guide at the top of the stairs, the corridor was empty. "I wonder where everyone is," said Victoria. "We saw a few people downstairs, but not as many as I would have thought."

"It's a big house and it's a beautiful day. I expect lots of people are enjoying the garden and the rest will be scattered about."

"Or they may have gone to the café," said Victoria. "It's almost lunchtime and I'm getting hungry. I had an early breakfast. How about we check out this floor, then find the café? We can see the rest of the house after lunch. As nice as the posh rooms are in places like this, I always find the kitchens and servants' quarters more interesting."

They spent a few minutes admiring the furnishings in the next bedroom, the largest and grandest, and then moved on, pausing to check their floor plan in front of a small set of three cordoned-off stairs that led up to a short corridor. A couple of pale grey canvas drop cloths were piled loosely at the foot of an open stepladder in the middle of this hallway. Several WET PAINT signs sat on the ladder's lowest rung, and a roller brush on a long handle resting in a paint tray and three unopened paint cans were lined up against the wall.

"Looks like somebody's getting ready to go to work," mused Penny. "I wonder if that's where Andrea is working. She mentioned she was going to be painting at Speke Hall, but I don't know if she's here today."

"If she is, we might bump into her," said Victoria.

They moved on until they reached the end of the main corridor, then turned to their right.

"Oh!" said Victoria. The door to the Green Bedroom was closed, a faded red velvet rope affixed to two brass stanchions stretched in front of it. A printed sign taped to the door read WET PAINT. "It's odd the guide didn't mention this. He said all the main bedrooms were open. You'd think he'd know that one of the bedrooms is closed."

"And not just any bedroom, either," said Penny, "but the one most people, including me, want to see, because that's the bedroom with the priest hole that the outdoor guide mentioned. I've always wanted to see a priest hole." She checked her map, peered into the next room, and the one after that. "Yes," she said, gesturing at the closed door. "This is the Green Bedroom all right. Oh, this is so annoying."

She pressed the door lever, opened the door a few inches, glanced in, then closed it. "The room looks normal, although it's pretty dark and I couldn't see much, but there's no smell of paint."

"Maybe they blocked off the room because they're going to get it ready to paint," Victoria said.

"Maybe," said Penny. At the sound of voices drifting down the corridor from the direction of the stairs, she told Victoria, "Wait here. I'm going to ask the guide about this."

She returned a few minutes later with the guide, who rubbed his hands together nervously. "I knew there was some cleaning, hoovering, window washing, and the like going on, and the painting in the hallway that's cordoned off, but I wasn't told about painting in any of the bedrooms," he said. "Certainly not the Green Bedroom. And all this"—

he indicated the red rope and WET PAINT sign—"wasn't here earlier this morning when I started my shift. I'd better find out what's happening." He pulled a portable two-way radio out of his pocket, spoke into it, then shook his head. "No, they don't know anything about any painting. Someone's coming up to sort it."

"I don't think we need to wait until somebody comes," said Penny. "There's no reason why we shouldn't go in there now. If there's no painting planned for this room, maybe someone got it mixed up with another room that was scheduled for a bit of refurbishment and closed this one off instead."

"Well, I'm not sure that we should . . . I mean, surely it would be better if we . . ." muttered the guide, but Penny was already opening the door, with Victoria looking over her shoulder. They edged into the Green Bedroom. The guide lingered in the doorway for a moment and then returned to his post at the top of the stairs to await the arrival of a site manager.

As in the previous bedrooms, this dimly lit, dark-panelled room also featured an elaborately carved bed. A tin hip bath with a rough, scratchy-looking towel draped over the side was positioned in front of the unlit fireplace. To the left of the fireplace, a carved wooden panel, which when in place would have blended invisibly into the rest of the room, had been removed to reveal a cleverly concealed cavity the size of a small walk-in closet, tall enough for a man to stand up in and stretch out his arms. A persecuted priest could have hidden here during a search of the building. And in the heart-stopping event the priest hole was about to be discovered by the queen's soldiers, a functional, rustic wooden ladder that presumably led to a labyrinth of secret passageways deeper inside the building was attached at a ninety-degree angle to the chimney flue, which formed one wall of the hiding place.

"This'll be the priest hole," Penny announced, imagining the hem on the black robe of a terrified priest vanishing up the ladder.

Victoria rested her hand on Penny's shoulder to steady herself and, leaning over, the two scrutinized the priest hole.

"Oh no. There's someone in there!" exclaimed Penny, pointing to the floor. What looked at first glance like a bundle of discarded navy blue clothes piled on the rough, unvarnished floorboards moved slightly and emitted a faint groan. "Tell the guide that we need help," Penny panted over her shoulder. As Victoria turned on her heels and dashed out of the room, Penny managed to grasp Barbara Vickers by her shoulders and lift and pull her a few inches out of the priest hole.

"Barbara," she said, "what happened to you? Who did this to you?"

Barbara's eyes fluttered open. She opened her mouth to speak but could not shape the words. Her eyes closed and her head lolled to one side.

"Hang in there, Barbara. Stay with me. Victoria's gone to get help and they'll be here in a minute."

Barbara held up a hand and Penny took it and gave it a gentle squeeze. "That's right, Barbara," she said. "Just hang in there."

Once more Barbara's eyes opened and she met Penny's with a clear, determined gaze. She raised her left hand to her chest, and once more her lips parted. She sucked in a deep breath and then turned her head slightly.

Penny crouched over her and turned her head so her ear was close to Barbara's mouth. "You were going to tell me something, Barbara. Please tell me now what it was. I'm listening," she said. "Tell me."

"It wasn't hers. It was someone else's," she whispered. Her breath was coming in short wheezes.

"What wasn't hers, Barbara? What was someone else's?"

"The marmalade. It wasn't hers."

"Who's 'her,' Barbara? It wasn't whose marmalade?"

Barbara did not speak again, and all Penny heard was ragged, laboured breathing.

Eighteen

The sound of footsteps pounding up the stairs and running down the corridor signalled the arrival of paramedics and the police. Penny let go of Barbara's hand and stepped back to give the paramedics space to work, then joined Victoria in the hall.

"Who is it?" Victoria asked as they waited outside the Green Bedroom. "Did you recognize her?"

"It's Barbara Vickers."

"What happened to her? Who could possibly have done this to her? And why?"

"I think it had to do with what she was going to tell me. She could have seen something, or heard something on the Friday night of the agricultural show that didn't make sense at the time but now she's realized its significance," Penny said.

"It's too bad she didn't have a chance to tell you whatever it was before she was attacked."

"She did manage to tell me something. She said, 'The marmalade wasn't hers.' I asked her who she was talking about, but she couldn't tell me. Oh, you have no idea how much I wish I'd gone to the loo with her so I could have heard everything she had to say," said Penny.

"'The marmalade wasn't hers,'" Victoria repeated. "I wonder what she meant by that."

"When we got off the bus, she said she'd remembered something that could have to do with Florence's missing marmalade. Did she mean the marmalade wasn't Florence's? But what marmalade is she talking about?" Penny clenched her fingers into a fist and tapped it lightly on the windowsill. "Oh, this is so frustrating!"

"Well, let's hope she's better soon, and then she can tell you," said Victoria.

A uniformed police officer emerged from the Green Bedroom. "Do you happen to know who that lady is?" he asked.

"Her name's Barbara Vickers and she's here with us on a Women's Guild outing," Penny replied. The police officer asked a few more questions, took their names and contact details, and then told them they had to leave. "We're securing the area and we need the corridor clear so we can take her downstairs. Time for you to move along."

"How is she?" Penny asked before she and Victoria turned to leave.

"They're doing everything they can for her," he said. His blank, official face gave nothing away. "Look, why don't you go to the café and have a cup of tea? If we need you in the next little while, we'll find you there." He escorted them to the stairs and stood at the top, feet firmly planted and arms folded, watching Penny and Victoria make their way to the ground floor. Penny looked back at him and he gave her an encouraging nod that delivered a "Keep going" message.

"I'm certainly not in the right frame of mind for strolling in the garden just now," Penny said, taking a deep breath of fresh air in the courtyard. "We might as well go to the café and have that cup of tea the police officer recommended, and some lunch, if you still feel like eating. Although I'm going to have a coffee."

They entered the café, to find several members of their party having lunch. Mrs. Lloyd and Florence, who were seated at two tables that had been pushed together, waved them over.

"We've just heard that something's happened at the Hall," Mrs. Lloyd said. "Have you just come from there? Can you tell us anything?"

"You sit down, Penny," said Victoria. "I'll get us a couple of coffees." Penny slid into the empty fourth chair.

"It's Barbara Vickers," Penny said cautiously. "There's been some sort of accident."

"Accident!" exclaimed Mrs. Lloyd. "What sort of accident? Did she fall? I often say the stairs in these old places aren't always what they should be. Worn, they are, and narrow. People must have had smaller feet back then." She turned to Florence. "You've heard me say that, haven't you, Florence?"

"Yes, I certainly have," said Florence with a small sigh. "Many times. Now let's just listen to what Penny has to tell us."

"Of course." Mrs. Lloyd gave a small apologetic smile. "Sorry."

"I don't know exactly what happened," Penny said, "but we found Barbara injured in one of the bedrooms. The paramedics are with her now, and they'll be taking her to hospital."

"Perhaps she collapsed," offered Florence. "She wasn't feeling well earlier, while we were at the garden centre. Is she going to be all right?"

"I hope so," said Penny.

Victoria returned with two coffees on a tray and set them on the table. As Penny took a comforting sip, the café door opened and a woman with blonde hair clipped on top of her head entered.

"Oh, there's Michelle Lewis," said Penny. "I didn't realize she was along on the outing today."

"I noticed her on the coach," said Mrs. Lloyd. "She was sitting at a window seat, about halfway along."

"I expect after all she's been through, with her mother dying the way she did, and having to look after her little girl, a nice day out is just what she needed," said Florence.

Michelle collected a tray and selected a few lunch items. After looking around the seating area and catching sight of Penny, she made her way toward her.

"May I join you?"

"Of course," said Penny, gesturing to the chair beside her.

"Something's happening at the Hall," said Michelle as she slid a bowl of soup and a plate with a bread roll off the brown tray and onto the table, then leaned the tray against her chair. "I've just seen an ambulance leave. I hope nobody in our group has been hurt. Does anybody know what happened?"

"We're not exactly sure," said Mrs. Lloyd. "These two"— she tipped her head at Penny and Victoria who were sitting across the table from each other—"found Barbara Vickers injured in a bedroom."

"Barbara Vickers? Oh no. Is she all right?"

"Well, we don't know. We hope so," said Penny.

"What happened to her?"

"Not sure. She was in the Green Bedroom, and it had been closed off with one of those red velvet ropes across the door and there was a sign," said Victoria.

"What kind of sign?"

"A sign that said 'Wet Paint.' But that was strange, because there was no painting going on. We thought maybe another room had been scheduled for painting."

Michelle sighed deeply. "Well, I hope she's all right."

"We hope so, too," said Penny. "I'm glad you were able to join us today, Michelle."

"Well, it wasn't me who was supposed to be here today, but since Mum had already booked and paid for the trip, and Macy's spending the day at a friend's house, I thought I might as well come along." She broke off a piece of bread and buttered it. "Mum would have loved being here today. She really enjoyed visiting these old houses. Especially the kitchens. She loved looking at the cooking utensils and the big old cookers, and thinking what it must have been like to work in such a place."

The women maintained a sympathetic silence and then Florence spoke. "You must miss your mother very much." Remembering what Joyce Devlin had said about Gaynor's tendency to criticize other people's relationships and knowing Michelle was no longer living with her partner, Penny waited to see how she would respond to Florence's kindly meant comment.

"The fact that she's gone hasn't really sunk in, to be honest. I'm still trying to get my head around it. And the way it happened . . . Well, you see things like that on the telly, but you never expect something like this to happen in your own family, and when it does, you just cope the best you can."

"And are they any further along in finding out what happened to Gaynor?" Mrs. Lloyd asked, displaying just the slightest hint of a little too much eagerness.

"I don't know," said Michelle. "The police asked a lot of questions about her. They wanted to know everything about the people she knew, and her relationships with them. They asked if I could think of anyone who might want to harm her. There were women she didn't get along with, but I can't think of anyone who actually hated her enough to do something like that to her. Of course the police also asked a lot of questions about the family, searched her house, all the usual police stuff."

"Looking for clues, no doubt," said Mrs. Lloyd.

"They were especially interested in my aunt. Wanted to know all about her, how my mother felt about her, and so on. I don't know all the details, but apparently there were bad feelings between them going back a long way."

"When you say the police were interested in your aunt, do you mean Andrea or Joyce?" Penny asked.

Michelle seemed taken aback. "Why, Andrea, of course. I suppose Joyce is technically my aunt, being married to my uncle Daffydd, but I don't really think of her in that way."

"Oh, right. It's only that . . ." Penny was about to mention what Heather Hughes had told her on the drive home from the agricultural show banquet about seeing Andrea and Gaynor arguing in the café in Betws y Coed. But after catching a glimpse of Mrs. Lloyd leaning forward, eyebrows raised and lips slightly parted, Penny decided it would be more prudent not to mention this. "Never mind. You were seated at Joyce Devlin's table at the agricultural show banquet, though."

"I chose to think of it as sitting with my uncle Daffyd, my mother's brother. He's always been really nice to me, and I feel comfortable with him. Joyce I can ignore."

"So you don't like her, either?"

"'Either'?" Michelle repeated with a touch of frost in her voice that caused Florence and Mrs. Lloyd to exchange a quick glance.

"Sorry," said Penny. "Bad choice of words. Only, someone mentioned that your mother and Joyce had had a falling-out and your mother wasn't too keen on her, which is why I wondered which aunt the police were interested in."

"There was no love lost between Joyce and my mother, for years. Everybody knows that. But now that my mother's murder has brought every last bit of the family's business out in the open, I expect the police are interested in both Joyce and Andrea."

"That soup looks delicious," said Victoria. "I think I'll get some. Penny, how about you?" Penny didn't know if she was changing the subject so abruptly because she genuinely fancied some vegetable soup or because she felt the conversation was straying into uncomfortable territory. But uncomfortable for whom?

"No, nothing for me, thanks, but you go ahead." Victoria tapped her with her knee under the table. "Oh, okay, on second thought, maybe I should have something." She stood up. "I'll go with you."

"If it's something sweet you're after, you might want to try the Wet Nelly," Florence suggested.

"What's that?" asked Penny.

"Have a look at the sweets on offer, and you'll see."

"Was there something you wanted to say to me?" Penny asked when she and Victoria were about halfway to the food-service area and far enough away from the table so Florence, Michelle, and Mrs. Lloyd couldn't overhear.

"Michelle seemed really uncomfortable with your questions, so I thought you should stop. And the way Mrs. Lloyd was looking at her, almost greedy for details, made me uncomfortable," Victoria replied.

"I know we always say Mrs. Lloyd has a good heart, but I do wonder sometimes if she doesn't take too much delight in other people's misfortunes. She seems to relish the details of the bad things that happen to people."

"Still, she can be a useful source of local knowledge," said Victoria.

They had reached the counter and were examining the sweets. "There's that Wet Nelly thing," Penny said, pointing to a slice of what looked like a brown bread pudding. "And here's a card with a recipe on it, telling us what it's all about." She picked up the card and the dessert. "Might as well give it a try. What about you? You said you wanted soup. Are you going to get some?"

"Yes, I think I am."

When they returned to the table, Mrs. Lloyd and Florence were preparing to leave, and Michelle Lewis had just about finished her lunch.

"We'll catch up with you later," said Florence. "I want to see something of the garden before it's too late." As they

190

opened the door to leave, Mari Jones, Delyth Powell, and Elin Spears arrived for lunch. Mari's black trousers, which pulled across her thighs, and her pudgy feet crammed into extra-wide sensible shoes with over-the-foot straps, contrasted with Elin Spears's youthful, stylish look. She wore expensive-looking jeans, a cropped black leather jacket, and a bright scarf in turquoise and pinks swirled around her neck.

"At least there are plenty of tables now," said Michelle Lewis, "so they won't have to join us."

Mari, Delyth, and Elin surveyed the food, made their choices, and found a table at the opposite end of the room. Michelle let out a small sigh of relief.

Penny raised an eyebrow.

"Sorry," said Michelle. "I'm just not up to talking to them now."

"I can see all this is hard for you," said Penny. "I apologize if I said things earlier that upset you. I didn't mean to pry."

"That's all right," said Michelle. "My mother wasn't easy to get along with. I know that. But Elin's different. Mum and Elin were friends, until Elin broke up my parents' marriage, so it's difficult for me to be around her."

Penny remembered that Mrs. Lloyd had mentioned Elin's involvement in the breakup of Gaynor's marriage. "How long ago was this?" Penny asked.

"Oh, over ten years ago now. Maybe twelve," said Michelle. "I was just finishing high school. I wasn't aware of what was going on, and one day my mother told me she and I were moving into town and that my father was going to stay on at the farm. So we left, and shortly after that, Elin moved in with my father. For years they pretended their relationship started after my parents had broken up, but people always know what's really been going on, don't they? The timing was just a little too convenient."

"That's the thing about villages and towns, isn't it?" Penny agreed. "Everybody knows all your business, or thinks they do. And when something like that happens, unless one of the couple moves away, the people involved have to live with it every day. Seeing your ex-partner out and about with someone else, and dealing with them at social events."

Michelle nodded. "I'm going through something like that myself right now. My partner and I broke up fairly recently. He still lives in town because he wants to be near our daughter—that's Macy," she said to Penny. "You met her at the agricultural show."

Penny nodded. "Yes, I remember her. She was so upset when her grandmother wasn't there to see her win the competition. And she and her little dog looked so sweet in their costumes. How is she doing?"

"The police Family Services officer told me to try to keep everything as normal as possible for her, so that's what I'm doing. We're sticking to our routine. But Macy knows that she can't go to her *nain's* house for tea anymore, and she really misses that. She's very clingy with her granddad now and is spending more time with him. She loves his beautiful chickens. She's almost as proud of them as he is."

Victoria had remained silent and her face was soft with sympathy.

"Macy doesn't know the circumstances about Mum's death, though," Michelle continued. "We've all agreed to protect her from that for as long as we can. I just hope some bully at school doesn't take it upon himself to tell her what happened and then taunt her with it. You know how cruel some kids can be. Macy's eighth birthday's coming up, so that's going to be hard for her. For me, too. Mum always made the most beautiful themed and decorated cakes, really special they were, just for her Macy."

As tears welled in Michelle's eyes and she blotted them with a paper napkin, Penny thought about Elin Spears winning Best in Show for her elaborately decorated cake. The rivalry between Elin and Gaynor probably included baking, too, as well as the Women's Guild presidency and Carwyn Lewis.

"Sorry," Michelle said, with an embarrassed shake of her head. "All this talk about Mum . . . sometimes it all just gets to me. Anyway, Macy also gets upset when the police come round, although they're nice to her. She just associates them with something bad happening. I've asked them to let me know when they're coming, so I can make sure she's somewhere else."

Michelle dabbed at her eyes again as the door opened, admitting the uniformed police officer who had spoken to Penny and Victoria outside the Green Bedroom. He didn't look as if he was there to grab a late lunch. He scanned the nearly empty room, then, catching sight of Penny and Victoria, took a few steps in their direction. A ripple of silence trailed in his wake as the few remaining diners became aware of the presence of the officer, and conversation stopped.

"This doesn't bode well," said Penny in a low voice. Michelle glanced over her shoulder to see what Penny was looking at. As the police officer reached their table, all three women looked up at him.

"I'm glad you're still here," he said to Penny, opening his notebook. "I was wondering if you can help us. We need to know more about Miss Vickers. Can you tell us if she has any family or if you know of anyone we should contact?"

"We're not the best people to talk to," said Penny, indicating Victoria. "We just recently joined the Women's Guild, and although we all come from the same town, we don't know everybody."

"What town is that?" asked the police officer.

"Llanelen. It's in North Wales."

"Yes, I know it."

"But this lady should be able to help you," Penny said, nodding at Michelle.

"Barbara Vickers isn't married, and if she has family, I don't know about it," said Michelle. "Her closest friend, as far as I know, is Joyce Devlin. Joyce owns a dog kennel and Labrador retriever breeding business just outside the town. She can probably help."

The officer made a few notes and then nodded his thanks.

"Can you tell us how Barbara is doing?" Victoria asked him.

"No, I'm sorry, I can't say too much. This Joyce Devlin, is she here with you today?"

"No, she's not a member of the Women's Guild." Michelle thumbed through the contacts list on her phone until she found what she was looking for, and then, without looking at the officer, she held up her phone. "Here's her number. Her husband is my uncle Daffydd."

"Oh, I see. That's helpful," he said, copying the number into his notebook. "Right," he said, handing the phone back. "Well, that'll be all for now. Thank you."

Michelle frowned as he departed, the watchful eyes of almost everyone in the room boring into his broad blue back.

"It seems like we're all finished," said Penny. Let's clear the table and then maybe explore the garden or finish the house tour."

Michelle picked up the tray that had been leaning against her chair, placed it on the table, and they loaded it up with everyone's used dishes and cutlery. "That's better," said Penny as Victoria disappeared with the tray to the food-service area.

Michelle cleared her throat, clasped and unclasped her hands, then stood up. "I'm going out for a cigarette. I'm sorry to say I started smoking again when Mum died."

On the way out, she passed Victoria, who was headed back to the table, carrying a cup of coffee.

"Just saw Michelle leaving."

"She said she was going out for a cigarette."

"Everybody else seems to have gone, too. Maybe I should have got this coffee as a takeaway. What time is it?"

Penny checked her watch. "Let's go. And I'm sure if you ask, they'll put that in a takeaway cup for you."

There was no sign of Michelle when they got outside.

"We're running out of time," said Penny. "We spent so long in the café that I think we'll have to leave the gardens, kitchen, and servants' quarters for another day."

Under the shade of mature trees, and accompanied by the sound of cheerful birdsong, they strolled along the walkway that led to the car park. Others with the same idea had arrived before them, and the coach was almost full when they boarded. Within minutes, the stragglers arrived and Carwyn Lewis walked down the aisle, counting heads. When he had returned to the driver's seat, Elin Spears rose from her seat at the front of the coach and accepted the microphone he handed her.

"I hope you all enjoyed your day here at this beautiful property," she began. A murmur of agreement rippled up and down the rows of seats, and she held up her hand for silence. "Unfortunately"—as this word dropped, an immediate silence settled over the group—"there was an accident of some sort involving one of our group, Barbara Vickers, and I'm sorry to have to tell you that she's been taken to hospital."

Everyone began talking at once, and shouting out questions. Finally, above the clamour, one question became clear: "What happened?"

"I don't know," Elin replied.

The drive back to Llanelen was silent and sombre. Penny sat hunched in her seat, staring unseeingly out the window while she pondered the words Barbara Vickers had whispered to her: "The marmalade. It wasn't hers."

Nineteen

The day out at Speke Hall had turned out nothing like Penny or anyone else had expected and she arrived home exhausted and emotionally drained. She had just finished feeding Harrison and was thinking about her own supper when Detective Inspector Bethan Morgan rang, asking to speak to Penny as soon as possible. Penny agreed, and twenty minutes later, Bethan was at her door.

Penny showed her into the sitting room. "I've just made some coffee. I need some, and thought you could use some, too."

Bethan thanked her and sat down. "It's good of you to see me, Penny," she said as Penny handed her a cup of coffee. "I expect you're knackered. You had an eventful day."

"Oh, you mean Barbara Vickers?" Bethan nodded. Penny thought about that for a moment. "Oh, I see. Merseyside police were in touch with you," Penny said, referring to the police service covering the greater Liverpool area.

"They were. It's their case, of course, but they informed us what happened today, as Barbara comes from our area, so there will have to be cooperation between the two police services. Merseyside's going to need our help. They told me that you and Victoria were the ones who found Miss Vickers in a bedroom at Speke Hall."

"We did."

"Now, you see that's of interest to us, because, frankly, our investigation into the death of Gaynor Lewis has stalled. While we've found a few people who didn't like her, we haven't found anyone with a good motive, so we're hoping that if there is a connection between the two deaths, we might get some leads into the Lewis killing."

"Wait. Did you say two deaths? Does that mean that Barbara Vickers has died?"

"Oh, I'm so sorry. How insensitive of me. I thought you'd been told, but yes, I'm sorry to say she succumbed to her injuries."

"Injuries?"

"We won't know for sure until we get the postmortem results, but it looks as if someone tried to strangle her. It's possible the killer was interrupted and then fled, leaving her for dead. She was still alive when you found her, I was told."

Penny's shoulders drooped as she slumped forward and rested her chin on her hand. "I'm so sorry to hear this. We knew she was in a bad way when the police officer asked about her next of kin, and we feared the worst, but we really hoped that somehow she would pull through. I feel as if I let her down."

"You did everything you could have done, Penny. In fact, the police officer was really impressed with the way you and Victoria handled the situation. Nobody could have done more for Barbara than you did." She remained silent for a moment to allow Penny to pull herself together, then continued. "The Merseyside police would like me to ask you a few questions. Would that be all right? Do you feel up to answering a few questions now?"

"Of course," said Penny.

"Besides the details about what happened at Speke Hall, I'm also really interested in exploring with you the connection between Barbara's death and that of Gaynor Lewis."

"That makes sense. So you do think they could be connected?"

"The victims are certainly connected. They were both at the agricultural show, and they were both members of the Women's Guild. So there's that; plus, they knew many of the same people. But it's the timing of the two deaths, so close to each other, that raises a red flag and makes it seem likely that there's some connection. And it's my job to find out what that connection is." After a moment, Bethan continued. "Let's start with this. Tell me everything that happened when you found Barbara Vickers. Probably easiest if you start at the beginning and work through everything in order, as it happened."

Penny straightened in her chair, took a deep breath, and in her mind tried to sort out the series of events. She wanted to get this right, and make it easy for Bethan to understand what happened.

"When Victoria and I reached the top of the stairs, a volunteer was sat there, and he told us all the rooms were open and to take our time looking around. So we wandered around for a bit, looking in the bedrooms. As we made our way down the corridor, we noticed some drop cloths on the floor of a little hallway that led off the main one. It was roped off. And then when we reached the Green Bedroom, the room was cordoned off with a 'Wet Paint' sign stuck on the door, but there was no paint smell. So I opened the door a little and peeked in."

"And that's when you found her."

"Right."

"She was still breathing when I dragged her out of the priest hole. She was just a small woman, so it wasn't difficult. I got her onto the carpet and I asked her what had happened to her and who had done this to her, but she didn't say. All she said was, 'It wasn't hers. It was someone else's.' When I asked what she meant, she said, 'The marmalade. It wasn't hers.'"

"Do you have any idea what she meant by that?" Bethan asked.

Penny shook her head. "Not exactly, no. But I think it might have something to do with Florence's missing marmalade."

"Florence's missing marmalade?"

"Oh, it's just something that happened that has us all puzzled. On the Thursday night before the show, Florence got a phone call telling her to bring in her entries for the show on the Saturday morning, but that would have been after the entry deadline. Victoria and I were at the show on the Friday night, accepting all the entries into the competition, and when we realized Florence's entries hadn't been submitted, we rang her, and she and Mrs. Lloyd hurried over and they got her entries in on time. But we want to know who rang Florence and told her not to bring her entries, and why. So I'd asked Barbara Vickers just this morning on the coach if she could shed some light on that. She was the agricultural show's general secretary, you see, and she'd been there on Friday night with Joyce Devlin, supervising things and making sure everything was ready for Saturday."

"So you asked Barbara about the marmalade while you were on the coach?"

"Yes, we'd arrived at Speke Hall and I moved across the aisle and sat beside her while the others were getting off. And then Elin Spears told us we needed to leave, too, so Carwyn Lewis could lock up. So we got off, Barbara and I, and while we were walking from the car park to the Hall, Barbara said she had noticed something—not on the Friday night, but later, on the Sunday morning after the show. She said something like, it seemed odd and might have to do with Florence's marmalade. Oh, and then she added that she checked, whatever that means."

Penny ran her hand over her face and winced.

"And then she had to go to the loo and said we'd catch up later, and Victoria and I went off to see the Hall. I was dying to know what she had to tell me. If only I'd followed Barbara, or waited for her to come back from the loo," she said. "I can't tell you how awful I feel."

"It's all right, Penny," Bethan said, trying to reassure her. "You weren't to know, and besides, there's nothing you can do about it now. So just out of curiosity, what were Florence's entries? Besides the carrot cake, I mean. We know all about what happened to that. The forensics people tell us Gaynor Lewis must have pulled it off the table with her when she went down and that the assailant then chucked it under the table with her to get rid of the mess."

"Oh, poor Gaynor. It's hard to imagine how frightened she must have been," said Penny.

"And Florence's entries," Bethan gently reminded her.

"Yes. Well, besides the cake, Florence entered jam and marmalade in the preserves category. Her raspberry jam won first prize, but the marmalade wasn't there on Saturday morning when we checked the entries to see how she had done. But Victoria and I logged it in ourselves the night before, so we know it was entered in the competition, fair and square."

"Well, I don't know enough about how the competition works, but could Florence's jar of marmalade have got broken? Knocked off the table, maybe, and smashed on the ground, and whoever broke it—a volunteer, a judge—didn't know how to handle the situation or what to do, so she just cleaned up the mess and hoped the problem would go away? Maybe it was Barbara Vickers herself. Could the explanation be as simple as that?"

Penny would have liked to agree with Bethan, but she couldn't.

"That theory doesn't really fit with the phone call Florence got that seemed designed to keep her entries out of the competition. I think it more likely that somebody who really wanted to win that category saw Florence as a serious competitor and found a way to make her marmalade disappear. How, I don't know. This is my first experience with the show, and the fierceness of the competition has been a bit of an eye-opener. I didn't realize everyone took it so seriously. It means a tremendous amount when people win, and I've realized that some people will go to astonishing lengths to make sure they do."

"I bet. So tell me, whose marmalade won?"

"Gaynor Lewis's." Bethan's eyes drifted to a corner of the ceiling and she made a small back-and-forth movement with her index finger while she considered what she'd just been told. "Do you think it's important?" Penny asked.

Bethan sighed. "I don't know. This whole case is confusing and complicated, but at this point, everything that concerns Gaynor Lewis is of interest to us. It's hard to see, though, how Florence's marmalade can be of any significance, and if her jar was stolen or switched or broken, it's hardly a police matter. As you say, it could come down to a jealous competitor wanting to keep her entries out of the competition. And I don't see how this connects to the death of Barbara Vickers." She gave Penny an indulgent smile. "But by all means, if it's that important to you, and you really want to know what happened to a jar of marmalade, keep digging."

"That's the thing," said Penny, ignoring what she could have taken as a hint of condescension in Bethan's reply. "At first, that's all I thought it was, too. A missing jar of marmalade. But as I thought more about it, I realized there's something critically important to the Gaynor Lewis case attached to the marmalade."

"Now you've got my attention," said Bethan. "What is it?"

"The timing."

"Explain."

"It's like this," said Penny. "The marmalade was in the marquee just at the deadline, and shortly after that, almost everybody went home. Me, Victoria, Mrs. Lloyd, Florence, the people who had been setting up the refreshment area . . .

as far as I know, we all left. But Joyce Devlin was still there, and according to Joyce, shortly after we left, Gaynor Lewis came rushing in with her marmalade, and Joyce Devlin entered that in the competition, even though the deadline had passed."

Bethan frowned as she attempted to follow Penny's reasoning.

"Stay with me here. Gaynor Lewis is now in the marquee, but she does not leave the marquee alive. The marmalade is in the marquee. By now, it's getting late, and it's getting dark. Joyce Devlin leaves the tent. And when I asked her, 'Did Barbara leave the marquee with you?' she said yes."

"So if Barbara *left the marquee,* she must have been *in the marquee,*" Bethan reasoned slowly. "She would have had to have been in the marquee to leave it."

"Exactly," said Penny. "So I'm wondering if she saw or heard something while she was there, something that she didn't realize at the time was important, and then later came to understand its real significance. And I can't stop thinking about what she said to me when I found her in the Green Bedroom. She said, 'It wasn't hers. It was someone else's.'"

"Very cryptic. I wonder what it means."

"I don't know," said Penny, "but it must be important. Barbara must have known she was gravely ill, and yet that's what she chose to tell me, so those words must have been terribly important to her."

Bethan opened her notebook. "Tell me again," she said. "Tell me exactly what Barbara Vickers said when you asked her what she meant by 'It.'"

"'The marmalade. It wasn't hers.'"

"I wonder where the emphasis lies," said Bethan. "'*It*

204

wasn't hers,' meaning something else was hers, or 'It wasn't *hers*,' meaning the marmalade belonged to someone else."

"I took it to mean that the marmalade belonged to some-body else."

Twenty

All right," said Bethan. "Let's talk about the Green Bed-room itself. Of particular interest to us was the way the bedroom was blocked off. Merseyside police forensics are testing the rope and sign, of course, so we hope we'll get something from that. You and Victoria told the officer at the scene what you saw and did, but now that you've had a bit of time to reflect on it, has anything else occurred to you? Anything that seemed out of place, anyone you noticed somewhere you wouldn't have expected to see that person?"

"No," Penny replied.

"Did you happen to see Andrea Devlin at Speke Hall? When you saw the paint drop cloths on the floor in the little hallway, did you happen to see her?"

"No. I'd heard that she might be working there, and

Victoria and I even wondered if we might bump into her, but we didn't see her."

Bethan did not reply. And as it dawned on her what Bethan was thinking, Penny said, "Oh, you don't think she killed Barbara Vickers, do you? What possible reason could she have to do that?"

"Andrea Devlin is a person of interest in the Gaynor Lewis murder. And you know as well as I do that the second murder is usually committed by the same person who committed the first. We've just been talking about that—whether Barbara saw something or someone. We have a witness who saw Andrea in Betws, arguing with Gaynor Lewis on the Friday night of the agricultural show, the night she was murdered. And quite heated that discussion was, too, by all accounts."

Oh, that's right, thought Penny. Heather Hughes saw them in the café.

"So you see, when a person of interest lies to the police, or withholds information, or tries to mislead us, that person becomes even more of a person of interest."

"What did she lie to you about?" Penny asked.

"She wasn't exactly forthcoming with us about how long she'd been in the area. She led us to believe that she only arrived here after she was notified about Gaynor's death, but it turns out she was here before that."

Penny processed this information.

"And there's something else. Whoever put Barbara Vickers in the priest hole had to have had some strength."

"Oh. Strength like a man, you mean?"

"Well, yes."

"But surely two women could have done that. Or maybe

208

even one woman. I mean, I managed to get her out on my own." The tone of Penny's voice rose a little in disagreement and frustration.

"Yes, but by the time you got Barbara out, she was considerably weakened and wasn't fighting you off," Bethan said gently. She folded her notebook. "Look, I can see you're tired, you've been through a lot, and you've had enough of my questions for today. Let's leave it there for now. We can talk again soon." She got to her feet.

"Before you go, Bethan, there's something I wanted to ask you. It's personal." Bethan sat. "About Gareth. How's he doing?"

"I don't really know. I haven't heard from him, and I don't think any of the other officers have, either. He seems to have moved on. I'm not even sure he's around much anymore."

"Oh, because of Fiona, you mean. Yes, well, she told us after the agricultural show banquet that he's moving to Scotland. I was thinking, though, after the body of Gaynor Lewis was discovered, he must have felt awful. He was supposed to be in charge of security."

"No one would have expected that to happen. He was looking after the grounds, and the animals. He wasn't responsible for the people. He was interviewed, of course, but he couldn't really tell us anything."

"No, it's only that I know what he's like, and I hoped he wasn't blaming himself for what happened." Bethan gave a dismissive shrug, then rose to her feet once again. "Must go."

Penny showed her out, then poured herself a glass of water and carried it through to her sitting room. Harrison curled up on her lap and she stroked him while she thought about her conversation with Bethan. They'd covered a lot of ground and touched on a lot of topics. The thought and accompanying image that bothered her the most was that someone had placed Barbara Vickers, still breathing, still living, still holding on, and probably begging for her life, in that horrible priest hole. Penny's breath came quicker and she closed her eyes against the image.

And someone, or possibly two people, had had the time to lift or drag Barbara's body into the priest hole, and then taken the time to cordon off the room and put up a WET PAINT sign before escaping. What kind of person could do that?

Penny yawned and checked the time. Bethan was right. It had been a long day, she was tired and hungry, and her head was filled with swirling, disconnected ideas and questions. She made herself a cheese and tomato sandwich and then, after checking to make sure both front and back doors were locked, scooped up Harrison and carried him upstairs to bed.

Mentally exhausted, she fell quickly into a deep, dreamless sleep, with Harrison tucked neatly in beside her. But as the heavy blackness of night lightened and lifted, giving way to the grey that would become dawn, and to the sound of birdsong from the garden below, she awoke with a sense of unease. As she remembered the events of the day before, the death of Barbara Vickers, and her conversation with Bethan Morgan, she turned over in her mind everything that had happened at the agricultural show. And the one thing that kept coming back to her was the marmalade. At first, her goal had been to discover what was behind the telephone call to Florence, so she could put Florence's mind to rest. But now she was determined to do it to put her own mind at rest.

She checked her watch. Much too early to get up, although she enjoyed this time of day, when everything was quiet and a beautiful new day lay in front of her. She turned on her side, disturbing Harrison, who let out an indignant cry at the disruption.

And then she lay there, her mind whirling, until she realized there would be no more sleep for her that night, so she got up and made herself a cup of coffee and a piece of toast.

Twenty-one

The next morning, Penny set a pretty cardboard box from the local bakery on Rhian's desk at the Spa. "Brought you a little something to share with Eirlys and the rest of the team to thank everybody for holding the fort yesterday while Victoria and I were off on the Women's Guild outing."

"Oh, thank you, Penny." Rhian admired the pink striped box with *Llanelen Bakery* written in chocolate brown script across the top, and untied the matching brown ribbon. "Oh, lovely!" she exclaimed as she opened the lid, revealing half a dozen elaborately decorated cupcakes. "Do I have to share them?"

"Well, not if you don't want to, I suppose." Penny grinned.

"Did you have a good day?" Rhian asked, closing the lid on the cupcakes. "Enjoy yourselves, did you?"

"Well, the building was interesting, what we saw of it anyway, but unfortunately, one of the ladies on the outing, well, it seems she was attacked, and I learned last night that she died."

Rhian's jaw dropped. "What? That's awful."

"I know. It was awful." Penny lowered her voice. "Victoria and I found the woman in one of the bedrooms."

"Oh no! Really? What happened to her?"

"We don't know for sure yet."

"Oh, that's too bad. And who was it? Anybody we know?"

"Barbara Vickers, her name was."

"Oh, no, not Miss Vickers." Rhian took a step away from her desk and her arms dropped to her side. "Really? I can't believe it."

"You know her?"

"Yes, I do. She's a bookkeeper. She did the accounts at the last place I worked, and she does the books for lots of small businesses in the area. She was very good. A real stickler for detail. Her books always balanced. Never heard any complaints. In fact, if Victoria didn't take care of the accounting for the Spa, I'd have recommended Barbara to you."

"A bookkeeper. And a good one, too. Well, that's very interesting."

"It is?"

"Yes. Oh, it's too complicated to go into here, but thanks for telling me that, Rhian. It could be very useful. And by the way, there's something else I've been meaning to ask you. Do you know any of our clients who use the word *pet*?"

"*Pet*? I'm not sure what you mean."

"Instead of saying *love,* for example, at the end of a sentence, as in 'I saw you coming out of the shop, love.' Do you know anyone who would say, 'I saw you coming out of the shop, pet'?"

"Oh, right. I see what you mean." Rhian placed one hand on the desk and leaned forward slightly. "I don't think so. Not off the top of my head anyway. Let me think about it, and if anyone comes to mind, I'll let you know."

Penny sped off down the hall to the manicure salon in her quick, light steps and asked Eirlys the same question.

"I can't think of anyone, Penny," Eirlys replied. "But you might want to ask Alberto. He sees clients in his hair salon who never set foot in our manicure studio. So I'd ask Alberto, if I was you."

"Ask Alberto what?" asked a tall man with hair just starting to grey at the temples. He stood in the doorway, carrying a chocolate cupcake on a white plate in one hand and a pink cupcake on a plate in the other. He held both plates out to Eirlys, who chose the one with the pink cupcake. "What do you want to ask me?" he repeated.

"Alberto, can you think of a client who uses the word *pet*? You know, like . . ."

"As in 'I don't want it too short, pet, just a nice trim to even up the ends.'"

"Yes, exactly like that."

"No."

Penny sighed.

"I don't know exactly who it is. But I can point you in the right direction." Penny perked up. "It's either Mari Jones or the other one. I can never remember her name. They both look alike, dress alike, and wear their hair the same. Like two peas in a pod, those two. They book their appointments for the same time, and one waits while the other gets her hair done, and then they switch places." He made a little movement across his shoulders with both hands, indicating hair all the same length. "But they only come here about once a year. It looks to me as if they cut each other's hair the rest of the time. I know all our regular clients' names, of course, but hers escapes me. Shouldn't be too hard to find out what she's called, though."

"Oh, I know who you mean," said Penny. "It's Delyth Powell."

Alberto savoured the last bite of his cupcake and turned to go. He was about to leave, taking his empty plate with him, when Eirlys reached out for it.

"Oh, give it here," said Eirlys. "It's my week for doing the washing-up and keeping the kitchen tidy."

"That's it!" exclaimed Penny. "They were doing the washing-up at the WG meeting, and Mari was on the left, and Delyth on the right. And it was Delyth who said to Mari something like, 'You'd almost think she liked her, wouldn't you, pet?'"

Eirlys and Alberto exchanged a slightly puzzled but amused look, and Alberto escaped to his salon across the corridor. "I have no idea what you're on about, but if you say so, Penny," said Eirlys, placing her empty plate on top of Alberto's and disappearing in the direction of the staff kitchen.

Penny hurried down the corridor toward the reception area and was just about to turn down the hallway to Victoria's office when the door opened and Inspector Bethan Morgan entered.

"Oh, Penny. Just the person. Got time for a quick word?"

"Yes, of course." Penny led the way to the quiet room, and when they were seated, Bethan Morgan pulled a sealed plastic bag out of a dark blue tote bag with the North Wales Police logo on the side.

"We might have found Florence's marmalade," she said, handing Penny the plastic bag.

Twenty-two

W here did you find this?" asked Penny, examining the glass jar with its silver lid.

"In Barbara Vickers's kitchen. We've been combing through her flat, and when I saw this in the fridge, I thought I'd show it to you, just in case it's Florence's marmalade, the one you were on about. The stuff's obviously homemade—there's no commercial label on it."

Penny turned the jar upside down and smoothed the stiff plastic of the bag over the bottom of the glass jar.

"Yes, I'm pretty sure it is Florence's," she said.

"How can you tell?" Bethan asked.

"Because there's a little sticker on the bottom with a number on it, and the number is 398, which is high. This is one of the last items we took in for the agricultural show competition. If the number had been three, say, then, no, it wouldn't be Florence's. But there is a sure way to confirm, and that's to compare this number against the list of entries Victoria and I logged in that evening. Barbara was the show's secretary, and she took the lists and put them on her clipboard, so unless Joyce Devlin has the list, it's probably somewhere in Barbara's flat." She held the jar, still in its plastic bag, with two hands in her lap. "When Florence entered this"—she lifted the jar slightly—"it was wearing a little red-and-white gingham topper. I guess that's just for decoration and most people toss it when they actually start eating the contents of the jar." She peered at it. "I can't really tell if any's been eaten. It looks full, but it's hard to tell through the plastic. What will happen to it?"

Bethan reached out for it. "We'll hang on to it, in case it needs to be tested."

"Tested?"

"Nothing is really clear at this point. The investigation is still in its early stages, and the Merseyside police haven't uncovered a motive yet. So it's hard to say what's important. Until we know what isn't important, we'll hang on to everything, just in case."

"May I tell Florence we found her marmalade?"

"Best hold off on that until we know for sure. PC Chris Jones is still at the flat, so I'll ask him to look for the clipboard with the entries. What's the sticker number again?" She checked the bottom of the jar, then sent a text.

"Can you tell me how Barbara Vickers died?" Penny asked.

"The postmortem hasn't been completed yet, but the hospital said she died from heart failure. The pathologist says it was likely brought on by attempted strangulation."

"Oh, I'm so sorry to hear that. How awful for her."

"Of course, Merseyside is still piecing the events together to determine exactly what happened."

"And hopefully who did that to her. She was such a quiet, unassuming soul. Wouldn't-say-boo-to-a-goose kind of woman."

"We'll get whoever did this. Anyway, thought you'd like to know about the marmalade. I'll let you get on now." As they left the room, Bethan's phone chimed to indicate an incoming text. She read the two-word message, then showed it to Penny. *Numbers match.*

"I'll let Florence know we've solved the mystery of her missing marmalade," said Penny. "I'm glad you were able to check the numbers so easily."

Check the numbers, thought Penny as Bethan left. That must have been what Barbara had meant when she said, "I checked." For some reason, she had checked the number on the bottom of the jar against the entry documents and had realized the marmalade was Florence's. And now we have to find out how it ended up in the kitchen of Barbara Vickers.

Client appointments kept Penny busy for the rest of the morning. Finally, hungry and in desperate need of the restorative power of freshly brewed coffee, she and Victoria headed upstairs for lunch in the spacious, airy flat on the top floor that had been created for Victoria when the building that was now home to the Llanelen Spa had been renovated.

When they'd taken on the project—against the advice of just about everybody—the only things the grey, three-storey stone structure had going for it were its solid outer walls and its location. Situated on the bank of the River Conwy, with beautiful views to the richly forested hills beyond, the building was in need of much restoration. Its windows were boarded up and weeds sprouted in the mortar that barely held the place together. The abandoned rooms were filled with rubbish left behind by squatters, the plasterwork was crumbling, and the wooden window frames and sashes were rotted beyond repair.

Nevertheless, they'd seen past all that, right down to the building's beautiful bones, and recognized the potential, not only for business possibilities but as a property investment, and they'd been right on both counts. The business they created was thriving, and the value of their real estate holding had more than doubled.

Victoria unlocked the door to her clean, uncluttered flat, decorated in soothing neutral colours, accented by splashes of bright accessories, and Penny followed her in. Schedules permitting, they tried to have lunch together in the flat at least once a week. Penny set the second box she had brought from the bakery on the kitchen worktop, and then, as she always did on every visit, she went straight to the sitting room window that overlooked the river and peered out. Victoria headed to the kitchen, and a moment later came the sound of rattling dishes and cutlery. Penny drifted back into the kitchen to see what she could do to help.

"Here," Victoria said to Penny, handing her a tray, "You can set the table whilst I make a salad."

Ten minutes later, they sat down to lunch.

"Looks lovely," said Penny. "I'm starved."

"Me, too." Victoria offered the salad to Penny, then served herself. "What was Bethan doing here this morning?"

Penny explained that Florence's marmalade had been found in Barbara Vickers's kitchen. "But what's really got me thinking is something Rhian told me this morning—that Barbara was a bookkeeper and handled the accounts of lots of small businesses around here. Remember she was the treasurer at the Women's Guild meeting we went to?"

Victoria nodded. "Are you back to thinking about Joyce? That Barbara might have discovered some discrepancies in the finances related to the kennels?"

Penny nodded. "Barbara might have discovered discrepancies in the kennel accounts, or she might have wondered, as we did, where the Devlins got the money to pay for them. And maybe she realized that Joyce, and/or Dev, had been stealing from the agricultural show's account, used the money to finance the kennels, and then she confronted one or both of them about it."

"She might have told Joyce that if she paid the money back, the matter would go no further, but Joyce couldn't do that, because she's in too much debt," said Victoria.

"So poor Barbara had to go."

"People have been killed for a lot less. There is one thing, though. Neither Joyce nor her husband were on that trip to Speke Hall, so I don't know if they had the opportunity. But still, it might be helpful to know about the funding for the kennels."

"I agree," said Penny. "And it would be interesting to know if funds are missing from the agricultural show's account. I wonder if there's some way to find out. And I've just thought of something. If Barbara was a bookkeeper, why would she be the show secretary and not the treasurer? Why would Joyce's husband be the treasurer? That doesn't make sense."

"I don't know. But I don't see how you can ask Dev. You've got no authority or reason to be poking your nose into the show's finances, but Bethan could. As part of her investigation, she can ask anybody anything. Why don't you mention this to her?" said Victoria.

"I did mention it to her earlier and she just said something like 'Oh, farm financing is so complicated.' So before I bring it up with her again, I need to be able to give her more details. Everything just seems so half-baked at this point. We've got absolutely nothing to go on, just vague suspicions," Penny replied.

"Mrs. Lloyd is on the agricultural show committee, but we agreed earlier that it would be a mistake to involve her in this. Who else do we know?" asked Victoria.

"Can't think of anyone off the top of my head. Have you still got your copy of the program? It lists the directors." Victoria set her fork down and left the room, returning a few minutes later with the familiar blue program booklet. She slid it onto the table. Penny put down her fork, picked up the program, flipped to the back page, and scanned the list of names.

"Let's see. Executive committee . . . Joyce, Barbara, Daffydd; members at large . . . Evelyn Lloyd . . . some I've never heard of . . . oh, here's somebody we know."

"Who?" Victoria picked at her salad.

"Haydn Williams."

"Oh, right, our old friend the sheep farmer. He might be

a good one to talk to. He'd know all about how complicated farm financing is."

"I'll add him to my list. I've got a few people to speak to. First, there's Delyth Powell. She was the one who rang Florence and told her to bring her entries to the show Saturday morning, and I'm just going to come right out and ask her why she did that. She must have had a reason."

"That seems like a reasonable approach."

"And of course I've got to let Florence know the police found her missing marmalade in Barbara Vickers's kitchen."

"I wonder how it got there."

"Well, that's the question, isn't it? And I suspect once we know the answer to that, a lot of other questions will be answered, too."

"Who are you going to speak to first, Haydn or Delyth?"

"Haydn, I think. He might be easier. He usually comes into town on market day for the sheep auction, and that's tomorrow, so I'll stroll around at lunchtime and see if I can spot him."

"Good. Now, moving on. Let's talk about the Spa. Anything you want to say about that? Any problems we should discuss?"

"Not a problem, but I've had an idea. Remember when Michelle said her little girl's eighth birthday is coming up? I thought that's something we could do for the business. Birthday party manicures."

"For children?"

"For any age, really."

"At the Spa? Wouldn't that disrupt our Saturday-afternoon trade?"

"We do wedding hair and makeup services at home, so why not this? And we could do birthday parties on Sunday afternoons, when the Spa is closed anyway, so it wouldn't interfere with our day-to-day operations. And home-manicure birthday parties might be really popular with senior ladies."

"That's not a bad idea."

"Why don't I reach out to Michelle Lewis and see if she'd be interested in having us do one for Macy's birthday."

"Good idea. I'll give you a pricing estimate as soon as we get back to the office. And now I'd better get us that coffee you were so desperate for." Victoria disappeared into the kitchen.

"I left a little something for you on the worktop," Penny called after her. As she spoke, Victoria let out a little squeal of delight. "Oh, I guess you opened it."

Victoria returned with two cupcakes on plates, two mugs, and a French press of freshly brewed coffee.

"I was thinking," she said as she set the tray down, "I really like the birthday party idea. It could be a really nice earner for us. Every little girl at Macy's party would want one for her birthday, and it wouldn't take long for word to get around, so that could really grow. And I suspect parents are always looking for new, fun things to do at birthday parties. But we want to get it right the first time, so if you don't have any appointments this afternoon, and if Michelle is available to talk to you, why don't you go and talk to her? As a mother with birthday party experience, she knows more about kids' parties than we do, and can probably tell you exactly how it should be run, and what the parents and kids want. And that way, we'd be able to deliver a great party the first time, so the little girls at Macy's party will want their mothers to book one for them."

"Good idea. I'll ring Michelle as soon as we finish lunch." She turned her attention to the cupcakes. "Which one's mine?"

Twenty-three

Michelle Lewis's grey pebble-dash house was located at the end of a row of identical modest properties on a quiet, narrow street tucked in behind the community swimming pool. It was an easy walk from the Spa, and Penny arrived on time.

Michelle answered the door and invited her into the sitting room.

"Sorry about the mess," she said, gesturing at cardboard boxes stacked three and four high, "but there's still room on the sofa."

"Are you moving house?" Penny asked as she sat down.

"No, not now," Michelle replied. "We were going to move to Spain, Macy and I and Mum, who had a cousin out there with a pub. It was meant to be a fresh start, but then Mum died, so we're staying put. All this"—she waved at the boxes—"is for the charity shop. Kids' stuff. Clothes and toys. They pile up fast."

"I can imagine," said Penny. "There's a lot. Must be, what, a dozen boxes? If you think it's too many, I'm sure Bronwyn would welcome some for the church jumble sale."

"That's a good idea," Michelle replied. "I'm not a church-goer, so I didn't think of that. We can see what my dad says. He should be here in a few minutes with Macy, and he was going to take some of it away with him."

"Well, maybe we should have our discussion now, before Macy gets here," said Penny. For the next fifteen minutes, Michelle explained what she had in mind for her daughter's party and how many guests there would be, and when she'd finished, Penny showed her the contract Victoria had drawn up.

Michelle read it over and then remarked, "That looks great. I'm sure Macy and her friends will love it." She signed the contract, then handed it back to Penny. "I'm just going to stick the kettle on," said Michelle. "Dad should be here any minute and he'll want a cup of tea. I'll make some for everybody."

"Can I help?" Penny asked, following her into the kitchen.

"Well, you could pour a glass of orange juice for Macy."

Penny opened the fridge and pulled out a carton of juice. "Michelle, did you happen to see Andrea anywhere that day we went to Speke Hall?"

Michelle looked startled. "Andrea? No, I didn't see her there. Was she there?"

"I'm not sure," said Penny. "She mentioned to me at the agricultural show banquet that she had some work lined up at Speke Hall, so I just wondered."

Michelle shrugged. She carried the tea tray through to the sitting room just as the front door opened and Macy ran into the room, followed by her grandfather, Carwyn Lewis.

"Had fun, did you, love?" Michelle asked Macy. The little girl nodded and looked at Penny. "You remember Penny from the agricultural show?" Michelle asked.

"Hi, Macy," said Penny. "You look different."

"It's my new glasses," Macy replied.

"Well, I like them," said Penny. "Those purple frames really suit you. Make you look even smarter." While Michelle handed Macy her orange juice and explained the manicure party to her, Penny brought Carwyn Lewis a cup of tea. He was wearing a green puffy vest with a cluster of small enamelled metal pins of the sort worn and traded at conventions. One pin was shaped like a chicken, and others featured logos of Welsh farming organizations. He looked at the boxes piled around the room and sighed. "I'll just finish my tea and then start loading those up."

A little squeal of delight from Macy let Penny know the manicure party had her approval. Macy got up from the table, ran to her grandfather, and sat beside him on the sofa. He put his arm around her and listened carefully while she explained all the arrangements for her birthday party.

"And I was so upset I couldn't have a bouncy castle, but you see, Granddad, this is going to be so much more fun. I'm going to get my nails done!"

"Oh, very good," said Carwyn. "Now, then, after I've had my tea, are you going to help me carry out the boxes to the Land Rover?"

"I could try," Macy replied, looking up at him with great

231

sincerity. "I do like to help you when I can, but I'm not sure I can lift those boxes. I'm not even eight yet."

Penny laughed and said good-bye.

"See you at the manicure party. It's going to be lots of fun."

Twenty-four

The next day, country market day, saw the cobbled town square filled with covered wooden stalls from which traders sold seasonal fruits and vegetables, home baking, artisan cheeses, eggs, preserves, crafts, and plants for indoors and gardens. The atmosphere was almost festive as townsfolk wandered from one display to the next, stopping to chat with a stall holder, or buying a teatime treat.

Penny stopped at the preserves stall and was reading the label on a jar of chilli jelly when a familiar figure emerged from the bank, leading a black and white Border collie. She handed the stall holder enough coins to cover her purchase, tucked the jar in her bag, and set off in pursuit of the man she wanted to speak to.

"Hello, Haydn." Penny smiled at him but gave his dog a

bigger smile and leaned over to stroke him. He returned her greeting with a vigorous wagging of his tail.

As she straightened up, Haydn's lips parted in an open, generous smile. "Hello, Penny. Kip's always so glad to see you. How are you?"

"Very well indeed, thanks. And you?"

"Oh, you know. Always the same, Kip and me. Aren't we, old boy?" Kip wagged his tail in agreement.

"I was wondering if I might have a word. It won't take long."

"I'm in no rush," Haydn replied. "Meeting a few of the lads in the pub in about half an hour or so, and I'm just heading over there now. Care to join me?"

"I'd like that very much."

Although Haydn was dressed in the rough working garb of a Welsh hill farmer—worn trousers, heavy boots, faded checked shirt, and a quilted vest—Penny had learned a long time ago that in these parts, farmers' looks could be deceiving. They often dressed like they didn't have two pennies to rub together, but in fact, many were sitting on large landholdings, ran profitable businesses, lived in comfortable stone houses with stunning views, and were custodians of priceless antique furniture and clocks that had been handed down through generations. And Haydn was one of them.

They strolled along the High Street to the Leek and Lily, the local pub. Haydn pulled on the brass handle and held the door open for Penny as she stepped into its warm, relaxed atmosphere. Horse brasses and sporting prints hung on its whitewashed walls, and its low-beamed ceiling ensured a lively noise level.

"What can I get you to drink?" Haydn asked.

"A white wine, please." She gestured to a small table in the corner. "That table all right for you?"

"I'd rather we get a bigger one, so there's enough room for the lads when they get here." He gestured to the one he wanted. "I usually come along early to hold the table."

The pub was not yet busy, but it would soon fill up with hardworking farmers who had spent the morning at the livestock auction held on the outskirts of the town.

Penny settled herself on a bench, with Kip seated beside her, and Haydn returned a few minutes later with two full glasses. He placed a white wine in front of her and took a deep draft of his beer, then asked, "What was it you wanted to talk to me about?"

"I wanted to ask you a couple of questions about the agricultural show committee," Penny began. "I wondered how the finances work."

"What do you mean, 'how the finances work'?"

"Well, the treasurer, is he responsible for the money?"

Haydn frowned. "Of course he is. Isn't that what a treasurer does?"

Penny sighed. "Well, yes, but, and this is a little difficult, I just wondered if you've noticed any discrepancies in the show's funds."

"Discrepancies? What kinds of discrepancies?" The conversation wasn't going well. Even to her, the questions seemed clumsy and badly worded, and Haydn's responses were sluggish and defensive. Normally a man with an easygoing, low-maintenance personality, he seemed on edge.

"Look," said Penny trying to reassure him, "I'm not suggesting anything, so please don't take this as criticism, but I just wondered, well, if you, as a committee member, have noticed any money missing."

"'Have I noticed money missing?' Well, no, I haven't, and if I had, I would have done something about it. But I wouldn't know. The committee members don't have anything to do with the books. We just know what the treasurer tells us."

"But does the treasurer manage the books?"

Haydn laughed. "You mean Dev? He signs cheques, and is the official treasurer, but really, that's in name only. Barbara Vickers manages the money. Managed, I should say. Still can't get my head around that. It's too bad what happened to her."

"Yes, it certainly is. But she looked after the books, did she?"

Haydn took a sip of beer. "For all practical purposes. And then the accounts are professionally audited every year."

"Why would Dev be the treasurer, then, if Barbara Vickers was really looking after them?" Penny persisted.

Haydn sighed. "Look, it's not really common knowledge, and I don't want to say too much, but Dev's not as with it as he used to be. He's getting forgetful, and he comes across as a little confused sometimes. You tell him something, and five minutes later, he can't remember what you told him. So Joyce, bless her, not wanting to upset Dev, thought it would be a good idea if he continued on as the treasurer, in name only, really, but Barbara did the real work." He shrugged. "Lots of organizations have what they call a secretary-treasurer, so there's no harm in it. And yes, most of the committee members are aware of Dev's condition, but out of respect to him, no one mentions it."

"Oh, I see," said Penny, remembering the unpaid bills piling up on the Welsh dresser in the Devlins' kitchen. Dev's forgetfulness suggested that they weren't being paid because he forgot about them. "I'm sorry to hear that."

Haydn shrugged. "But everything's on the up-and-up, if that's what you're getting at, although I have no idea why you would be. Everything's shipshape."

"Oh, I'm just exploring possibilities, that's all."

"Possibilities?"

"The deaths of Gaynor Lewis and Barbara Vickers trouble me."

"They trouble everyone around here, Penny," Haydn replied with quiet dignity.

"Yes, of course." She took a sip of wine and they sat in silence until Penny said, "Victoria and I visited the Devlin farm the day after the agricultural show and Joyce gave us a tour of the new kennels. They're really something."

"State-of-the-art, from what I hear."

"You haven't seen them yet?"

He shook his head. "No, but I will, one of these days. All Joyce's idea, of course, and Dev insisted she should have them exactly the way she wanted them."

"They must have cost a pretty penny."

"Oh, I know they did." Haydn took a sip from his almost-empty glass, and then a slow smile spread across his face. "I paid for them."

"What! Why would you pay for them?"

"Because I was looking to expand my acreage last year, and Dev sold me one of his fields. The money from the sale paid for the kennels."

"Oh, I see." Well, there goes that theory, thought Penny. It had seemed plausible enough that Joyce and Dev needed money for the kennels, and had defrauded the agricultural show to get it. And that Gaynor had found out about it and threatened to go to the authorities, so Joyce or Dev, or possibly both, had killed her to silence her.

Penny admitted her theory didn't really allow for how Joyce and Dev could be implicated in Barbara Vickers's death, though, but that didn't matter now. And then, as she had another thought, Penny couldn't resist a little smile. Bethan Morgan had been wrong when she said farm financing was complicated. This transaction had been remarkably simple, and farmers had probably been doing the very same thing for centuries.

As Penny finished her wine, the door opened and a group of farmers burst in. One or two headed for the bar to get their drinks in while the rest made for Haydn's table.

Penny picked up her handbag, and after thanking Haydn for the drink, she nodded to his friends, then returned to the Spa.

"Well, we can cross Joyce and Dev off our list," Penny said to Victoria after she'd explained that the Devlins had sold a parcel of land to Haydn to raise money for the kennels. "We thought money might be a motive, but it isn't."

"No," agreed Victoria, "the money motive seems to have disappeared, but can we be sure Joyce didn't kill Gaynor Lewis for some other reason? After all, they were in the tent together on the Friday night and she must be one of the last people to have seen Gaynor alive."

"True enough," said Penny. "But I don't see how she could have been involved in the Barbara Vickers killing. She isn't a member of the Women's Guild and she wasn't on the outing. We just can't get around that."

"Could there be two killers?" Victoria asked. "What if the killings are unrelated?'

"There could be two killers, I suppose." Penny hesitated. "But that makes everything so complicated. Probably better to keep things simple, assume there's one killer, and see where that gets us. And besides, we've got lots to link the two murders."

"Such as?"

"Everybody who was on the coach trip, and everybody who was at the show ground, after, say, eight o'clock." She was interrupted by the ringing of her phone. She glanced at the screen, then frowned. "It's Florence. She wouldn't be ringing if it weren't important."

"Better see what she wants, then." Victoria prepared to return to her office, but Penny gestured with her free hand, urging her to sit. Penny listened for a moment, then ended the call.

"There's been a development, of sorts. Andrea Devlin was over at Mrs. Lloyd's, painting the dining room, and while she was there, the police rang to ask Andrea to come to the police station to help them with their inquiries. Mrs. Lloyd's upset. She's afraid Andrea is going to be arrested for the murder of Gaynor Lewis."

"What does she want you to do?" asked Victoria. "I hope they don't think you should go over to the police station and try to help. If the police are questioning Andrea, it sounds as if she needs a solicitor, not you."

"You're right," said Penny. "I can't do anything to help Andrea, but speaking of Florence, there is a bit of unfinished business to sort out. Let's get the marmalade issue settled once and for all."

Twenty-five

The address jotted on a scrap of paper led Penny to a small, beige pebble-dash house, optimistically called Cornell Manor, on Watling Street, just across from the bus stop. She knocked and waited. A moment later from inside the house came the sound of footsteps, then the click of the lock being turned.

"Yes?" Delyth Powell peered suspiciously around the side of the door.

"Well, hello, pet," said Penny. "I'm Penny Brannigan. Our paths crossed briefly at the Women's Guild meeting, at the banquet, and then again on the Speke Hall excursion, but we haven't really been properly introduced."

Delyth frowned and pursed her lips as a glimmer of recognition flashed across her face.

"Oh, yes. I remember you now. You'd better come in,

then." She led the way into a sitting room of unrelieved brown: sofa, chairs, carpet, curtains, cushions. A popular tea-time quiz show blasted from a giant flat screen television. She picked up the remote control and muted the program, closed the door to the hall, gestured to a chair, and waited.

"I'll get right to the point so that you can get back to your program," Penny said. "Did you call Florence Semble and tell her to bring her agricultural show entries to the marquee on the Saturday morning, rather than the Friday evening?"

"Bring her entries in Saturday morning? To the agricultural show?" Penny recognized repeating the question as a classic stalling technique to buy a few more seconds for a whirling brain to come up with some kind of answer.

"Yes. That's what I'm asking you," Penny said.

"Now why would I want to do a thing like that?"

"I don't know. I'm just asking if you did."

Delyth's chest rose and fell rapidly, but before she could reply, there came the sound of the front door opening, followed by footsteps in the hall. "Only me," a woman's voice called out. The door to the sitting room opened, and Mari Jones entered. Penny was struck once again by how much the two retired schoolteachers resembled each other, and she wondered if they had deliberately adopted the same look, or if they had just grown to look alike over the years, the way long-married couples are sometimes said to do. She also wondered how it was that, with their strikingly similar looks, she hadn't noticed them out and about in the town. It must be, she thought, that we just move in different circles.

"Oh, Mari, pet. I'm so glad you're here. I've landed myself in a bit of a pickle, I think."

"Why? Whatever's happened?" Mari set down two carrier bags filled with groceries, slid onto the sofa beside her friend, and, after giving Penny a cold glance, fixed concerned eyes on Delyth and asked, "Has she said something to upset you?"

"I did something rather foolish, I'm afraid, and she found out." Delyth glanced at Penny, who gave her a nod of encouragement. "I rang Florence Semble and I told her to bring her entries for the agricultural show to the marquee on the Saturday morning."

"Oh, Delyth, why did you do that? How many years have we been entering in the competition? You know the entries have to be brought to the tent on the Friday night."

"Because others at the Women's Guild meeting had been talking about how good Florence's baking is, even before she joined our group, and I thought if she didn't have a cake in the competition, you might be in with a chance. You work so hard on your cakes and never win. It hardly seems fair, and I thought winning might boost your confidence."

"How did you get Florence's phone number?" Penny asked.

"I saw the notice in the village hall about the cooking classes she gives to new mothers, and her phone number's on it."

"I see."

"I realize what I did was wrong, pet, but after all, in the grand scheme of things, it's not a big deal, is it?" said Delyth. "I mean, really, when you think about it, what harm was done? She did get her entries in on time, and one of them, if I remember correctly, came in first."

Bloody hell, thought Penny. This must be the third time

243

I've heard someone say it doesn't really matter that Florence almost didn't get her entries into the competition, because it all got sorted in the end, so where's the harm? What kind of thinking is that? And it didn't all come right in the end, because Florence was denied entry into two categories, which she very well might have won.

"Yes, her raspberry jam came in first," said Penny in a tone almost as sharp as Florence's jam, "but her marmalade didn't make it into the judging, for some reason. And her cake was ruined and didn't make it into the judging, either, so as you can imagine, she was upset and disappointed. And who can blame her?"

Delyth looked at her hands in her lap and Mari did not reply.

"All right," said Penny. "You didn't want her entering a cake in the competition. I don't suppose you know anything about her marmalade, do you?"

"No, we don't," said Mari. "After we dropped off my entries, we went home, and we didn't go anywhere near that marquee until the next day."

"But, that's not—" Delyth began, but Mari stopped her with a thunderous look.

"And even if we had gone back to the tent," Mari continued, "how would Delyth have known which entries were Florence's? The judging's supposed to be anonymous, isn't it? Isn't that the whole point? And you were right there checking them in, so how would we have got past you?"

"I think you wanted to say something, Delyth," Penny said, as if Mari hadn't spoken. "Please finish what you started to say."

Delyth did not reply, so Penny prompted her. "'That's not

right? That's not how I remember it? That's not how it happened?' Were you about to say something like that? Is that
what you wanted to say?" She held her breath and waited.

"She was going to say, 'But that's not quite right,'" said
Mari, "because I did go back to meet someone."

"We've gone this far, we might as well tell her everything," Delyth said with a resigned sigh.

"All right," said Mari. "I met up with Elin Spears. She
wanted to find a way to get someone's entry out of the competition. She thought if we could get into the tent and take
the entry, we could make it look as if someone—Joyce Devlin or Barbara Vickers, or maybe even you"—she flicked a
hand in Penny's direction—"had dropped one of the jars.
And if it didn't break on its own, we would have helped it
along."

And then Penny understood. "It was you and Elin I heard
talking at the marquee on the Friday night, just after eight,
when the entries closed. I'd gone back to get something, and
I overheard two women talking about not wanting someone to win. So Elin wanted Florence out of the competition, too."

Mari looked puzzled. "Florence? No, not Florence," she
said with a touch of impatience. "Elin wanted Gaynor's entries out of the competition."

"Gaynor! So Florence wasn't the target, then?"

"No, Elin would have been happy if Florence had won.
She didn't care. Anyone but that cow Gaynor, really."

"So then it was you who took Florence's marmalade?"

"No, because when we got inside the tent, we could see
Joyce and Barbara over in the tea area, so we gave it up as a
bad job and left before they spotted us."

245

"And if you had been successful, how would you have known which jar was Gaynor's?" Penny asked.

"Because she always enters hers with those daft red-and-white metal lids. They're allowed. You can buy those jars at the local kitchen-supply store, so they're quite common. But no one else uses them."

"And did you see Gaynor Lewis while all this was going on?" Penny asked.

"No," Mari replied. "I didn't."

"And have you told this to the police?" Penny asked.

"No. Why would we tell them that we tried to steal Gaynor's marmalade?"

Now it was Penny's turn to show impatience. "It's not about the marmalade! You need to tell them you were at the marquee after eight o'clock on the Friday night. Gaynor Lewis died that night. You might have seen or heard something important, something that you don't even know is important. Tell the police everything you did, and saw, and heard, and they'll decide. You might have the one key piece of information that could help them find a killer." She let the words hang in the air, and when Delyth lobbed a fearful glance in Mari's direction, which she returned, Penny knew her words had done their work.

"And did you see Elin Spears leave the show grounds?" Penny asked.

"No, I didn't," said Mari. "She was planning to meet Carwyn somewhere, maybe over by his chickens, and they'd go home together. Or maybe she was going to go home and he was going to stop the night there with his blessed chickens, like the rest of the farming community. Anyway, she was waiting for him to come back."

"What do you mean, 'come back'?"

"Oh, she'd forgotten something important that was needed for the show, and he'd gone home to fetch it for her," said Mari.

"And what was that?"

Delyth laughed. "She'd only gone and forgotten the Women's Guild cake set! The cake stand and server for the Best in Show cake display. The winner takes it home every year, and is supposed to bring it back the next year. Elin had it because she'd won the previous year. Only she'd forgotten it, and it has to be returned the night before so that the judges can put the winning cake on it the next morning."

"And Carwyn went home to get it?"

"That's right."

"I suggest you tell that to the police, too," Penny said. She sighed. "Well, thank you. I appreciate your clearing up part of the mystery, anyway. At least we know now who made the telephone call to Florence." Now all we have to do is find out who removed Florence's marmalade from the tent and how it ended up in Barbara Vickers's kitchen, she added to herself.

Delyth and Mari exchanged worried looks. "What is it?" Penny asked. "If you know something, please tell me."

"Are you going to tell her?" Delyth asked. "Florence Semble, I mean. Are you going to tell her it was me who rang her and told her to bring her entries on Saturday morning?"

"She already knows it was you. Or at least she knows it was one of you. It was your calling her *pet* on the telephone that gave you away. And then we heard you say it again while we were having our coffee at the refreshment stop on the way to Speke Hall. But you were sitting behind us, so we weren't exactly sure which one of you it was. We were curious about your use of the word *pet,* by the way. I'm not an expert on accents, by any means, but you don't speak like someone from the North of England. I wondered why you use the word *pet?*"

"Do I?" Delyth's eyebrows shot up. Penny and Mari spoke at the same time, assuring her she did.

"It must be something I picked up from my mother, then. She used to call everyone *pet.* She came from Newcastle upon Tyne."

"Well, you've certainly given me a lot to think about," said Penny as she stood up. Delyth showed her to the door, and when she returned to the sitting room, Mari said, "Never mind the shopping for a minute. It'll keep. Come here." She patted the seat of the sofa beside her, and Delyth sat.

"You do realize what you did was very wrong, don't you?" Mari said. Delyth nodded miserably. "I know you did what you did because you wanted me to win, but if you think for one minute that I'd be happy knowing I'd won because of what you did, then you don't know me." As Delyth started to cry, Mari put her arms around her. "Don't you see, if you have to cheat to win, you haven't won at all?"

Twenty-six

O n the walk back to the Spa following her conversation with Delyth and Mari, Penny reflected on what she'd heard. Her mind raced as she tried to put all the pieces together.

The door to the Spa was unlocked, but Rhian, the receptionist, had left for the day and the remaining staff were tidying up and getting everything ready for the morning. Penny headed down the short corridor to Victoria's office and slipped into the visitor's chair.

"You're welcome to sit there as long as you like," said Victoria, "but I'm leaving. If you'd like to come upstairs and have a glass of wine with me, let's go."

They locked the main entrance behind Eirlys and Alberto, then headed back through the empty, silent space and upstairs to Victoria's flat. Victoria poured each of them a glass of white wine and they moved to her sitting room. Penny took an appreciative sip as she glanced out the window.

"It amazes me how fiercely competitive the women are who enter their preserves or baking in the agricultural show," said Penny. "It's all so confusing, who wanted who out of the competition and who wanted to win."

"Everybody wanted to win," said Victoria. "That's why they enter."

"Well, true. But it seems that some wanted to win more than others."

Penny explained what she'd learned during her visit with Delyth and Mari.

"I'm so confused," said Victoria. "Tell me again about the jars. Help me get my head around it."

"Well-meaning but misguided Delyth rang Florence and told her to bring her entries on Saturday morning. She did this because she thought if Florence missed the deadline, her entries would be out of the competition, and her chum Mari's cake would be in with a chance. But although Florence did get her entries in on time, her carrot cake didn't make it into the competition because it ended up under the table with the body of Gaynor Lewis, and Elin Spears won the cake competition anyway, so poor Delyth's scheme was all for nothing. And that's the end of her involvement.

"The voices I heard at the tent when I returned to get the program were those of Elin Spears and Mari Jones. Elin wanted Gaynor's marmalade out of the competition. Are you with me? But when they saw Joyce and Barbara in the refreshment area of the marquee, they lost their nerve and beat a hasty retreat. And in fact, unbeknownst to them, Gaynor had arrived late, and at that point, I don't think her marmalade had been accepted yet into the competition. That probably happened a few minutes later, after Elin and Mari had left, when Gaynor arrived at the tent, met up with Joyce Devlin, and Joyce allowed Gaynor's entries into the competition. You know all about that because you were there when Joyce explained that bit. And Joyce and Barbara left, and at that point, Gaynor must have been alone in the tent and met the killer."

"And Florence's marmalade disappeared."

"Right. Florence's marmalade disappeared, and ended up in Barbara Vickers's kitchen. So as I said to Bethan, it seems to me that what connects the two murders is Florence's marmalade. It was in the tent, where the first victim died, and the police found it in the kitchen of the second victim. Or do you think that's too much of a leap?"

"I'm not sure."

"Bear with me. I'm still trying to work this out. Gaynor . . . marmalade . . . Florence . . . marmalade. I feel I'm grasping for something that's just out of reach. It dances through my mind, and then it's gone." She closed her eyes and placed her hands over her face. A moment later, she lowered her hands and her face was transformed. "I've got it. At least I think I have. Here's what could have happened." Victoria set her wineglass down and leaned forward. "We've been going at this the wrong way. We'd assumed someone wanted Florence's marmalade out of the competition because of the phone call, and that's true, or sort of true. That was Delyth. But it wasn't the marmalade she wanted out of the competition; it was the cake. But that's not the reason Florence's marmalade wasn't in the competition. Oh, this is so complicated; I've got to try to explain it properly."

Penny took a moment to organize her thoughts.

"Florence's marmalade got taken out by mistake," she began. "Mari Jones said Elin wanted Gaynor's marmalade out of the competition. Whoever took Florence's was actually after Gaynor's, not Florence's. Think about it. Both jars looked the same. Florence's had a red cloth gingham top, but Gaynor's had the metal top with the red-and-white gingham pattern printed on the lid. Apparently, she uses that jar and lid every year and the locals know it's Gaynor's jam, but the judges don't know, because they come from out of town. Wrexham or somewhere, I think it said in the program."

"So you think someone took the wrong jar?"

"I do. We just have to work out who that was."

"Well, the obvious person is Elin, isn't it? You said she was the one who wanted Gaynor's marmalade out of the competition."

"Elin's the obvious one, but did she have the opportunity? Mari said she and Elin left when they saw Joyce and Barbara in the marquee."

"She could have come back."

"She could have."

"Yes, because someone entered the tent and murdered Gaynor Lewis."

"Maybe we'll see Elin at Macy's birthday party on Sunday. I hope so. If she's there, maybe we'll have the chance to ask her a few questions."

Twenty-seven

Michelle Lewis's house was easy to spot. Half a dozen helium-filled balloons in graduated shades of pink were tied to a gate. They bobbed and swayed in a light breeze as Victoria drove slowly down the narrow street, lined on both sides with parked cars. Unable to find a parking space in front of the house, they continued on to the swimming pool car park, where they left the car; then, carrying their manicure supplies, they walked back to the house.

Penny's assistant, Eirlys, who had come along to help with the manicures, knocked on the door, and seconds later it flew open, revealing an exuberant Macy. She raised both hands to straighten the silver-coloured tiara with its glued-on coloured stones, then politely welcomed Penny, Victoria, and Eirlys to her birthday party and invited them in.

The happy sounds of little girls at play greeted them as

they entered the small sitting room off the entry hall. The cardboard boxes that had been piled up on Penny's last visit were gone. Michelle Lewis sat on a slightly faded red sofa with a woman about the same age. The women's chatter fell away as the newcomers entered the room, and when the two women stood, the string of *Beauty and the Beast*–themed pennants taped to the wall above them fluttered slightly. "Right. Time I was on my way," Michelle's friend said. "Sorry I can't stay to help with the party, but I'll be back at five to pick up my two. Have fun!"

"I'll be off, as well," said Victoria to Penny, handing her a case filled with supplies. "Just ring me when you're ready to leave."

"I'll see you both out," said Michelle. "If you wouldn't mind just keeping your eyes on that lot," she said to Penny, "I'll be right back." When she returned, she pointed to a table covered with a *Beauty and the Beast* paper tablecloth at the other end of the room. "I thought you could work here," she said, raising her voice slightly to be heard above the girls' laughter. "When you're finished, we'll clear everything away and then I'll set up the table for their tea."

Eirlys and Penny laid clean white towels on the table, then arranged their manicure equipment and chairs so they could do two manicures at the same time. "There's just six children, so it shouldn't take long," Penny said.

"I'm so glad you suggested manicures as the birthday party entertainment. So much more fun than the usual clown, and we don't have a garden for a bouncy castle. You've really lifted Macy's spirits," said Michelle as Eirlys disappeared into the kitchen to fill the two soaking bowls. "She's thrilled to be getting her first manicure." She choked on the last couple

254

of words. "Sorry. I've been thinking about Mum, and her not being here today, and all the rest of Macy's firsts she's going to miss. When all's said and done, she was still Macy's grandmother, but I told myself I wouldn't go there today. Don't want to spoil it for the girls."

Michelle pulled herself together as Penny murmured all the right sympathetic noises and then commented, "It's been a long time since I was at a child's birthday party, so thank you for having us."

When Eirlys had placed the soaking bowls on the table, Michelle called out, "Right! Who's first? Who thinks the birthday girl should go first?" The little girls squealed their approval, Michelle told Macy to choose a friend to have a manicure with her, and the two girls raced to the table.

"What colour would you like, Macy?" Penny asked. "You can choose any colour you like." Macy rested her chin in the palms of her hands as she surveyed the range of pinks, greens, blues, and purples in the bottles of nail varnish in front of her. Penny pointed to a bottle of pale pink with added glitter. "This one's called Princesses Rule! What do you think of that one?"

"Yes, please!"

"Right. Now just dip your fingers in the water and we'll get started."

"My *nain* isn't coming to my party," Macy said. "She can't be here. But my *taid* is coming after he's fed his chickens. He's still got them, you know."

"Oh, I'm glad to hear that."

"Yes, me, too, because my *nain* said they were going to take them away from him."

"Who was going to take them away?"

255

Macy shrugged. "I don't know. He's bringing Elin to my party. I don't like Elin."

"Do you not?" Penny asked. "Why is that?"

Macy shrugged. "I don't know. I just don't, that's all. They're coming for tea. Elin and my *taid*. Do you like cake?"

"I do. It's my favourite thing, especially if it's chocolate and has lots of icing."

"Me, too!"

When she'd finished the manicure, Penny warned Macy that her nails would be sticky for the next little while, so she'd have to be very careful not to touch anything. Macy promised to be careful, and skipped off to show her glittery pink nails to her mother.

She stopped at the sound of a loud knocking on the door. "You'll have to answer the door, Mum," she said. "My nails are still wet."

Elin Spears entered the sitting room, carrying two large recycled gift bags with wrinkled pink tissue paper spilling over the tops. "Where should I put these?" she asked Michelle.

"Oh, just over there with the other presents, thanks. Macy'll open them after they've had their tea."

"And remember to save all the bags and wrapping," replied Elin. "There's no point in wasting good money buying more gift bags when you can reuse these. I can't bear waste. And here's a jar of my strawberry jam that Macy likes on her toast. I'll just put it in the kitchen."

At the mention of the word *jam,* Penny looked up from the set of little fingernails she was painting. Elin, jar of jam still in her hand, looked trim in a pair of black trousers paired with a white blouse topped with a black-and-white-striped sweater. Penny's gaze wandered to her partner, Carwyn

Lewis, who was standing in the centre of the room admiring his granddaughter's painted fingernails. He wasn't dressed in typical farmer's clothes, but in a smart pair of well-pressed trousers and a pale blue shirt, open at the neck. Over the shirt was his puffy green vest with the pins on it.

"Thanks, Elin," Michelle said. "Did you make the jam yourself?"

"Of course I did. Do you think I would give you someone else's conserve?"

Someone else's.

The words danced through Penny's mind, teasing her, taunting her, bringing her back to the time she'd heard them spoken by a broken woman lying on the floor of the Green Bedroom in Speke Hall.

"Penny?" The small voice from the child in front of her snapped her attention back to the upturned face, a frown creasing the child's forehead.

"Sorry. I was just trying to remember something."

"Well, you have to leave it alone," said the little girl. "And then, when you aren't thinking about it, it will pop right into your head when you least expect it. That's what my mum always tells me."

"That's good advice. I'll do that."

Just as Penny finished the child's manicure, Macy let out a loud wail. She ran to Penny and held out her hand, revealing a fluffy white feather stuck on the freshly painted fingernail of her right hand.

"It's all smudged," Macy cried. "We'll have to do it all over again."

"No we won't," Penny assured her. "We can fix this. Would you like to see a bit of magic?"

"I would!"

"Where did you get that feather?" Penny asked as she lifted it gently off Macy's fingernail with a pair of tweezers and wiped it off onto a towel.

"Off my granddad. It was on his vest. I guess from when he checked up on the chickens before he came here. It's a new vest. He hasn't had it very long. I liked the old one better. It had a red lining. But the pins are the same, so that's good."

Penny glanced at Carwyn, who was seated on the sofa. "So, Macy, how long has your granddad had this new vest?" Penny asked as she removed the cap from a bottle of nail varnish remover and poured a drop into it.

"I don't know," said Macy. "Not very long."

"Well, let's think now. Did he have it before or after the agricultural show?"

She dipped a cotton-tipped swab ever so lightly into the cap, then used it to gently smooth the roughed-up nail polish on Macy's fingernail.

"After the show, because it was too hot for him to wear his old vest at the show."

"That's right. It was warm in the tent, wasn't it, when we went to see him. Remember? We walked over to the tent together after the pet show, you and I and Haydn Williams."

"That's right," Macy agreed. "We did."

After giving the newly applied nail varnish remover a moment to dry, Penny applied another coat of Princesses Rule! nail polish.

"There!" she said. "All done. What do you think of that?"

Macy held out her hand, examined her fingernail, declared it perfect, and ran back to join the party. With the last manicure done, Eirlys began packing up their supplies, while Penny had a word with Michelle.

"I'm going to stay and help with the tea," Penny told Eirlys. "I'll call Victoria to let her know. Would you like her to give you a ride home?"

"No, I've got a friend lives near here, so I'll just walk over to hers."

"Okay. Leave everything here and I'll take it all away with me when I go."

They left the house together, so Penny could call Victoria from the relative quiet of the street, away from the party noise. She waved good-bye to Eirlys as she set off, and after making arrangements with Victoria, she returned to the house, where Michelle was setting the table with paper plates and napkins that matched the tablecloth.

"I'm not sure how this works," said Penny, "but as I recall it's children only at the table. Is that right?"

"It is. And the grown-ups eat later. You're welcome to stay for that."

"Oh, thanks, but I'll be off as soon as the children are sorted."

"I do appreciate you helping me," said Michelle as they moved into the kitchen. "I'm sure Elin would, but, well . . ."

"You want to keep her out of the kitchen?"

"Exactly. She's got such definite ideas about how things should be done, and I'd really rather just be left to do things my own way."

"Well, tell me what you need me to do."

Michelle switched on the cooker. "Just give that a few minutes to warm up, and then you can pop in the sausage rolls."

"I'm curious to know more about your father's chickens," Penny said as she unwrapped the packet of sausage rolls and set them on a baking tray.

Michelle scoffed. "His chickens. Honestly, you'd think they laid golden eggs, the way he goes on about them. They're called Silkies and they're so fluffy, they look like they've got fur, not feathers. And they moult like crazy. Apparently, they're what's known as an ornamental breed; they exist more for their good looks and show. My mother hated them, but he just adores them. You should see where they live. It's the Taj Mahal of chicken coops. He even brings in special ones to breed here."

"When you say 'brings in,' do you mean imports?"

Michelle nodded as she released a set of *Beauty and the Beast* paper cups from their cellophane and handed them to Penny.

"I expect that's a terrific amount of paperwork, with all the EU regulations governing every aspect of farming," Penny remarked. "I've heard farmers complain about that before. How complicated and difficult it is trying to get anything done."

"That's true."

"And does Elin ever look after them?"

Michelle laughed. "Are you kidding? As if he'd let anyone else near his Silkies. He does let Macy hold one occasionally, though."

Clutching the paper cups, Penny turned to find Elin standing in the doorway. "What are you two talking about?" Elin asked.

"The European Union regulations regarding the importation of chickens, would you believe," said Michelle.

"Oh, how interesting." She surveyed the kitchen work-top, and at the sight of a pink-and-chocolate-brown-striped box from the local bakery, commented, "Well, I wish you'd have let me bake Macy's cake. I do make a rather nice celebration cake, you know, having won Best in Show, in case you'd forgotten."

"I know," said Michelle, "and I'm sorry. It's just that Mum used to bake Macy's cakes, and I thought it would be less upsetting for Macy if she got to choose a store-bought cake this year, and she opted for a *Beauty and the Beast* cake to go with her theme. But it was kind of you to offer, Elin, and I do appreciate it."

"Maybe you could have brought the WG silver cake server," Penny offered. "Or perhaps you were going to but you left it at home."

Elin crossed her arms and glared at Penny but said nothing, and after a moment, she wandered back to the sitting room.

"That was a very naughty thing to say," Michelle said with a lopsided grin as she took a plastic container filled with sandwiches out of the refrigerator. She arranged them on a small platter and handed the plate to Penny. "Here you go. Can you manage that with the cups? And then, if you wouldn't mind, you can pour the drinks. Just half a cup, so there's less danger of a spill. You'll find a bottle of orange squash in the fridge."

Penny set the platter of sandwiches on the table, then made her way around the table, placing a drinking cup at each place. She returned to the table with the bottle of orange squash and circled the table, filling each cup halfway.

The girls were seated in a circle on the floor, playing a

board game, as Elin and Carwyn sat on the sofa, talking quietly. As one child rolled the dice and the others leaned forward to look at the numbers, Penny overheard Elin say to Carwyn, ". . . talking about EU regulations and chickens." Penny moved on to the setting at the end of the table, and with a sidelong glance, she watched as Carwyn turned slowly toward her and returned her gaze. Their eyes met briefly, and for a reason she couldn't explain, her heart began to pound. Her hand trembled as she filled the last cup.

Michelle emerged from the kitchen, a tea towel over her shoulder, and announced, "Tea's ready." The girls cheered and scrambled to find their places at the table.

"We were just saying we think we'll be heading home," Elin remarked.

"Oh, but *Taid*, you have to stay!" cried Macy. "You have to watch me open my presents!"

"Your granddad's going rock climbing tomorrow morning, and he's got a lot to do to get ready."

"For God's sake, Elin, she's only a little girl," Michelle hissed through clenched teeth so that the children couldn't hear. "It's you who wants to leave, not Dad. Can't you even let him be with Macy on her birthday?"

"You should talk!" Elin retorted. "You and your mother were planning on taking her to live in Spain. Do you have any idea how that upset him? She always just thought of herself, Gaynor did. She never cared how her actions might hurt someone else. Or maybe she did, and that was the whole point."

Someone else. There it was again. Penny wasn't sure, yet, how all the pieces of the murderous puzzle fit together, but she knew where the starting point was.

Taking extra care with the towels that had been used during the manicures, she gathered up her supplies, thanked Michelle, and wished Macy the happiest of birthdays. A few minutes later, Victoria picked her up and they set off for home.

As she put the car in gear, Victoria asked how the party had gone.

"The person who killed Gaynor Lewis and Barbara Vickers was there," Penny replied calmly. "Or maybe I should say *persons*."

"I wasn't expecting to hear that," Victoria sputtered. "I was expecting you to say that a group of noisy little girls drove you mad and you couldn't wait to get out of there!"

"Oh no. The girls were adorable. But a couple of the grown-ups, not so much. I haven't worked out all the details yet, so I'd rather wait until I've got it all straight in my mind before I explain it to you. But I can tell you, the mix-up over Florence's marmalade set in motion a cascade of unfortunate events. But before that happened, Elin Spears forgot to bring the silver cake service."

Twenty-eight

First thing Monday morning, carrying a plastic bag, Penny entered the Llanelen police station and asked to speak to Inspector Bethan Morgan. She was shown into an interview room and told that Bethan would be with her soon. After several minutes, Bethan entered the room and closed the door quietly behind her.

"Penny. What can I do for you?"

"I've come to share my theory with you, and if I'm right, you could be making an arrest before lunchtime."

"That's what I like to hear," said Bethan as she took the chair opposite Penny.

"But first, let's get something out of the way," said Penny. "Andrea Devlin had nothing to do with either murder. I heard she'd been brought in for questioning. Mrs. Lloyd was worried about her. You didn't find anything, did you?"

"No. She wasn't at Speke Hall on the day Barbara Vickers died, and the mate she's staying with in Betws said she was at home on the Friday evening Gaynor Lewis died, from eight o'clock onward. She's in the clear. But we wanted to talk to her again about something Gaynor Lewis said to her during that conversation they in the café. So now that you're reassured on that score, tell me what you think happened."

"The chain of events started when someone took Florence's marmalade by mistake, and after that, everything got out of hand. I never knew entering cakes and jam in an agricultural show could be so competitive and cutthroat, but apparently it is."

"Only not usually to this extreme."

"We thought an insecure rival wanted Florence's marmalade out of the competition, but it wasn't that at all. You see, Florence's marmalade was taken by mistake—Elin Spears wanted Gaynor Lewis's marmalade out of the competition but was unable to get it. So she rang her partner, Carwyn, who had gone home to fetch the cake stand set that she'd forgotten, and asked him to get Gaynor's marmalade for her. 'The jar will have a red-and-white top,' Elin told him. But what she didn't know was that Florence's jar had a red-and-white gingham fabric topper, whereas Gaynor's was just a red-and-white metal screw-on lid.

"When Carwyn got to the tent, Joyce and Barbara had just left, but his former wife, Gaynor, who'd arrived late with her entry, was still there. I don't know what she was doing, but probably she was looking at the entries. She wouldn't have known which entries belonged to the members of the

Women's Guild, but she would have wanted to have a good look at them anyway."

"Hold it there, Penny," said Bethan. "I'm just going to switch on the recorder."

On Bethan's signal, Penny continued.

"So while she's stood there looking at the entries, in comes Carwyn with the Women's Guild cake stand, server, and knife that Elin had asked him to fetch from home. She'd won the Best in Show award for baking the year before, so she got to keep the silver set for a year, and then had to return it for this year's show.

"Gaynor and Carwyn had a hard breakup. Gaynor hated him, and Elin and Gaynor hated each other. Even after all these years, there was a lot of bitterness festering among all three of them. And I believe Carwyn and Gaynor got into a terrible argument because Gaynor was about to take away the most precious thing in Carwyn's life."

"Which was?"

"At first, I thought the murder might have something to do with his chickens, which he loved so much, and then I realized it was something more precious."

Bethan's eyes widened.

"Macy. His granddaughter, whom he loves more than anything. Gaynor and Michelle were planning to move to Spain, and naturally they'd take Macy with them."

"So Carwyn and Gaynor get into a violent argument," Bethan said, picking up the narrative. "He begs her not to take Macy away. She taunts him, and as she turns to walk away, he snaps, grabs the Women's Guild cake knife off the table, and stabs her."

"And now, of course, he's panicked," said Penny. "He's horrified by what he's done. He's got to do something with the body, and quick. Joyce could return at any minute to lock up. So he stuffs the body under the table and tries to hide it, along with Florence's cake, which Gaynor had put her hand in when she grabbed at the table as she collapsed."

"Yes," Bethan said. "That matches the forensics."

"And then Carwyn grabs the jar of marmalade with the red-and-white top that Elin told him to get, and he legs it. He can't get out of there fast enough. But he's grabbed Florence's marmalade by mistake, not Gaynor's," said Penny. "Because when Joyce accepted Gaynor's marmalade into the competition, she didn't put it with the others. She told Victoria and me that she left it at the end of the table. Maybe she intended to put it with the others later, when she locked up, and maybe she did, and that's where the judges found it in the morning."

"So Carwyn took a jar of marmalade with a red-and-white top home to Elin, just as she'd asked him to do," said Bethan.

"Right. And as soon as she saw it she knew it was the wrong jar. You can imagine how annoyed she must have been after all the trouble she'd gone to, that Carwyn had taken the wrong jar, and at the show the next day, Elin discovers that Gaynor has won after all. And instead of throwing the jar out, as she probably should have, she's too thrifty and can't bear waste, as she said at Macy's party, so she gives the marmalade to Barbara as a little gift, passing it off as her own," explained Penny.

"And Barbara realized the marmalade wasn't Elin's, probably because it was better," said Bethan. "And poor Barbara was starting to realize what had happened, and Elin over-heard her telling you on the way to Speke Hall that she had noticed something odd, and she realized Barbara was on her way to working out what had happened, because Elin had given her Florence's marmalade—so either Elin or Carwyn had been in the tent after the deadline closed. And all it would take would be a conversation with Joyce and she and Barbara would work out what must have happened."

"Exactly. So Elin alerted Carwyn, who followed Barbara into Speke Hall, confronted her, and tried to kill her to keep her quiet," Penny concluded.

"The scene set up at Speke Hall bothered me," said Bethan. "It seemed cumbersome that the killer would attack Barbara, grab the cordon and 'Wet Paint' sign, set all that up, then risk being seen while he escaped. But after talking to Mersey-side, we discovered there's a simple explanation, as there almost always is."

"Let me guess: He set up the cordon and 'Wet Paint' sign before he attacked Barbara," said Penny, "thinking it would keep people out and he wouldn't be disturbed. And how did he get away? He used the ladder beside the chimney flue. His hobby is rock climbing. Scrambling up that thing would have been easy for a fit person like him."

"So how did you put all this together?"

"Well, the thing that struck me about both murders is that they weren't planned. You can just imagine the killer pan-icking, trying to hide the bodies, and knowing they'd soon be discovered. So I thought about who could pull off some-thing like that."

"The second murder," said Bethan, "was one murder too many. It was really sloppy. When killers are trying to think on the fly, they always make mistakes. Mistakes that cost them dearly."

"And there's something else," said Penny. "Something that might connect Carwyn to the Gaynor Lewis murder. On the morning of the show, he wasn't wearing his green puffy vest that he always wears. I think he couldn't wear it because there was blood on it from when he killed his wife the night before."

"He probably got rid of it," said Bethan. "Too bad."

"But he didn't get rid of everything," said Penny. "It had little pins attached to it. Farming pins and chickens. I'll bet if you were to have them tested—"

"Gaynor's DNA!" exclaimed Bethan, interrupting Penny.

"Yes," said Penny. "But I don't have anything that actually places Carwyn in the marquee at the time of the murder."

"Maybe you don't have to."

"I'm not sure what you mean."

"We have something. A piece of evidence we held back from the public. When we analyzed the carrot cake Gaynor Lewis took down with her, we found a feather stuck in the cake. Could be a chicken feather."

Penny opened the bag she had brought with her and removed a rolled-up white towel. She carefully unrolled it and pointed to the fluffy white feather with a dab of pink nail varnish on it.

"Did it look like this, by any chance?"

Bethan grinned. "Where did you get that?"

"I did a birthday manicure for Macy Lewis, and she touched her granddad's vest and got this feather stuck in her nail varnish. It was still tacky."

"Well, I can't use that one—there's an issue with chain of

270

custody—but I will send someone to his farm to collect feathers from his chickens and we'll DNA them. And once he's been fingerprinted, we can see if his prints are a match to the sets Merseyside were able to recover from the bedroom at Speke Hall. The handle of the cake knife had been wiped. Even the most amateur of murderers would know to do that."

"I'm sure you interviewed Carwyn Lewis about his whereabouts at the time Gaynor was killed."

Bethan sighed. "Of course we did. He lied to us. But that's not unusual. Everybody lies to us."

"And Elin?"

"Quite likely an accomplice. We'll dig deeper to see if she assisted in the cover-ups. We'll be bringing both of them back for questioning, and as you said, we could very well be charging the pair of them by lunchtime. Or by this evening at the latest."

Carwyn Lewis was arrested that afternoon and charged the next morning with the murders of Gaynor Lewis and Barbara Vickers, and Elin Spears was arreseted on suspicion of being an accessory in the murder of Barbara Vickers.

"Why couldn't Gaynor have left us in peace?" Carwyn said. "All we wanted was to be happy. She should have just stepped aside and let us be happy."

Twenty-nine

"Remember that time we went to see puppies at Joyce Devlin's kennels and how adorable they were?" Penny said to Victoria a few days later over lunch.

"I certainly remember seeing the puppies, but I think the real point of the visit was so you could do a bit of sleuthing," Victoria replied.

"Well, how would you like to go and see some kittens this afternoon? With no sleuthing involved."

"Kittens! What do you want with another cat?" Victoria took a sip of wine. "Maybe I should get a cat."

"Maybe you should! Everybody should have a cat! Because Florence is about to get one."

"She is?"

"Mrs. Lloyd rang to say Florence's birthday is coming up and Florence has been pining for a cat for the longest time.

But Mrs. Lloyd insists it must be a better class of cat, like my Harrison, and she's asked me to find one."

"And you found one?"

"I found six!"

Victoria laughed. "And where did you find these kittens?"

"Emyr's cat had another litter and they're ready for their new homes. He's delighted Florence is going to take one."

"I bet he is."

Emyr Gruffydd's home, Ty Brith Hall, was situated high above the town of Llanelen and offered stunning views over the valley to the Snowdonia range of mountains. Sometimes snowcapped, sometimes wreathed in mist and low-lying clouds, but always beautiful, the rugged mountains filled Penny with awe. She never tired of their majestic grandeur and never took them for granted. She stood for a moment in the afternoon sunlight admiring them, and then, when the sound of footsteps crunching on the gravel announced Emyr's arrival, she and Victoria turned to greet him.

"Hello. Here for a kitten, are you? They're in the greenhouse. Let's go see them."

He led the way around to the back of the house, past beautifully tended gardens, to a large greenhouse. He opened the door and about halfway down, beside a screened opening where one of the panes of glass had been removed for ventilation, sat a large shallow box. In it, a black mother cat fended off the playful advances of her frisky brood of five kittens, including a little grey one that looked like Penny's Harrison, a black-and-white one, and a tabby.

"I thought there were six," said Victoria.

"The first one left for her new home this morning," said Emyr. "But I'm sure there's one here for Florence. Does she want a girl or a boy?"

"I'm not sure," said Penny, "and I don't think it matters, because we know the one we're taking, don't we, Victoria?"

"We sure do," said Victoria, pointing to one. Emyr picked it up and handed it to her. "It's a little girl."

Victoria cuddled it, rubbing her chin on its soft round head. "This'll do for today," she said, "but I may be back to get one for myself."

"I'll give you a little box to put her in," said Emyr.

Penny held the box on her lap as they drove to Rosemary Lane.

"Is Florence expecting you?" Victoria asked.

"Mrs. Lloyd is, but Florence isn't. It's meant to be a surprise."

Penny cradled the box as they walked up the path to the front door.

"I'll get it, Florence," Mrs. Lloyd called out in response to their knocking. A moment later, the door opened, and Mrs. Lloyd stood there, her blue eyes twinkling as she rubbed her hands together.

"Oh, girls, have you got it? Come in, do!" she said, leading the way to the sitting room. "Have a seat. I'll just get Florence." She bustled out of the room, and a moment later her voice carried into the sitting room. "No, never mind that right now, Florence; it can wait. Penny and Victoria are here and they've got something to show you."

Florence entered the sitting room and smiled a cheerful hello. "Sit yourself down, Florence," Mrs. Lloyd said, gesturing at the sofa. "You're going to want to be sitting down for this." Florence did as she was told, and Penny placed the little brown box on her lap. "Go on," Mrs. Lloyd urged, barely able to contain her excitement. "Open it."

Florence pulled the flaps apart, peered into the box, and gasped. She reached into the box, and as she lifted out a marmalade kitten, Victoria leapt up and pulled the box away. The marmalade kitten crouched on Florence's lap as she steadied it with one hand and stroked it gently with the other. "It's a female," said Victoria.

"What do you think you might call her?" Mrs. Lloyd asked.

"Oh, I really have no idea, but thank you all so much." Florence's blue eyes glistened with unshed tears and the contours of her face, softened with love, and the uplifted corners of her mouth made her look twenty years younger. She cradled the kitten and, holding it high on her chest, rubbed her cheek against its soft striped orange-and-white fur. "Oh, she's adorable." She admired the kitten's front paws, then looked at Mrs. Lloyd, then at Penny, then at Victoria. "Are we keeping her? Is she really mine?"

"She is," said Mrs. Lloyd, dabbing her eyes. "Goodness me, Florence, if I'd known how happy this was going to make you, I would have got you a wee cat ages ago. She'll make you a lovely little pet."

"That's it!" exclaimed Florence. "Let's call her Pet!"